Praise for Lynne Connolly's *Yorkshire*

"This grips you from page one and you will not want to put it down. I was teased with just a taste of what is to come from this first in a series and cannot wait to see what happens next with Richard and Rose. Ms. Connolly has completely captured the essence and ambiance of the period including some of the religious fanatics back then. ...To sum this up never underestimate a woman especially when under duress, you will be surprised and cheer along as I did."

~ *Lainey, Coffee Time Romance & More*

"...As Richard and Rose bravely face each obstacle thrown their way under the diabolical pen of author Lynne Connolly, we readers are skillfully drawn into a finely crafted tale in which surprises abound. As we speed towards the finale of this gripping novel, the fate of this resourceful couple, Richard and Rose will keep us engrossed until the very end."

~ *Nadine, Romance Junkies*

Look for these titles by
Lynne Connolly

Now Available:

Triple Countess Trilogy
Last Chance, My Love (Book 1)
A Chance to Dream (Book 2)
Met by Chance (Book 3)

Secrets Trilogy
Seductive Secrets (Book 1)
Alluring Secrets (Book 2)
Tantalizing Secrets (Book 3)

Richard and Rose Series
Yorkshire (Book 1)
Devonshire (Book 2)

Coming Soon:

Richard and Rose Series
Venice (Book 3)
Harley Street (Book 4)
Eyton (Book 5)
Darkwater (Book 6)

Yorkshire

Lynne Connolly

A Samhain Publishing, Ltd. publication.

Samhain Publishing, Ltd.
577 Mulberry Street, Suite 1520
Macon, GA 31201
www.samhainpublishing.com

Yorkshire
Copyright © 2009 by Lynne Connolly
Print ISBN: 978-1-60504-423-1
Digital ISBN: 978-1-60504-269-5

Editing by Angela James
Cover by Natalie Winters

First Samhain Publishing, Ltd. electronic publication: December 2008
First Samhain Publishing, Ltd. print publication: November 2009

Dedication

To my dad, for all his encouragement and love.

Prologue

I sat in my best riding habit in the dirt at the side of the road, a man I hardly knew sprawled next to me, his head in my lap. I looked ruefully at my skirts as blood seeped into the material. I'd bought it especially for this visit, and now it was ruined. Mr. Kerre and the coachman kicked and pulled at the overturned roof of the stricken vehicle. The canvas covering was peeling away with age; its thin top splintered when the men aimed hard kicks at it. Mr. Kerre had pulled out his brother, the man whose head now lay in my lap. They had more difficulty reaching the other occupants.

Our horses were safe enough, their reins thrown over the branches of a nearby tree. The unhurried shifting of their hooves matched the movements of the coach horses standing close by, cropping grass.

Blood saturated my riding gloves as I held the gaping wound together in what seemed increasingly like a vain attempt to stop the bleeding. I daren't move in case the outpouring worsened. Cramps spread across my back, and the hard pebbles of the road dug into my legs.

My breath misted in the crisp autumn air, and I feared my patient would begin to shiver in that uncontrollable way I'd seen before in others. He might have lost so much blood he wouldn't recover before we got him back to the Abbey. The thought, rather than the cold air, made me shiver. I hardly knew this man but I might not get to know him any better.

He opened his eyes and looked directly at me, staring

uncomprehendingly until he recovered his senses. I saw intelligence return to his face, and then something else. Something warmer.

I stared at him transfixed. No, oh no. This couldn't happen, to me, not sensible, shy overlooked Rose Golightly. But I had no way to stop it, and I couldn't look away now. This wasn't right, but my treacherous heart turned over when he smiled. "It's you," he murmured weakly.

How could a visit anticipated so eagerly, regretted so bitterly, end in this?

Chapter One

1752, one day earlier

"Rose, are you feeling quite well?"

I was tired from the long journey and I felt ill, certainly in no mood for polite disclaimers. "No," I snapped. The nausea didn't come entirely from the dreadful state of the drive leading to Hareton Abbey, but from my dislike of meeting new people.

I looked past my sister to glimpse Steven Drury, one of our two male escorts, riding by the side of the hired coach. I envied him. I'd have been much more comfortable on horseback and I wouldn't have had to talk to anyone. "I'll be well once I get out of this infernal coach," I said.

"When you hire them you can't inspect them," my sister-in-law said in her practical way. "And we sold our travelling coach years ago. When do we travel long distances?"

"This last week." I shifted on the worn leather seat, futilely trying to improve my position on the lumpy upholstery. I'd been trying to do that for days. The only respite had come when we stopped to change horses and we could get out for a time and stretch our legs.

Martha gazed out of the other window, at the overgrown trees bordering the drive. Fallen leaves, so prevalent in October, made our progress even more treacherous.

My sister, Lizzie, turned away from the gloomy prospect outside. "I believe Lord Hareton's trying to deter visitors."

"So why," Martha demanded, in an exasperated tone, "are we really here?"

"To witness the marriage of our cousin, the Honourable Edward Golightly to the only daughter of the Earl of Hareton," chanted Lizzie, quoting the letter we had received a month earlier.

Martha made a "Tch" of exasperation, turning to stare out the window again. The coach moved slowly, crawling and bouncing up the drive. It was bordered by overgrown lime trees, soaring far above where they should have been curving gracefully over our heads. The other routes of access were probably worse. "What kind of earl leaves his drive in this state?" Martha demanded.

"An eccentric one?" I suggested.

"What sort of man will let his only daughter marry into this?"

"Perhaps the Southwoods don't know about this either, my dear," said her husband, my brother. "They arranged the marriage in their children's childhood, after all. The last Lord Hareton wasn't like this, was he?"

"Far from it." Martha glanced again at the picturesque but treacherous scene outside the relative safety of our coach. "He's probably spinning in his grave. He planned everything for his sons before he died, even this marriage."

"What do you think Lady Hareton feels about this?" I ventured.

"I've never met her, Rose, and she's never written to us." I knew the lack of common courtesy irked Martha. "They married in haste. I thought she'd got in the family way, they married so quickly, but it wasn't so. They're still childless and my James is still the heir, after the brothers."

"Do you think he'll ever be an earl?" asked Lizzie, ever the social climber.

Martha glared at her. "Not for a minute. I wouldn't welcome it if he were. Just imagine the changes."

"Yes." A faraway look came into Lizzie's eyes. She gazed dreamily at the worn squabs and faded upholstery of our hired coach.

"I think they just want me to witness the marriage contract," James said. "Then we can go home and get on with our lives. There'll be an heir here soon enough."

"Do you think they want to inspect us?" Lizzie asked.

Martha answered her. "No. Why should they? They've shown no interest in the last ten years, why should they want to see us now? No, I think James is right. They want us to witness the contract, and to tell us we're out of the reckoning, as far as the succession is concerned. If the earl's marriage is barren, perhaps his brother's won't be. Thank God, I say."

Her voice reverberated around the small space for a minute or two, echoing dully.

"The papers say he's a recluse." Lizzie read every society paper she could lay her hands on. "They didn't say he was mad. I can't understand how there could have been such a change between then and now." The proposed country house party she'd dreamed of for weeks evaporated before her eyes.

"At least there won't be a house party like the last time," Martha observed, not without relief. "If he's a recluse, he won't want more people than necessary."

"You never know." Lizzie's pretty mouth turned down at the corners. "He might have invited a few more people."

Silently, I agreed with Martha, and fervently hoped her predictions would come true. I was as happy as I could be in our comfortable manor house, surrounded by familiarity. I hated meeting strangers. The sight of the neglect in the drive, the lack of any other tracks coming this way had been a relief, not a disappointment, though I was sorry for my sister's sake. Her angelic beauty deserved more than a provincial audience.

At last, we came to a juddering halt at the top of the drive, nearly throwing us out of our seats. We waited as the steps were let down, which gave me the chance to take a few deep breaths in preparation for the ordeal ahead. James got down and helped Martha, Lizzie and me to alight.

Silence fell, suddenly oppressive. Steven stood by his horse. We stood by the coach. No one spoke, appalled and awed in equal measure by the sight before us.

13

We stood in the courtyard, before the main part of Hareton Abbey. Two great grey wings stretched out on either side. Elsewhere, they would serve as a protective barrier against the bitter Yorkshire winds, but here they seemed more like a trap waiting for the prey to spring it. No life stirred behind the windows, dulled with begrimed years of neglect.

The house was rendered in grey Yorkshire stone, formidable and forbidding. It had not been cleaned except by the weather, nor repaired where pieces of the stone had shattered in the frosts of winter. Pieces still lay on the ground. They must have lain there disregarded for some time. The main part of the building towered in front of us. Its air of abandonment was almost tangible: you could almost hear the house crumbling.

"Rose..." Lizzie whispered.

I glanced at her. "Dear God. What have we come to?"

Her face reflected my own apprehension. "I don't know. This is Hareton Abbey, isn't it? We haven't come somewhere else by mistake?"

"It has to be," Martha said. We spoke quietly; afraid of awakening echoes. "Don't forget, James and I have been here once before, but it didn't look like this the last time we came."

"Lord, no." James murmured. Martha clutched his arm as if she might never let go. "It's supposed to be one of the show houses of the county; whatever can have happened?"

The rumble of wheels on the drive behind started us out of our shock. We stepped back to see what was coming, and to get out of its way.

Into the dilapidated courtyard bowled two travelling carriages, as different from our hired vehicle as possible. They were clearly private vehicles, bang up to date in style, bearing emblazoned crests on their doors. The shiny new black paintwork contrasted strongly with the dull, weathered finish on our carriage. The windows were glassed in, but despite their fashionable comfort, the bodies of the vehicles jolted and swung just as much as ours had. The horses pulling them were matched thoroughbreds. They must have cost a fortune.

They came to a brisk halt in front of the house. We watched liveried footmen leap down and run to let down the steps. "The Southwood party," Lizzie whispered, awestruck. The cream of society, the top of the tree. Her ideal, her dream.

From the first coach alighted a figure that made my mouth drop open in disbelief. A vision of male gorgeousness, a sumptuous feast of a man. Lizzie gasped, but I didn't turn to look at her. I kept my gaze fixed on the mirage before us.

He wore scarlet velvet, dressed for the Court. He would be sadly disappointed here. His white powdered wig was set just right, his waistcoat was a dream of embroidered magnificence. He swung around to help a lady descend from the vehicle, and when I again glanced at Lizzie, I saw she had temporarily lost all faculties of speech. No doubt remembering her manners, she closed her mouth.

This younger lady was attired—dressed would have been too clumsy a word—in a French sacque of blue watered silk, embroidered down the hem and the robings in fine floss. Frills and furbelows seemed to take on a life of their own, romping over her petticoats. Pearls gleamed at her neck. "Dear God," whispered Lizzie.

Behind these visions of fashionable excess, another man climbed down. He wore his fair hair simply tied back; his clothes were just as well cut as the other gentleman's though not as extravagant, and his attitude far more natural. "They're twins," Lizzie told me, back in control of her voice.

"I know," I said. "You told us. More than once."

To see the Kerre brothers was a different experience to merely reading about them.

The only identical twins in polite society, they made themselves more conspicuous still by creating scandal after scandal. Lizzie's information continued, "The younger went abroad after eloping with a married woman. He's only lately returned, after twelve years away. I wonder which one it is?"

"The peacock." It had to be. The other looked far too sensible.

They glanced at us. The gorgeously dressed gentleman

15

turned back to the coach, and said something only his brother could hear. His twin spun on his heel, the gravel grating under his foot and stared at us for one impolite moment before he looked away. I guessed the popinjay had said something like "country bumpkins", and I resented the comment while at the same time agreeing with it. We were in a hired coach, and hadn't thought to make a stop to change into better clothes as the other party obviously had. I smoothed my hand over my worn, brown wool gown.

With a leisurely gait, the peacock approached us and bowed. "You, sir, must be Sir James Golightly. Lord Hareton informed us you would be here." His voice was faintly musical and touched with a low burr I found unusually attractive.

James bowed in response, and introduced us. The gentleman in turn introduced his party. The beautiful gentleman was Lord Strang, heir to the earldom of Southwood and not the one who had caused the scandal after all. The other gentleman was Mr. Gervase Kerre, Lord Strang's twin. Despite Lord Strang's heavy maquillage, the resemblance between them was remarkable. Perhaps smallpox or his sojourn in the tropics had marked Mr. Kerre's face, but Lord Strang's makeup was fashionably thick, and his skin could be similarly rough underneath.

"From—Devonshire?" Lord Strang's voice held a fashionable drawl, but the tones were soft and low.

"Indeed," Martha answered. "It's been a long journey."

"Only to find this at the end of it?" With one elegant gesture, he indicated the hall behind him. "Hardly the gold at the end of the rainbow."

"Hardly," I said.

His clear blue gaze rested on my face, making the hot blood rush to my face, heating my skin. I wasn't sure why, unless my reticence was getting the better of me. "Miss Golightly. The elder daughter?"

"Yes." I replied too shortly for politeness. In truth, my sensitivity on this subject bordered on the obsessive. I'd reached the ripe old age of twenty-five and hadn't raised hopes in any male breasts that I knew about, while Lizzie, five years younger, was sought by all. My dark looks couldn't compare to her golden loveliness and I was too tall for the petite beauties currently in fashion.

"Have we met?" This from Miss Cartwright, the lady in blue.

"No; I would have remembered." Miss Cartwright raised a haughty eyebrow, but smiled frostily as if I'd paid her a compliment.

Lord Strang looked at the tightly closed front door. "Do you think they'll let us in?" His frown and sharp tone clearly showed his displeasure. "Or should we just get back in the coaches and return to York?"

I wondered where his father was. This gathering was, we understood, to celebrate the nuptials of Lord Southwood's only daughter. At first, I had thought she was the lovely lady, but she had been introduced to us as Miss Cartwright, Lord Strang's affianced bride. The older lady who had stepped down unaided from the coach was her duenna, another Miss Cartwright, presumably an aunt or more distant relative.

As though set in motion by his lordship's words, the front door creaked open. Its once smart black paint was peeling away; the double flight of steps leading up to it were crumbled, stained and cracked. Nevertheless, it seemed to be the only other alternative to returning to York, so we moved towards it.

We, the Golightlys, followed closely by Steven went up the steps first; cautiously, as the stone was none too safe. At any moment a piece of decayed stone might break, crumble away, and take the unfortunate person with it.

We walked into the Great Hall. Or something that had once been the Great Hall. It took some time for my eyes to adjust to the relative darkness inside. The great space felt gloomy and cold, clammy with disuse. Martha had described Hareton Abbey's great marble entrance hall to us, but this couldn't be the same place.

The staircase with its crimson carpet soared in front of us. Myriad life sized marble statues ranged around the upper storey. Dirt obscured the finer features of the marble, and turned the pure white on the gods and goddesses of a different age to a murky grey. Cobwebs stretched from fingertip to hipbone in a weird parody of the fine lace sported by the Southwood party. The once smart black and white tiles, laid in a chequered pattern, were blurred with dirt. Shuddering in revulsion, I took Lizzie's arm. We held each other tightly and looked around in silence; all affected by the tomb-like silence of the once Great Hall.

Suddenly, shockingly, the stillness shattered. "My God, I wonder which bedroom Sleeping Beauty rests in." A male voice, quiet, low but penetrating. I knew without looking that it was Lord Strang.

The man who had let us in waited for us by a small door at one side of the hall. He must be a servant, but his role wasn't easily identifiable either by his appearance or demeanour. He wore no livery nor the quiet, smart clothes of an upper domestic, but a rough country coat, such as a gamekeeper might wear.

Lizzie glanced at me, eyebrows raised in a tacit comment. When I looked at her, I caught Lord Strang's glance. He smiled. I looked away.

We moved towards the servant, who led the way through the door and along a passage, where we entered another world. The magnificence and filth changed to Puritan cleanliness. No paintings hung on the wall here, no ornaments adorned the well-polished country furniture, just plain, gleaming floors and whitewashed walls. Our feet clattered on the uncarpeted wooden floor.

The manservant led us to a door at the end that opened onto a modest parlour. Here the Earl and Countess of Hareton and the Honourable Edward Golightly waited for us. The men stood while the lady sat in a hard chair before of them. They were all completely rigid. No smiles marred their stern features. They wore perfectly plain garments, the men simulacra of the manservant, the lady in dark blue and white with no lace, only plain linen cuffs to her sleeves and no jewellery.

Nothing approximating comfortable domesticity spoiled the austerity of the little room. No ornaments decorated the old fashioned carved oak mantelpiece, no cushions added comfort to the hard chairs. I found the obsessively spotless parlour as disturbing as the abandoned magnificence we had just left.

Our hosts bowed rigidly, and the lady stood and curtseyed with an awkwardness that indicated she didn't do it very often The answering bows from the Southwood party were awe inspiring, especially Lord Strang's, which combined precision and elegance in one graceful gesture. It seemed more elaborate than the bow he had given us in the courtyard, mocking the Haretons with its perfection.

"Welcome," said Lord Hareton. I felt anything but welcome here. The door opened to admit the manservant returning with a large wooden tray. It held a large teapot and several tea dishes.

There weren't enough chairs for everyone in this small room, so the ladies sat and the men remained on their feet. Lady Hareton saw to the tea, practically and without comment. The brown teapot, like the one we had in Devonshire for the servants to use, contained a weak infusion, but we found it welcome all the same. The heated cup warmed me in this unfriendly place. Despite the chill outside, the fireplace was cold, the fire unlit.

"I am pleased to see all of you. I thank you for coming." Lord Hareton's tones were exaggeratedly formal, perhaps a legacy of his childhood. The formality of the Hareton household had been famous in the last generation; the children forbidden to sit in their father's presence.

"I am surprised not to see Lord Southwood and his daughter."

Lord Strang gave him an easy smile. "He sends his apologies. A minor disposition has delayed his arrival with my sister, but he sent me ahead as a token of his good faith."

Lord Hareton nodded, his mouth a tight line of disapproval. "It is to be hoped that he doesn't keep us waiting long. I have made arrangements for our family lawyer, Mr. Fogg, to visit us tomorrow. Also, my minister will arrive. I intend to collect him personally in the morning. He uses public transport. He deems private carriages an extravagance, and I tend to agree with him. I do not wish for a long betrothal period, and I would like the contract fulfilled as soon as possible."

His glance at Lord Strang asked for complaisance, but he didn't find it.

"Can the lawyer's visit be deferred?" the younger man asked calmly, but I could hear the passion beneath. Lord Strang was in a temper.

"No, sir, it cannot. There is—"

Lord Strang lifted his chin. "I don't know if my sister would be content here."

"Contentment is in God's hands, not ours."

Lord Strang ignored the comment and continued to speak. Although his demeanour was rigidly polite, his low tones quivered with the anger beneath. "The betrothal was never a done thing; your father and my grandfather arranged it, but left it to my father and you to fulfil it. I am here as my father's representative, and if I dislike what I see, I fear I cannot recommend the betrothal to him."

Hareton smiled. It appeared malicious, but this interpretation surely must be wrong. I preferred the stern look; Lord Hareton had lost most of his teeth, and what remained weren't in good condition. "Perhaps you need some time to reflect." He used a soothing tone that made me want to slap him. "I would welcome an opportunity to bring your sister to God's family. I hope, once you have met Mr. Pritheroe, our minister, you will come to see the error of your ways and join our family."

Lord Strang stared, his eyes wide in anger and astonishment, momentarily transfixed. Abruptly Lord Hareton turned away and smiled at James. Now our turn arrived.

"I am pleased to welcome you back to my house, Sir James. I'm sorry not to see all of your family, as I requested, but it is not entirely necessary."

"My younger brother, Ian, had a fall and injured his foot. He sends his apologies." Lord Hareton nodded in response to James's explanation. "My younger sister, Ruth, is barely out of the schoolroom and my children are too young to embark on such a long journey."

Not the whole truth, but it would do. Ian's injury was far from serious, Ruth was too headstrong and excitable and the thought of those lively children in a coach on a long journey made me shudder. Not to mention the odd rumours we'd heard about the state of the Abbey. We hadn't imagined matters would be as bad as this, but it had given Martha and James pause.

Lord Hareton continued to speak. "I have asked you here as a witness to the betrothal, and to give you the opportunity to do something for God's people." James remained silent. Hareton ignored the rest of us. As women we were probably beneath his notice. I sipped my tea in an effort to appear unconcerned, waiting for the next bombshell. I had no doubt it would come.

"I have asked Mr. Fogg here for another reason. I wish to break the entail." Seemingly oblivious to the sensation he caused, he continued calmly, "I do not wish to be known as the earl, and I do not wish for the wealth and privilege that go with it. I wish to live as a private citizen. If the entail on the estate is broken, I am free to do that. I cannot prevent or deny the earldom, but I do not have to use it or encourage people to use the title."

James couldn't speak. He stared at Lord Hareton rather in the way a rabbit watches a snake, fascinated, waiting for the final, killing stroke.

"Mr. Fogg informs me that in order to break this document, it must be signed by the heir, and the next heir, in line. That is my brother, and you, Sir James." Our host smiled, as if this explained everything.

"And you want my sister to marry into this?" Mr. Kerre, who had up to now remained silent could no longer keep his indignation to himself. "Not only to live in a mausoleum, but to lose her standing in society, the privileges she has a right to expect?"

21

"Only by birth," Lord Hareton responded.

"That is true." Lord Strang's quiet, low voice cut through the air, like the voice of reason. "And among those men born to high state, there are a few who deserve it. I don't want to leave Maria here because it would make her unhappy. She wasn't born to this. From what I have seen here, I don't think I can recommend that my father brings her here."

He paused, glancing around the comfortless room. "I, however, am strangely intrigued by your minister, and I'd like to stay a little longer, if I may." His brother shot him a sharp glance, but remained silent.

"I am delighted to hear that, sir," Hareton replied. "Perhaps I can persuade you to change your mind."

Hareton's brother, the prospective bridegroom, showed no emotion at all. Intrigued, I wondered what other surprises this strange place held.

Hareton excused himself, saying it was time he went to pray. He looked askance at Steven in his dark clerical garb, but Steven said nothing, avoiding his gaze. I didn't blame him.

After they left the room, we breathed a collective sigh of relief, and looked around at each other. Lizzie and I exchanged a smile, then a laugh as we felt the oppressive atmosphere slide away. The exotic Kerres seemed normal, next to the extraordinary figures of our cousins.

"When did you last come here, Martha?" I knew, of course, but needed the confirmation. Something to remind me of my normal life, my normal home.

"Ten years ago. The last earl sent for us when we were married. It was different then. Our rooms were magnificent, even though we didn't have the best ones and a footman stood at every door."

"A stickler for ceremony by all accounts," said Lord Strang. "I have to confess there is no indisposition. My father sent us ahead to form an opinion. He has heard some odd rumours about Lord Hareton, and has serious doubts about the match. Society thinks Hareton is a recluse—they don't know the half of it."

"Indeed," agreed Martha. "It's all very shocking."

James looked up from silent contemplation. "I don't know what to do about this entail. If I refuse to sign it, will it still go through? It's not that I expect to inherit. Indeed, I don't wish for it, especially now I've seen the property, but I don't think it's right. I've never heard of such a thing before." I hated to see my beloved brother so worried. I would gladly have consigned the Haretons and the Abbey to perdition, if it would help him.

"I'm sure I'd feel the same." Mr. Kerre studied James, his finely shaped lips pursed in thought. "In truth, sir, from what I've seen, I think the Hareton estate is bankrupt. He may talk of God and his minister all he likes, but I think his father bankrupted the estate with his extravagance."

"I'm not so sure," said Lord Strang. "Why would they leave all the treasures in the Great Hall to rot if that's the case? I'm sure they could fetch a good price. What's the rest of the house like?"

James frowned. "You have a point, but on the way here I studied the land. Some of the fields are uncultivated, the animal population is scarce and what buildings I saw are sadly in need of repair."

"Yes," agreed Mr. Kerre, "I saw that too. I think you're right, sir. The Hareton estate is bankrupt."

My brother heaved a sigh. "So you think I should sign the entail away?"

"I would never presume to tell you what to do, sir," said Strang, "but in your place, I would seriously consider it. The situation intrigues me. I want to see more of it, but be assured, sir, there will be no wedding. Please feel free to shake the dust of Hareton Abbey from your heels as soon as you wish."

A maid chose that moment to come in and offer to show us to our rooms. It was early, but we accepted. When I passed James, he murmured to me, "Don't unpack."

I nodded.

My room was spotlessly clean, but contained no comforts,

and the fireplace was distressingly bare of kindling. All the drapery had gone, just like the parlour downstairs, and when I looked under the bed, it was as spotlessly clean as the rest of the room. I didn't know which I preferred; the decayed luxury of the Great Hall or the obsessive, bare cleanliness of this wing. Both chilled me to the bone.

My luggage stood in the middle of the floor completely untouched; a very unusual thing in a well-regulated household. However, I wasn't entirely helpless. I lifted the lid of the trunk and began to unpack. Remembering my brother's warning, I left most of the items in the trunk. I sighed when I looked at the gown I had bought in Exeter for this visit, and decided to leave it, after fingering the fine silk regretfully. This was no place for finery. Not for me, at least.

When two o'clock arrived, I could dress properly for dinner with some semblance of respectability. I wanted to go down with my sister, but at half past two, I was still waiting for her. It never took me long to dress; I didn't think overmuch about my appearance any more. I'd reached the advanced age of twenty-five without raising any hopes, but my sister, at twenty, was at the centre of the marriage market. I left her in front of the spotted mirror in her room, as she primped and pouted at her undeniably lovely reflection.

Only when I left the room did I recall that dinner wasn't for another half hour.

I didn't want to meet all those strangers on my own, so I decided to explore a little instead.

I wanted to see more of the Abbey. Like Lord Strang, I felt sure there was a mystery here; this great house held more than bankruptcy. Deliberately, I turned in the opposite direction to which I had come. My romantic soul demanded it and my curiosity rampaged across my more sensible emotions.

At the end of the passage, it turned dark. I soon discovered why. The windows here hadn't been cleaned for an age. They were begrimed with years of dirt, misting the light that fought its way through them. I wished I'd brought a candle, but someone might see me, and realise I shouldn't be there. Who would have thought I would need a candle at this time of day?

I turned a corner and opened a door at random, drawing a deep breath when I saw what lay inside.

I recalled Lord Strang's earlier comment because this room came straight out of Sleeping Beauty's castle. No neat covers hid any of the fine furnishings from the obscuring dust. It hadn't been a State Room, but a small room which contained some fine objects, the sort of treasure room often found in great country houses. Cobwebs covered the chandelier above me, adding their own ghostly comment on the scene below. The air smelled of damp decay. I drew my handkerchief over a small round table, revealing the elaborate, expensive marquetry that decorated it. Damp had raised the fine woodwork to irreparable ruin. Even the ornaments remained in their places on the mantelpiece, dotted about the room in casual, gruesome disarray, as if their owner had just stepped out, never to return.

I went to the window, careful not to let my skirt touch the exquisitely filthy furniture and rubbed a viewing hole in the window.

Suddenly, a pair of hands seized me from behind. One went round my waist and the other over my mouth. I froze in terror.

Chapter Two

"I saw you come in here," a male voice murmured. "Don't shout out."

I breathed out in relief when I recognised the voice, and then tensed again when I remembered what lay between us.

He released me and I turned around to confront him. I didn't like him so close. Not any more. Steven's garb of sober, clerical black only served to accentuate his dark good looks. So confident, so sure of himself. I moved hastily out of his reach.

"Not here, Steven." My voice still trembled in shock. When he heard it, he smiled. "Someone might come along."

"We can always close the door." He moved toward it. His look spoke of stolen kisses and dalliance.

"No," I replied, uncomfortably aware of his meaning. I had no wish to be alone with Steven, with the door closed.

He came back to me, took my hand and smiled in the heart-stopping way I had loved so much mere months ago. "What's made you so missish?"

Even now, I found his smile immensely attractive, but now I knew about the vanity and ambition beneath.

When Steven had arrived at our parish twelve months ago, the young ladies of the district vied for his attention—not all of them in ladylike ways. However, none of them took him too seriously after they discovered he was penniless; so, twenty-five and desperate to be off the shelf, I won. Now I knew my family connections, rather than my looks or personal appeal drew him to me, although at first I let myself think he'd fallen as passionately in love as he'd told me. I was wiser now.

Steven used his grip on my hand to swing me into his arms in a way that knocked the breath out of me. It had excited me once, but now I found it oppressive. He bent his head to kiss me, but I made this impossible by chattering at him, caught in panic. "A strange place, this." My voice came faster and higher than usual, as I tried desperately to put off the inevitable. Steven ignored my attempts at conversation, my obvious desire to be free.

When he pulled me closer I tried to push away but he only smiled, and I grew worried. My voice rose, "Please, Steven, let me go, I don't think—"

We heard a sound, footsteps close by, easily discernible in the hush of this desolate house. Steven released me, leaving me breathless, ruffled and tremulous. Whoever approached had heard us, because the footsteps quickened, coming closer.

To my deep embarrassment, into the room strode Lord Strang and Mr. Gervase Kerre, both dressed for dinner in the most up to date, finest fashion. They filled the gloomy room with their vitality, the jewelled colours of their attire bright against the room's muted tones. I was mortified.

Steven didn't seem in the least disturbed by their entrance, but I coloured up and turned my heated face to the window.

"Good afternoon," said Lord Strang. "I trust we haven't interrupted anything."

"Not at all," Steven replied in the same urbane tones, volunteering no explanation. I tried to recover my composure, but couldn't face anyone yet. I felt so ashamed, though I'd done nothing really wrong. Being discovered here, as though I had arranged a tryst, was enough.

"The gardens are a little overgrown, are they not?" Mr. Kerre strolled to the window and stood by my side. I smelled his perfume, an unusual rich, musky scent I hadn't noticed before. It was a welcome change from the dankness.

"Any more and they'll be positively fashionable." His brother must be referring to the current rage for "wildernesses". He came to my other side, not standing too close. He smelled of

27

something citrus and floral. I breathed it in.

They had neatly boxed me off from the curate. Steven couldn't come anywhere near me. I felt even more ashamed to be discovered in such circumstances, but grateful for their assistance. We looked out of the clean patch on the window I'd made with my handkerchief.

"I don't think our stay will be protracted, but while we are here, I should like to see more of this house." Lord Strang drew one delicately manicured finger across the dusty pane, before drawing the digit away and regarding it thoughtfully, as if surprised to see the dirt. I gave him my soiled handkerchief, which he accepted with a small smile. He wiped his finger, returning it to me after carefully folding the soiled part inside the cloth.

"I'll have to change it before I go downstairs," I said, grateful to find an excuse to leave.

"If you'll allow me, I'll escort you." Lord Strang didn't gave me a way out of the situation that I was thankful to take. He moved past Steven to the door, opening it for me. We walked out of the room, leaving Mr. Kerre and Steven behind.

When we were out of earshot, I drew a deep breath of relief. "Thank you, my lord."

"Think nothing of it. But I should take care in the future who you find yourself alone with, if I were you."

My face glowed, but I couldn't take offence at his reproof, because he was right. I tried to explain to this vision of a demigod, masklike and perfect in his immaculate costume, how I found myself in such a situation. I didn't know why I should explain anything to him, but I might feel better if the Kerres knew I wasn't the hoyden I appeared to be on this evidence. "Mr. Drury is our curate. He's been pursuing me for six months or so now. I—I'm having difficulty—"

We had reached the inhabited part of the house, and I shut my eyes to get rid of the humiliating scene. I dared a look at Lord Strang through lowered eyelashes. He didn't seem shocked.

"You wish to depress his pretensions?" My escort gave me a

perceptive look, but spoke with no particular emphasis or even interest. His eyes were such a startling blue. They held a warmth and humanity, totally at odds with his formal, fashionable appearance. His indifference made my situation more bearable, less embarrassing, somehow. I resented Steven fiercely for putting me into such a position.

"Yes, but I'm having difficulty doing so."

"If you persist he might come to realise you mean it. If not, there are other ways."

When we reached my room, I left the door open while I fetched a clean handkerchief. "Is your room like this, my lord?" I said, from where I stood by the chest of drawers.

He glanced inside, taking in the lack of drapery and ornament in one swift perusal. "Very much so. But our group of rooms was more hastily cleaned. I've set my man to improve matters. I live in hopes that Carier may be able to make them habitable."

A sharp clatter on the ceiling made me crouch down, afraid the ceiling was about to fall on my head. When I looked up again, Lord Strang stood next to me. I hadn't heard him move.

"I beg your pardon for startling you. I'm afraid this house will fall apart if it's left like this much longer."

I smelled his scent now he stood close to me. I felt his humanity, jarring something inside me and his warmth when he held my hand to help me to my feet. It shook me, in a way I could not explain. Before this incident I could regard him and, to a lesser extent, his brother, as interesting people to study, people we wouldn't meet again after our few days in this house. Now he became human, and his presence jolted me in an uncomfortable way.

We left the bedroom and I waited while he took snuff; a procedure worth watching. It must have taken him a long time to perfect it, and then by another miracle he made it look natural. He used one hand to flick the box open. Taking a tiny amount of snuff, he applied it to his right nostril with one hand, while snapping the box shut and returning it to his pocket with the other. All the while he showed off his long, beautiful fingers to their greatest advantage. Such a simple gesture, done with such finesse. He met my eyes, smiling, before holding out his arm for me. I felt the hard muscle beneath the satin sleeve of his green coat when I put my fingers on it. I could no longer ignore the man beneath the glossy exterior.

He took me downstairs to a small drawing room. At the door, he released me with a smile at Lizzie's side, and then moved off to join his betrothed. Lizzie nudged me. "You sly thing."

I blushed. "It wasn't like that." She wore her fine gown. Poor Lizzie, I thought. There should be a house party here for her to show off to.

Dinner was dismal. The food was cold, the company depressed under the influence of Lord Hareton, his wife and his brother. I kept my head down, still ashamed of the compromising situation in which the Kerre brothers had discovered me. Even Lizzie failed to sparkle. I went up to my room as soon as I could and read a book until bedtime.

Despite my fatigue, I couldn't sleep that night. The blankets on my bed were thin and few in number. Although I put my heavy travelling cloak on top, it made little difference to the chill filling my bones. I tossed and turned for an hour or more. Just as I was about to give up and get up, my door opened.

Sitting up quickly, I stifled a scream, immediately aware of the strangeness of my surroundings and my own vulnerability within them. My trembling fingers felt for the tinderbox on the nightstand.

"Rose, I can't sleep."

Steadying my hand, I struck a light. "Come in then," I said to my sister. "And bring your bedding with you." While she fetched them, I recovered from my shock. I didn't like this house. The sooner we went home, the better.

We enjoyed the plenteous expanse of the generously proportioned bed, and with Lizzie's blankets, we had a much more comfortable night.

When we woke in the morning, I got up with her. I saw the speculative looks she had cast at Mr. Kerre the day before and didn't want her to be alone with him. I was afraid my flirtatious, innocent sister might tumble into trouble with these worldly wise guests. She needed my company.

The fire hadn't been laid or lit, so we shivered in the chilly rooms. It might be colder indoors than out, with the damp from a long-unheated house and the roof most likely in a state of disrepair, letting in the rain. Our rooms faced away from the sun in the morning, which made matters worse. We found the garments that were easiest to get into—yesterday's riding habits. Shivering in our underwear we managed to climb into the warm woollen cloth, and tied each other's laces and tapes at the back as quickly as we could.

Hurrying downstairs, we tried to find somewhere warm. We checked a couple of rooms and found their fireplaces as bare as the ones in our rooms.

Eventually, in the small parlour, we found fresh bread and cheese laid out on a table. Used plates were stacked upon a sideboard, while clean ones stood on the food table. The evidence showed someone had been here before us. We helped ourselves to the food and a nearby pitcher of water. There was no chocolate or tea, nothing to warm us.

We ate in silence; both overwhelmed by the silence of the Abbey and the oppressive atmosphere it engendered. However, we left the room a little more satisfied in body. Then we had to find a way out, since we were determined not to stay in this gloomy, dank house a moment more than we had to.

We doubted the Great Hall would be open at this time of day and decided to try to find a side door. It took some time. We traversed up and down several narrow corridors, but eventually we found a door to the outside world, and luckily for us, it was unlocked. We hurried blissfully outside, as though we escaped from a prison.

This side of the house was relatively well kept, the path clear and not pitted like the main drive. After we took a few deep breaths of the clean, autumn air, we decided to discover

31

where it led, perhaps to the stables.

Rounding a corner, we nearly collided with Mr. Kerre. Flustered, I smiled politely. My society manners had never been what they should be—at least that's what Lizzie had always told me, though I found they served well enough.

He smiled in a friendly manner. "I thought I might take a morning ride."

"You must have been up early." Everyone knew about, or thought they did, the late hours kept by members of polite society. I presumed the Kerre brothers didn't get up much before noon.

"I'm not used to sleeping in. Besides, there isn't much rest to be had on a lumpy bed."

We joined in his good natured laughter. "Lord Hareton told me he has been up since five," Mr. Kerre continued. "He says he rises to pray for guidance throughout the night if he cannot sleep."

We took the information with complete gravity, in the same way Mr. Kerre delivered it. After all, a man was entitled to his beliefs. "I don't think I've ever been awake at five," Lizzie said.

Mr. Kerre smiled. "Oh, I have, but recently it's been from the other end and I've been retiring, not rising. The few times I've risen at that time have been for a journey, not for prayer."

"Are such hours frequently kept in London, sir?" Lizzie was ever eager to be in the know. "We are to go next Season, you know, to visit our Aunt Godolphin." Knowing such exalted people might give her the entrée she needed next year. Aunt Godolphin never made any bones about informing us that we would be unlikely to obtain access to the ton if we stayed with her, although her contacts were most respectable, and we could expect to enjoy ourselves and perhaps make a few useful connections. But with the acquaintance of one of the privileged few, our chances went up.

Lizzie's eager innocence seemed to amuse him. "Such hours are regularly kept by some people. I can't say I know your aunt, but, of course, I've been away a very long time." That was a kind thing to say.

We turned and began to walk along the path toward the stables together. It seemed the only way we could go, apart from back to the house, as weeds and overgrown plants tangled every other path. This abandonment seemed malicious, as though something more than financial ruin had caused this desolation.

It was blessedly easy to talk to Mr. Kerre. His manners were not in the least condescending. "You went to India, I believe, sir," I said.

He smiled. His stern features softened, and at once underwent a change that persuaded me that I could talk to him without fear of ridicule. I imagined that he never ignored the more unfortunate girls at public gatherings. "It wasn't exactly voluntary, but I came out of it better than I deserved."

We hadn't expected him to be this frank. I found it refreshing, but from the look on her face, Lizzie found it disconcerting. "I think you're past all that now, sir," I said.

"Just so," he agreed cheerfully.

The stables were in much better repair than the main house, arranged in a U-shape around a central yard. There in the yard stood a large bay stallion, saddled and ready. The groom at his head struggled to control the animal, which appeared full of oats and eager for some exercise. Mr. Kerre looked at the beast with satisfaction. "I planned to go into the village to find some breakfast. Richard's already gone with Lord Hareton and his brother on their mission to collect their prophet." He grinned. "But I think a good breakfast was more of an enticement than the opportunity to meet the fabled minister." Much of Lord Hareton's conversation the previous evening had been of this man, who obviously inspired his lordship to adopt his present way of life. Would you ladies care to accompany me?"

I shook my head. "I'm afraid we didn't bring any horses." I would have loved to ride out. At home, I often did so, in the morning.

"That's no problem. Miss Cartwright and her aunt sent

their hacks ahead with our mounts. If you feel you could give them some exercise while you're here, they would greatly appreciate it. My brother's intended doesn't spend much time on horseback, although she likes to travel in state." His comments made it clear what he thought of the beauteous Miss Cartwright. And horses needed exercise.

I opened my mouth to refuse but Lizzie forestalled me. "That's very kind, sir. It would be a pleasure."

Bloodstock was expensive and clumsy riders could ruin a good horse. However, since Lizzie had accepted with such alacrity I had to accept too, and thanked him. The propriety of such an action troubled me, too. Before I could think it through, Mr. Kerre turned and gave the groom an order. The man went off to prepare the horses.

"I'm told the village is only four miles away, and boasts a comfortable hostelry," Mr. Kerre said. "I'm not sure we can expect much here, and I need sustenance, especially in the mornings. The others have quite a head start on us. They set off nearly an hour ago."

"I didn't think Lord Strang would keep such early hours," Lizzie said lightly. It was a forward comment, but Mr. Kerre didn't seem to mind.

"He's a law unto himself. He has few habits, changing from day to day. Indeed, I hardly recognised him when I returned from abroad, he'd changed so much. Besides, he had a poor night of it last night. He said he'd ordered every stitch of bedding he had brought with him put on the bed. Even then, he couldn't sleep, so he gave up and got up."

"We doubled up," Lizzie confessed. "The bed was large enough, but the bedding too thin."

Mr. Kerre smiled again. "I wish we'd thought of that." I found it difficult to imagine the haughty viscount sharing his bed with anyone except, perhaps, Miss Cartwright after they wed. Then, they would be at either side of a very large, grand bed. I couldn't imagine him with his brother in the same fashion as Lizzie and I had scrambled our bedding together last night.

In a remarkably short time, the groom had found the two horses and tacked them up with ladies' side-saddles.

"The groom is very efficient," I remarked. "More than I expected of this place."

"He's my brother's groom. We brought him with us." Mr. Kerre called to the man, "Did you sleep well, Bennett?"

"No indeed, sir," the man called back. He didn't seem to care who overheard. "It's very draughty, up by the roof in the main house. I'll try to find somewhere nearer to the stables, I think."

Mr. Kerre nodded to Bennett and helped us mount the horses, which were very well kept animals. The side-saddles must belong to the Kerre party too, as they were of good quality and not at all worn. I thought sadly of my well-used gear left at home, waiting for me to save enough from my pin money to replace it.

"We owe you our thanks for the loan of the horses and saddles," I said, when I'd settled my mount.

Mr. Kerre, now also mounted, held his huge animal's reins with wrists of steel. "Not at all, ma'am. They need the exercise, and I can see you're well accustomed to riding."

My horse was a well-behaved animal with a springy step, indicating good feeding and care. I loved to ride, relishing the freedom it gave me.

We followed the path out of the stables that led away from the house, heading for the gates and the outside road. Concentration was needed to avoid overhanging branches and avoid the occasional pothole. When we reached the gates, we turned on to the main road outside with some relief, as even this was in better condition than those within the estate. We could ride abreast and converse, something we had been unable to do on the narrow, rutted path inside the Abbey grounds.

Lizzie began with an easy gambit. "Is India so very hot?"

"Indeed it is," Mr. Kerre replied. I mentally castigated my sister for an idiot, for asking such a stupid question, but he didn't seem to mind. "It's hot enough to kill many Europeans. I saw many diseases caused by the heat out there. It is, however, a country of many changing scenes and very beautiful, indeed."

"Why did you leave it, then, sir?" I knew what Lizzie meant: wasn't it time he came home and found himself a wife?

"I thought I should come back and make my peace, and I think India had finished with me. My last venture was none too successful. Once I made myself a competence, the challenge went out of it."

His description of this country genuinely interested me, besides the differences between India and England. "Where did you stay, sir?"

"Calcutta, mostly. It's in the north, but still very hot." He looked into the distance, as though thinking of that hot country, and all the colour he had left behind, only to return to this pale day, in this bleak part of the world.

I almost forgot my manners, strangely, at ease with this man. "When did you leave, sir?"

"Last year." He didn't look at me. As he swayed easily with his horse's walk, he continued, "I'd done enough."

"There has been trouble there recently, but anything I know about it I read in the newspapers. I really know very little of India."

"Very interesting it proved to be." He glanced at me, and gave me one of his easy smiles. "I arrived in '46, just as the French captured Madras. They returned it in '48, but they're still jockeying for position out there. There are riches enough for everyone, for an enterprising person, but governments think otherwise. Still, I have every trust in Robert Clive, who seems to have the situation in control for the Company."

Such conversation fascinated me, but I heard so little of it back home. Devonshire people were more concerned with local matters. "Is Mr. Clive a great man?"

"I couldn't say for sure, ma'am. I've not met him above half a dozen times, but he seems to be the right man in the right place."

"Will you go back?" Lizzie asked.

He didn't answer immediately, but controlled his horse. The great animal fretted for a gallop, shifting restlessly. Mr. Kerre seemed to find the stallion easy to control. "I don't think so. India is for young, ambitious men. The climate is unhealthy for the English, and every day is a gamble, with health and with the financial ventures. I left while I was still winning."

These enquiries satisfied Lizzie for the present. Lord Strang's betrothal put him out of the picture, so his brother was the only eligible male in the party. If I knew my sister, she would try to make the most of it. His manners were so unaffected that he put me at my ease as few other men outside my own family had. I liked him, his easy manner, and his lack of condescension, but bitter experience had showed me that men looked on me as a friend, and a way to approach the delectable Elizabeth.

Lizzie shifted slightly in her saddle, to show the shape of her body under the riding habit. This trick had brought previous swains to their knees, but she had merely practiced on them, ready for our all-important visit to London. I had an inkling she would now try her well-practiced arts in earnest.

"The colours in India are most remarkable and the architecture is unlike anything you have ever seen before—" Mr. Kerre began, but cut short when he saw something in the road ahead. We were too far away to distinguish it completely, but we could see a coach, and a coach in trouble.

"Your parents—" I began in alarm, but he interrupted me.

"No, they aren't planning to arrive until we send word. This must be Hareton's coach—my God, Richard!" His voice rose with the realisation, and he spurred his horse forward. Lizzie and I kicked up our mounts and followed as fast as we could behind him.

Chapter Three

The vehicle lay on its side at the edge of the road, like a great dead beetle, the tracks of its sideways slide easily visible in the crushed grass and weeds. If it had travelled any further it would have plunged into the ditch. The noise of our horses' hooves masked any sound from the coach, but when we pulled up, we heard someone bellowing inside the vehicle. This came as a relief; it indicated at least one of the inhabitants still lived. The two horses that had pulled the coach stood quietly by the roadside, cropping grass, their traces severed. The coachman must have released them first; a sensible move, as otherwise they could have kicked and bucked, causing further damage.

The coachman lay on his stomach; flat on the top that had been until recently the side of the vehicle, with the door flung open and his hand inside. "You're too strong for me, sir. Please don't move so much. There are people beneath you."

Mr. Kerre dismounted quickly, flinging his horse's reins over a nearby branch. I did the same, while Lizzie stayed on her horse. "How far is the village?" she shouted.

The coachman looked up. "Oh, miss, am I glad to see you! The village? It can't be above a mile or two." He pointed down the road.

"I'll go for help." Without further delay, Lizzie spurred her horse to a gallop, disappearing in a dusty cloud. She'd forgotten about her lovely new riding habit and her pretty poses in this crisis.

Hastily, with some difficulty, but with as much haste as he

could muster, Mr. Kerre climbed to the top of the coach while I watched anxiously from below. He lay by the side of the coachman and looked down into the stricken vehicle. At once, he reached his arm into the depths of the coach, to the source of all the noise. "Take hold!" Between them, with a great deal of effort, he and the coachman slowly hauled up a large gentleman in a homespun country outfit. I'd never seen this man before. Perhaps this accident had happened to someone else. The other coach, the one from the Abbey, would be along in a moment on its way back from the village.

The man groaned and complained bitterly. He sat on the top of the coach. I could see his deep, steadying breaths, misting in the cold morning air. Looking over the side, he paled in alarm.

I shouted, "Take care!" and moved to help him down. With a sharp cry of alarm he slipped off his perch. It was a pity I was, by then, underneath him.

Gasping, I fell, winded but otherwise unhurt. Fortunately, I hadn't been directly beneath the man. His weight, falling that far, could have killed me. I struggled to pull my skirt from under him, ripping it in the process.

I stood, regaining my balance and my breath, then bent and examined the stranger for injuries. He'd gone silent and I feared the worst when I saw his eyes closed. I groped in my pocket for my necessaire. Putting a mirror to his lips, I saw it mist faintly. Sighing in relief, I examined at the rest of him, searching for any injuries he might have sustained. His leg had twisted under him in the fall, and it now lay at an unnatural angle.

"How is he?" Mr. Kerre called down.

"I think his leg is broken," I called back.

"It looks bad here. There's a lot of blood. Are you up to this, ma'am? If you feel you might faint, you'd better return to the Abbey and rouse what help you can."

I didn't hold out much hope of help from that quarter. "I can stand it."

"I'm very pleased to hear it," he called back. "What's the

state of the top of the coach? Is there any chance we can break through?"

I stood and tried an experimental kick at the coach. My foot went straight through the canvas and rotted wood, and I nearly overbalanced; it was a wonder it had ever kept the rain out. "I think it would be quite easy."

I moved aside while Mr. Kerre and the coachman climbed down. I didn't want to break anyone else's fall. While the coachman helped me to drag the fat man aside, Mr. Kerre began to break through the coach roof. He pulled off the canvas top, kicking at its thin supports and hurling them out of the way. He was heedless of where they might land, in his haste to reach the ominously silent occupants.

The coachman went back to help, and I did what I could for the stranger. I straightened his legs and looked for a stout branch with which to bind the broken one. One leg was obviously broken, although thankfully the bone hadn't pierced the skin. Such a serious injury might have led to a nasty, even fatal, infection later. I aided him while staying aware of the surrounding events, working quickly. I couldn't find a suitable branch, so I used a rope from the coach to bind his legs together, the good one to the injured. It would do until we got him to a physician.

By then, Mr. Kerre had managed to break through the roof of the coach. With the coachman's help, he pulled out a body from the grisly heap of humanity inside. I didn't need the stricken expression on his brother's face to recognise Lord Strang. That dashed my faint hope of a different coach carrying strangers. In that case, the stranger I'd attended to must be Mr. Pritheroe, the so-called minister they had gone to collect from the village.

Lord Strang lay unconscious, deathly pale, covered in blood. His brother carried him a little way from the ruined coach, laying him on damp grass. I hurried across to help. I was needed there more urgently than with the minister, who now breathed heavily, as if in deep sleep. Heedless of the effects of the damp grass on my new riding habit, I squatted next to the injured man.

"He's alive," Mr. Kerre breathed.

Without delay, I fetched a small pair of scissors from my necessaire and began to cut and tear his clothes away. Blood seeped through the cloth, and I knew I must find the source of the bleeding and try to stop it. I'd seen this kind of wound before in the fields at home at harvest time. Scythes cut deeply and this wound looked to be as bad as an accidental scythe cut.

I sat on the damp grass while Mr. Kerre lifted his brother's shoulders to put his head in my lap. I leaned over the inert body. "I've found it."

A deep gash on the upper part of the left arm bled profusely. It bled still, when I pressed my hands together on the wound's sides. The red liquid dripped through my fingers, far too fast for my liking, but it didn't spurt. Mr. Kerre glanced at me, his face pale and worried, as if I was his only hope.

I let go of the arm and took up the sleeve of the coat I'd just cut off, glancing up at Mr. Kerre. "I think I can manage."

Mr. Kerre still squatted beside me, staring and shocked. The sight of blood affected some people very badly, including my normally practical sister-in-law. I wasn't sure whether it was the gore, or knowing that it was his brother's, that shocked him into near-insensibility.

The coachman needed help with the other occupants of the coach and I didn't think Mr. Kerre would be of much use here. "I'll call you if I need you," I said firmly.

He stirred himself and stood, taking one last look at his brother. "Be sure you do." He left for the coach.

In truth, his hovering, anxious presence made me nervous. I could manage better, alone. As I gripped the edges of the wound tightly together between my gloved hands, I felt a movement under me and glanced down. Lord Strang had come to. He stared up at me, bewilderment clouding his gaze.

"It's you," he said. We gazed at each other, a moment out of time, caught in a net I'd never known before.

I felt a jolt somewhere in the region of my heart, but

41

decided to ignore it and attend to more urgent matters. "You've been hurt, sir. Please keep still and I'll do what I can to help you." Holding my breath, I released his arm and began to bind it tightly. This had better work. The man could die here if he bled much more. I pulled the makeshift bandage as tightly as I could, and waited. After a moment the blood flow lessened a little. I sighed in relief and concentrated on the task in hand.

He drew a deep breath, as if taking his first—or last. "Well, well. At last, you're here." At least, I think that was what he said. His words were indistinct.

I felt the movement when he turned his head on my lap. He watched as I bound his wound, pulling the improvised bandage firmly around the wound. Then I pressed down hard. A definite easing of the blood flow rewarded me.

Lord Strang kept completely still while I attended to him. I was grateful for that, but concerned that he might be too weak to do anything else. "I think that will do for now." I straightened, wincing at the crick in my back. Taken off guard, I looked directly into those deep blue eyes.

A chill made me shiver. I couldn't imagine where it had come from. Although late in the year, the sun shone brightly and I was well wrapped up against the cold.

I decided to assume it was shock. Lord Strang shivered, too, likely from blood loss. I tried to cover him with my riding habit's wide skirt. He smiled his thanks, faintly.

That smile gave me another jolt, and I realised I'd never seen him smile properly until this moment. I'd seen Mr. Kerre smile, though, but Lord Strang's was slightly different, an edge of realism, not the sunny smile his brother had bestowed on me. Odd, considering the ordeal Mr. Kerre had been through, publicly humiliated and sent away in disgrace.

Lord Strang wore no maquillage this morning, revealing clear, smooth skin. He had lost his hat and wig in the accident. His golden close-cropped hair gleamed in the morning sunshine, the same colour as his brother's. For the first time I wondered what had made them turn out so differently.

"A good angel." He gritted his teeth against his shivers. I

felt a responsive shiver pass through my body.

"No angel, sir," I said tartly, too sharply. "Merely someone who happened to be in the right place at the right time for you. Still, I'm glad I was."

I looked down, met his eyes again and knew where my shiver came from. I wasn't cold.

I looked away quickly, toward the still bodies the men had hauled from the coach. No solace there. Recovering my senses, I turned my attention once again to Lord Strang. "It's a deep cut, but a clean one, sir," I informed him in practical tones, as briskly as I could muster. "It should heal well."

"Thank you." Many people can't voice simple thanks, but he had no problem with it.

"Your fiancée will be pleased to see you whole," I used the word 'fiancée' deliberately, reminding myself as much as him that he wasn't available.

"If she were my wife, she would not. Widowhood would suit her." I stared at him; surprised and shocked by the cynicism toward someone he should feel cordial towards, at the very least.

The sound of galloping hooves heralded Lizzie's return from the village at full tilt. She pulled up skillfully as she reached us. "The landlord will bring men, a cart and rope. They'll be here at any moment."

She dismounted quickly, and went to see what she could do to help, but she paled at the sight of all the blood. "Shall I go back to the Abbey and warn them?" Her voice shook and she turned away from the gory scene. Mr. Kerre tersely agreed and helped her to remount. She galloped away. She would be of more use at the Abbey.

Mr. Kerre walked across to us and squatted by his brother. "The earl is dead, but his brother is alive. Most of the blood seems to have come from you, Richard. How do you feel?"

"I'll do," said Lord Strang, and promptly went off into a dead faint.

Much to our relief, we heard horses pounding the road and

soon the landlord of the inn arrived, driving a serviceable cart carrying several men. The casualties were immediately loaded into it. I hovered over Lord Strang. "Don't move him too much. You'll reopen his wound. It's a deep one." They were very careful and I was satisfied to leave him in their care. They laid him tenderly on the floor of the cart, next to the youngest Hareton brother, in front of the other two casualties, and covered with a rough blanket that would at least keep him warm until he got back.

They set off for the Abbey. The coachman said he would walk the coach horses back, so Mr. Kerre and I remounted and rode back up the road at a brisk canter.

I had something new to think about now. I would have to face this new feeling and identify it. Mr. Kerre's concern for his brother kept him quiet, so we didn't say much on the way back. However, he did compliment me upon my level-headedness, and thanked me for what I'd done to help his brother. I said it was nothing, lying to be polite. That morning the ground under my feet had shifted just a little bit.

Chapter Four

We arrived back at the Abbey before the cart, which had to go the long way around, up the main drive. The groom in the stable yard had his hands full with only the coachman available to help him, as the other men were carrying the injured into the Abbey. We threw him the reins of our horses and hurried inside, trusting the redoubtable Bennett to take care of them.

From the accounts I received later, I knew my family roused the Abbey into a frenzy of activity, the like of which hadn't been seen for years. Lizzie did her job well. She ran into the Great Hall and shouted and, as well as raising a great deal of dust, she roused the whole of the household. With a struggle, they managed to open both the doors at the front of the house, and awaited the arrival of the dead and injured.

Lady Hareton had been beside herself, collapsing when she first heard the news. Despite her protests that she never touched alcohol, Martha took her into the parlour and forced her to drink a medicinal draught of brandy.

Then my formidable sister-in-law invaded the kitchen. Although appalled at what she found there, she stirred the slovenly cook into action and got her boiling pans of water and making a decent breakfast for everyone. Martha always thought of people's sustenance in a crisis and she had rarely been proved wrong. I had seen Martha at work in a kitchen before and I pitied the servants who were not used to her exacting standards.

Steven opened up the chapel to receive the body of the late

Earl of Hareton. He found that all ornaments had been stripped away, but it was obviously one of the rooms in current use, clean and bare. He got some men to shift a large table in there to act as a bier, and busied himself in looking for the ornaments and vestments that would be proper in the circumstances.

By the time the cart arrived, preparations were well under way, and we all anxiously awaited it.

Martha looked sadly at the body of the late earl, and supervised the loading of the body on to a door, unscrewed from its hinges for the purpose. They took him to the place hastily prepared for him in the chapel, and someone else took his brother, now suddenly the fifth Earl, to his room to await the arrival of the doctor. I could do nothing for him other than make him comfortable. He had injuries beyond my simple skills; he was deeply unconscious with no obvious wounds that needed attention. We sent a man to sit with him, and inform us at once of any change.

Lord Strang had come around in the cart again, they said, but when they brought him into the hall, he lay pale and still, only just conscious. His valet and his groom waited for him. Between them, they gently placed him on a door and carried him up the stairs to his room. They allowed no one else to help, but I followed behind, in case I could do anything more for him. He was my particular patient, and I didn't want to leave him.

Miss Cartwright anxiously waited for him, dressed beautifully in a blue gown Lizzie would have given a great deal to own. No tear marred her pretty eyes; no trouble creased her features. I would have relinquished the care of Lord Strang to her, but she took one look at my appearance, covered in her betrothed's gore, and then the bloody bandage on his lordship's arm and went off into strong hysterics. She fainted into the convenient arms of her aunt.

I thrust the smelling salts from my necessaire at the elder lady and left them to it. Then I went where I was most needed. I caught a speaking look from Miss Cartwright that indicated her displeasure in receiving such cavalier treatment from me, but had more important things to deal with. I hadn't the time to be polite.

Steven had returned from the chapel by then. He seemed very concerned by Miss Cartwright's distress and immediately went to her side, and took her hand without once looking at me. "Why, madam, you must not let yourself be so upset." She moderated her hysterics. She looked prettier that way.

Steven patted her hand. "A gently nurtured female shouldn't see such things." I felt offended. What did he think I was?

"I think you should retire to your room. Would you allow me to escort you?" Miss Cartwright hesitantly put her hand upon his sleeve, gazing at him in gratitude. That melting look seemed to stop Steven, until he put his hand gently back on hers.

He smiled at her encouragingly, while she peeped through her lashes. Pretty to see, but completely inappropriate under the present circumstances. He led her out of the room, and said as he went, "I shall see about procuring some brandy for you, ma'am. There must be some in this house, despite his lordship's stated preferences."

I didn't know what to make of this little scene. Steven virtually ignored me to attend to Lord Strang's betrothed. Perhaps he would move on, I thought, hopefully. Then I recalled she held a binding marriage contract, and my heart sank again.

At least it left me free to go to Lord Strang, to see if I could do anything more for him. I met his valet, one Carier, an ex military man, he told me, and relief surged through me when I realised he was a capable man and could take proper care of his master, not one of the niminy-piminy gentlemen who often attended those of high rank. After laying Lord Strang carefully on the bed, Carier sent Bennett back to the stables to cope with the chaos there.

Between us, working carefully but quickly, Carier and I removed Lord Strang's ruined coat and tore away the shreds of fine linen that were all that remained of his shirt sleeve. Then we carefully unwrapped the makeshift bandage I had applied at the scene. Lord Strang came around while we were undressing him, but he remained silent and held his arm completely still for us.

Carier glanced at his master when he probed the wound, but apart from one wince, his lordship held himself stoically steady.

Blood still wept sluggishly from the wound. If Carier moved the limb too quickly, the blood would start up again. I came forward to hold his lordship's arm at the wrist, in case he should move, but he didn't. His wrist lay lax in my hand, worryingly cold.

Eventually, Carier sighed in satisfaction. He stood back. "I think it's just a deep wound, my lord. There's no debris here and no serious injury to the structure of the arm. It would be better stitched, or it will open up as soon as you move your arm. Would you like me to do it for you, or would you rather wait for the doctor to arrive?"

"I would a million times rather you did it, Carier," Strang murmured. "I don't want to risk permanent injury from a country doctor."

Carier nodded, and went away to find the materials.

I sat quietly on the edge of the bed as I waited for Carier to return, but, shockingly, Lord Strang gripped my wrist with his good hand. It must have taken a great deal of his remaining strength to do so. I looked at his face and met his cool, blue gaze once more, trying to clear the shards of sensation that always affected me when he touched me. "I must thank you. Your help has been invaluable. I'd have bled to death, if it hadn't been for you."

Mechanically, I smiled. "Thank you, sir. It must be my country upbringing. I do try to help. Harvest time brings many injuries." The polite response sounded trite and foolish to my ears. He closed his eyes, releasing me from his gaze.

In truth, I felt ridiculously shy. I sat here, alone with a complete stranger for whom I felt the most absurd degree of concern. I'd never been alone with a man not a member of my family before, except for Steven twice, not counting the distressing incident last night. I hardly knew Lord Strang at all.

Despite his weakened state I grew acutely aware of his virility and his presence. I longed to touch him, not just to heal. I shook the thought aside. This was worrying, and completely unknown to me. It was something I hadn't a name for yet.

I told myself not to be so missish, but couldn't ignore that strong inward pull. For now, I would excuse my response to him as a natural concern for the injured and hope that it passed quickly.

I started when he spoke. He'd been so still I thought he'd fainted again. "There is something else." He still looked at my face. "But I will, God willing, be able to speak to you another time about that."

Silent, I braced myself to meet his gaze again. I could lose myself there, but could read nothing in it. I tried to smile, to reassure him. Although I decided to answer him, to ask him what he meant, the manservant came back in and the moment was lost.

Carier returned with the materials he needed and a large glass full of brandy. He put his arm behind his master, lifted him, and made him drink the liquor. Strang drank it when told to without protest, and then lay back, but the brandy acted on him so quickly, I suspected there had been something else in the drink. He watched with an unfocused stare while his valet skillfully got to work.

I watched, fascinated, as Carier stitched up the wound, forgetting everything else in my interest. I'd never seen such an operation done before. I'd heard of it, but this was the first time I'd seen it done. Carier used a large needle and coarse, brown thread to draw the edges of the skin back together, working quickly. I winced when he pierced the skin, but his lordship bore it without complaint, watching the operation with an interest that matched mine. The sides of the gaping wound came together reassuringly to form a tidy, recognisable arm again as the valet pulled the stitches tight and tied them off.

The brandy, the shock, or the pain from the stitches made Lord Strang pass out again before his valet had done. It relieved me, as his conscious presence made me something more than uncomfortable.

After I helped to bathe the wound, gently swabbing away the blood. Carier poured some pungent liquid over the cut. He told me it was good gin, assuring me it would help in the healing process, inhibiting any infection that could prove so dangerous to a healing wound. It was as well Lord Strang wasn't conscious, as the application of the gin would certainly have caused him excruciating pain.

When he finished his work, the valet regarded me appraisingly. He must have seen my state of shock, because he made me sit by the fire and drink a smaller measure of the undiluted brandy. I didn't feel it as it went down, but the strong spirit improved my resolve. Busy winding a clean, white bandage around the wound, he turned his head to say, "You must go to your room and change, madam."

I looked down at my new riding habit, now grimed filthy with dirt, saturated with blood, and torn in one or two places. I doubted it could ever be put right, but hadn't even noticed it until now.

I took my leave, but not before I looked back at the bed to ensure my patient was comfortable.

I went wearily back to my room to find a simple gown I could struggle into without help. I needed time to reflect, to try to absorb all the things that had happened that day. After I had changed, I sat on the bed, and tried to think.

The emotions sweeping over me overwhelmed me, nothing like anything I'd ever felt before. They were just recognisable to me as desire, and maybe, love. But that way lay madness.

I must, at all costs, stay calm, keep my feelings to myself. They might well pass in a week or two, indeed they might even be the result of today's events. I stared at my ruined riding habit, cast on the floor ready for the maid to take away for rags or burning, not seeing it, thinking, thinking.

The intensity of all this, the helpless feeling, the confusion finally knocked the last nail in the coffin of my infatuation with Steven, so some good had come of it. I scolded myself for being so foolish. I had always been known for my sensible outlook: I should call on it now.

After a short mental struggle I managed to persuade myself my new feelings were only the result of shock. When I tested my theory, I found I could live with it. Mentally armoured, I went back downstairs.

I found James and Martha in the parlour, tucking into a hearty breakfast, together with a man introduced to me as Mr. Fogg, the family lawyer. He had come over from York that morning to draw up the marriage contract, the one which would not now take place. He'd kindly agreed to stay on for a while to clear up the current situation. With the earl dead, and the next earl lying unconscious upstairs, matters could change at any time. One glance at my brother's genial, handsome face told me he knew exactly what that meant. I instinctively trusted Mr. Fogg, neatly but expensively dressed, and of an age my father would have been, had he lived.

I couldn't eat much, but I was glad of the hot, strong coffee that restored some of the warmth to my chilled bones. I watched the others as they ate, having what might well have been the first decent meal to grace that table for many years. Mr. Fogg seemed to have no problem, and made a hearty meal in between telling us what we needed to know.

He studied James dispassionately. "The late Lord Hareton made a standard will, which he drew up while his father still lived. After his wife's disposition, the rest of the estate would pass to the next earl, with the title."

James looked interested but said nothing, so the lawyer continued. "However, last week Lord Hareton asked me to visit. I replied that I would arrive today, if that was convenient to him."

"You didn't see the overturned coach, sir?" I asked.

"No, ma'am." He turned his friendly grey gaze to me. "I came from York. That's the other way. The bend in the road would have prevented me seeing it."

I nodded while he continued with his narrative. "His

lordship informed me he was desirous of changing his will."

"Did he say in what way?" James held out his coffee cup for Martha to refill it, not looking at her until she had finished. His smile of thanks clearly showed his affection for his wife of ten years. People had wondered why such a handsome, well-off man as my brother should have married the plain daughter of an Exeter gentleman with an inferior estate to his. They should have seen that look. Then they would have known.

"He did, my lord," Mr. Fogg replied, evidently too discreet to elaborate. We all knew what it would have included—the breaking up of the estate, its dispersal to a doubtful cause.

"Last night, Lord Hareton told us that he intended to break the entail," James said. Mr. Fogg nodded. "It can't be broken now," my brother went on. "My son and heir is only ten years old. As I understand it, this entail requires the heir, and his heir to sign, and Walter is very much a minor."

"Sir James, I'm glad to hear it." The lawyer's expression hinted that a great weight had gone from his shoulders and James looked pleased, too. To break an entail was a serious matter, something he wouldn't have approved of under any normal circumstances. Ever the country squire, the status quo meant a lot to my brother.

To my surprise, I found the little I ate for breakfast very welcome. Since Martha had now taken temporary control of the household during Lady Hareton's indisposition, she'd had fires lit in all the occupied rooms and food taken up to all those people who preferred to stay in them, driving the remaining servants into an unaccustomed frenzy of activity.

Steven joined us, sitting down with a plate of food. It could almost have been a normal day in Devonshire, but for the lawyer's presence and air of tension. At home, Steven would often join us for breakfast if he'd visited anyone in the area of our Manor house.

"The sight of her fiancé put Miss Cartwright out a great deal. It wasn't at all, proper to allow her to see him in such a condition." Steven's disapprobation didn't seem to extend to me.

"Is she better now?" Martha asked.

"She seems to be, thankfully. Her aunt and I were seriously concerned by her distress, but we gave her some laudanum and she's asleep now."

Martha asked me. "How is Lord Strang? He looked so pale when they carried him in."

"He lost a great deal of blood, much more than can be thought comfortable." Trying to be tactful, I remembered Martha's squeamishness about blood and forbore to give her any more detailed information. "He'll recover. He had a deep, clean wound and his valet stitched it. He's resting now." Relief showed in the various faces. "I don't think he'll want to stay much longer, but I don't know what sort of patient he is. There's no reason why he shouldn't be up in a day or two, as long as he keeps the arm still and he doesn't do too much."

Martha smiled, and I felt sorry that my next news wasn't as cheerful.

I reached for my cup. "I met the doctor before I came down. The new Lord Hareton doesn't seem to be recovering as well." Martha's expression returned to one of serious concern. "He's not conscious. He seems to be deeply asleep and that's never good." I took a sip of coffee, relishing the bitter taste. "I couldn't find anything seriously wrong, there's no broken bones, but he's not well, Martha." Martha looked at James, her eyes wide with alarm. She knew what would happen if this Lord Hareton died. Neither wished for that. To give up a handsome estate and comfortable life for a broken inheritance, even if it included a title, wasn't a comfortable thought.

Mr. Kerre and Lizzie joined us after a time. While Lizzie had changed her clothes, she'd cajoled help from somewhere, as she was far more becomingly attired than me. I smiled, not jealous, long used to being cast into the shade by Lizzie's beauty. She was getting into her stride, using this sad situation to her advantage. It couldn't be helped, but none of this was our doing, so why not?

By the time we finished our meal, the doctor had arrived. I went out to the hall to meet him and found him with Lord Strang's valet. Carier assured the doctor Lord Strang wouldn't be in need of his services.

The same surly servant who showed us in the day before took the doctor straight up to the new earl's room. I accompanied them, to see if I could assist in any way. I seemed to be the unofficial nurse, for now.

Lord Hareton lay on his comfortless bed. Extra bedding had been procured, probably by Martha, and piled on top of the coverlet. A fire had been lit. The room's austerity startled me, even compared to the ones we had. I had thought the occupants of the house must have some extra comforts, but it was not so. No ornament or drapery lifted the mood here. A well-thumbed Bible by the cheerless bed was the only book in evidence.

The new earl was alarmingly pale. His breath came in small, shallow gasps. "There's no time to waste." The doctor lifted out his knife case. I was relieved to see the instruments were reasonably clean.

He rolled the man's sleeve up several turns, glancing at his face as he felt for a vein. Nodding, he directed me to the bowl on the nightstand. I picked it up and held it under the arm as the doctor cut deeply into it. I stood back as far as I could as I'd had enough of blood for one day. I had just changed my dress, and my supply of fresh clothes wasn't limitless.

The blood dripped into the bowl. The doctor watched it closely. Lord Hareton still slept, breathing heavily, not in the least disturbed by the bloodletting.

The doctor felt Lord Hareton's forehead with his free hand. "No fever. That's good." He staunched the wound, binding it tightly. I put down the half-full bowl carefully, watching the discarded blood leave small dots of intense colour where it swilled around. The doctor stood back, assessing his patient.

He put a hand up to his chin, and sighed heavily. "I can do little more for him. We must let nature take its course. Either he recovers, or he doesn't."

He examined Lord Hareton's head more closely, running his fingers over the scalp. "Ah. There's a bad wound here, but little blood. The poor man seems to have received a blow to the back of his head which has crushed part of his skull. It's soft and yielding."

Despite my lack of squeamishness, I paled at the thought and made no move to examine the wound. I could imagine it only too well. "Can we do anything?"

"No. We must keep him kept quiet and as still as possible." We stood by the bed and watched the shadow of a man laid out so straight under the thin covers.

The new earl took several deep, dragging breaths. The last ended on a choke, the kind I'd heard once or twice before in my life, and hoped not to hear again.

The doctor didn't need to tell me what had just happened. That sound only meant one thing, together with the eerie silence that followed it. The man died as he had lived—quietly, without fuss. I had barely heard him speak. The fifth Earl of Hareton was dead. Long live the sixth earl.

My God. James. My own breath nearly stopped at the thought.

The doctor went on to Mr. Pritheroe's room, but he could set a simple break on his own and tired now, I went downstairs to see my family. I left a tearful maid to do the laying-out. I wasn't sure how my family would take the news.

Mr. Kerre, James, Martha, Lizzie, Steven, and Mr. Fogg the lawyer all sat in the small parlour. It was crowded but warm now, unlike when Lizzie and I had found it earlier in the day. Chairs had been brought in from the dining room. I sat, gratefully. Mr. Kerre lifted his head and stared at me.

"There seems to be no danger to Lord Strang, but we must pray the wound doesn't become infected. They can kill so easily when that happens." I stopped abruptly, choked by the thought.

Mr. Kerre promised to send word to Miss Cartwright when she awoke. He added, "I wondered if I should leave to inform our parents, but I don't think there's any need if Richard is in no immediate danger. I'll write." That surprised me; I would have thought his mother would want to be present, but I supposed he knew his own family best.

"The minister's leg is broken," I continued. "The doctor is

setting it now." Martha nodded at the news. There were a few polite murmurs of sympathy.

When I thought of the news I had to convey to them now, I tensed. Martha must have seen the way my jaw clenched, something I knew I did when nervous, for she immediately put a hand to her mouth, her eyes wide in alarm.

"The new earl died a few moments ago." I was too weary to be tactful, to break the news gently. "So that leaves you, James. You're the Earl of Hareton now."

Chapter Five

A long silence fell as everybody absorbed the news. James looked horrified, dark eyes wide in his pale face. Inheriting a crippled title with a ruined manor and estate hadn't featured in his plan of life. We had a comfortable existence in a completely different part of the country. To leave all that, the estate he'd worked on so hard, all his friends, his whole life up to this point, would be a terrible blow.

Overcome, Martha indulged in no outward show, other than a short gasp. Only because I knew her so well could I interpret her stillness of expression as distress. As always, she thought first of her husband. She leant forward and laid her hand gently on James's arm. "Never mind, dear, we might be able to wind things up here and then go home."

James's face cleared. He smiled back at her, and his broad, handsome face took on its usual expression of contentment. After all, nothing had to change except the title he used, if he wished it.

Lizzie could barely hide her elation but, knowing her as well as I did, I saw the gleam of excitement in her eyes. If we'd been alone, she'd have clapped her hands together in delight, as she usually did when something excited her. This meant she had a stake in society, she didn't have to stay on the edge of things in Devonshire. When we visited Aunt Godolphin in London next year, we would have a new status. This gave her a chance, the opportunity she had longed for all her life.

I couldn't condemn her for her excitement, but I felt

nothing but shock and disbelief. I felt as if I stood apart, watching a very vivid dream and I wished with all my heart to wake up in my own bed at home.

The lawyer looked as pleased as a lawyer can. He knew James, a right thinking man, wouldn't wish to break the entail. He couldn't, even had he wished to. I thought of his son and my nephew, Walter, who now would one day be the Earl of Hareton, and this realisation went a long way to bring me back to normality. The thought of that scamp ever having the dignity to hold the title of earl lifted my spirits.

Mr. Fogg rose and cleared his throat. "I am delighted to be the first to welcome you into the Abbey as the new Earl of Hareton," he said formally, extending a hand to James. My brother stood and took it, still bemused, but beginning to come to terms with it all. James was a slow thinker, but he always got there in the end.

Mr. Kerre also got to his feet. "I presume there's a great deal for you to discuss, so I'll leave you to it. I'm sorry to impose my presence on you at such a time, but I should like to ensure my brother is perfectly comfortable before we leave."

"Please feel free to stay as long as you wish," said Martha, the new countess. "I shouldn't like to drive you away under any circumstances."

"You're very kind." Mr. Kerre gave her a small smile and bowed.

"I think I must see to the sad duties of a man of the cloth on these occasions." Steven got to his feet. He too had a glint in his eye, one I didn't quite like.

I'd forgotten Steven. I'd determined to break with him before we came here, and now I feared the task would be even more difficult. He must realise that I could further his career more effectively as an earl's sister than as an earl's cousin. He looked across the room, caught my attention and smiled meaningfully before he turned and left the room in the wake of Mr. Kerre. My stomach knotted tightly.

We turned our full attention to Mr. Fogg. He reached for a stack of papers that up to now had lain disregarded on a small table by his side. Sitting down again he cleared his throat portentously. "My lord."

Martha looked at James to see how he would take the new title, but he didn't move a muscle.

We waited tensely. I glanced at Lizzie. Her eyes were wide and excited. She sat forward in her chair, her elbows pressed hard on its arms. I hoped I didn't betray myself as clearly. I passed my tongue along my dry lips, not daring to not break the tension by pouring myself a glass of water from the pitcher on the sideboard. I felt as wrung out as a dishcloth.

"Both of the unfortunately deceased earls had only standard wills, which were drawn up in their father's time," began Mr. Fogg. "I was to have drawn up a betrothal contract and two very unusual wills, as well as bringing the necessary documents to break the entail." He glanced up at James. "I may take it this is no longer necessary, my lord?"

James answered in the affirmative. A silence followed, only broken by the sound of shuffling paper while the man of law sorted through the bulk of his papers and set them aside.

"Then we are left with the original wills. These are standard documents, only altered on the fifth earl's marriage. Adequate provision is made for his wife in the event of the earl's death without issue—that is a matter which we must be sure of, by the way—" He pushed his cup aside to make room for the growing pile of papers.

"You mean you wish to ensure Lady Hareton isn't with child?" Martha was indignant. "The poor lady is distraught. How do you suggest we do that?"

"I suggest that we wait," the lawyer replied. "No dispositions can be made until the wills have undergone probate, and by then we will know for sure. I shall, of course, expedite matters for you as quickly as possible."

There was a pause. Eventually, James asked the question we all wanted to know the answer to, interrupting Mr. Fogg's orderly flow. "Was Lord Hareton bankrupt?"

James clasped his hands tightly in his lap: I saw he feared the worst. The lawyer's next words shocked us all. "Dear me, no. Oh no. I can see how you would make that error, my lord, but I can assure you Lord Hareton was most comfortably circumstanced."

He cleared his throat again and I took the opportunity to pour some water out for both of us. I didn't spill any, but came near to it. I didn't think I could take many more shocks today. The lawyer accepted the glass with profuse gratitude, obviously more tense than he showed on the outside. I was glad of the drink too.

Mr. Fogg looked down at his papers once more. "The fifth earl disliked ostentatious display. When he fell in with this—ahem—new religion of his, he became determined to dispose of all his property and donate it to his minister." He looked up at us. "The greater bulk of the estate is covered by the entail, so he could not dispose of it. He salted away his income for years, instead of reinvesting it in the estate." The man paused, looking round with some satisfaction at the sensation he caused before continuing. We sat still, wide eyed, transfixed by his words. "I can grant you access to some of these accounts immediately, but most will not be free until probate is established. The late earl was possessed of a great fortune in cash, which could be reinvested if your lordship should wish it."

A stunned silence fell, while we took in the startling news.

Martha found her voice at last. "Why didn't he sell the treasures in the Abbey? Why did he leave them to rot?"

"He'd planned a grand sale, to rid himself of everything at once," Mr. Fogg replied. "I should also tell you that a great deal of bad blood existed between the late earl and his father. I think he took some—satisfaction in seeing the treasures his father had amassed so carefully go to rack and ruin."

So, the Abbey and all its treasures had been deliberately neglected. This whole affair had taken on a new, dreadful texture. Who would want to destroy such lovely things? What kind of insanity produced such a desire?

Martha must have been thinking along the same lines. "Then the third earl didn't bankrupt the estate with his building projects and style of living?"

"No, my lady." The man of law looked her straight in the eye. "He depleted some of the resources it is true, but he was a good and careful landlord and the estate is basically sound. Or was. In the last ten years many of the farms and manors have been kept short of funds for repair and maintenance, and I am informed more modern methods of husbandry would also improve matters."

James began to brighten up when he found something he could do. "Why, I've been interested in farming all my life. I can do a great deal on that head."

Mr. Fogg ventured a smile. "It is what the estate needs. And this isn't the only property requiring attention, nor is it the largest estate in the earldom. Of course, there is your own estate in Devonshire now, two more substantial houses, the house in London, and various other concerns. Most of the property is concentrated in the south of the country."

Lizzie caught her breath and I glanced at her sharply. Her face shone with new hope.

James saw the light, and perhaps a lifetime's work. "But it's like our own estate only larger." If he had been given an estate in perfect working order, I don't think he'd have taken the news so well. With this, something he could make his own, he'd be so busy that he could adjust to his new station in life without even noticing it.

"I will make an effort to bring this house into order. I will not send for my children, not yet. I don't wish to house them here, with the house in this state."

"And you will need new staff, my lady?" Mr. Fogg said.

"Indeed I will." Martha agreed.

"For the time being, I suggest your ladyship might find willing hands in the village. In old Lord Hareton's day many of his staff came from there. They were dismissed when the fourth earl inherited. If you leave word at the inn that you will interview prospective members of staff, I am sure the response will be both immediate and swift. If you wish to engage more senior staff members, I can recommend Thompson's in London. They provide high class servants for most of the major families in the country."

"Splendid." Martha brightened. I could see her mind racing ahead, as she too accepted the challenge thrown down by our sudden change in fortune.

I couldn't take any more, I'd heard enough. I wanted to be on my own. Martha looked concerned when I stood, forcing a smile. "It's been a long day. Do you mind if I leave you to it?"

Martha immediately stood and came to take my hand. "I'm sorry, Rose, I should have thought earlier. The shock, all you've done to help today—would you like dinner in your room?"

I shook my head; I didn't want any fuss. "No. Just a little time on my own."

I left the room, heading swiftly outdoors. I wanted some fresh air.

Leaning against the wall by the back door, I tried to think, but it did no good. My mind raced, taking me along avenues I had no desire to face. I feared Steven would redouble his attentions to me, that I would never see my comfortable home again.

And I'd fallen in love with someone impossible.

I turned and struck my fist against the unyielding wall, feeling the soft flesh lose the battle with the hard Yorkshire stone. I took it away and felt for my handkerchief, holding it against the blood welling up from the scrape. At least this was proper pain. It gave me something real to consider.

I shivered and turned to go in. I met James and Martha, coming outside to see Mr. Fogg to his carriage. Martha's gaze travelled to my hand, swathed in my handkerchief, but she said nothing. The lawyer refused an invitation to stay, saying he should get back to York and begin his work as soon as possible. I envied him his comfortable bed and warm house.

"Thank you for these papers, my lord." He motioned to a leather case in his hand. "I will contact you again as soon as matters are under way."

Then he fumbled in his pocket and drew out a piece of

pasteboard. "This is the address of Thompson's in London. You will find them invaluable in the provision of upper servants." He gave the card to Martha with a small flourish. She took it, with a smile. "I have had some dealings with them in the past. If you wish it, I can contact them for you. They'll send you a list of the servants they think are suitable."

"Most kind, Mr. Fogg," Martha replied. An impressively efficient man of law for such a ramshackle family.

He had an air of pomposity that probably came with his position in life. We watched his vehicle jolt down the drive, then returned to the house.

I found Lizzie and we went upstairs to rest, to my room, since all our bedding was there. We removed our outer clothes, loosened our stays, lay down together and slept like babies.

I awoke later when Lizzie turned over, taking most of the covers with her. When I pulled them back, it woke her, and we grinned at each other, like children waking from an afternoon nap. Lizzie got up and sat by the fire. Thanks to Martha, there were now coals in a bucket by the fire. She heaped them on the flames. It would take more than one fire to dispel the neglect, the dampness, but it was a great comfort.

My sister wiped her hands on a nearby cloth and turned a face of beatific bliss to me. "The world is our oyster now, Rose love. It's London and society for us."

I sat up in bed, stretching my arms high above my head. I felt much better for the sleep. "I can't help thinking something will change. I'm not sure I want all this."

Lizzie laughed. "You must be mad. We can enter society at the highest level now. We can have all the beautiful things we want. We can pick and choose, Rose. Pick and choose." Her voice trailed off, as her imagination took hold.

I interrupted her reverie, hugging my knees for comfort. "I'm not sure I want all that. After all, I'm twenty-five and all the clothes in the world won't hide that. I'll still be an old maid. Just a richer one."

"But you'll be a fresh face, Rose. You have maturity and grace and—things like that. And if you don't take, you'll be able to set up your own establishment, if you want to."

That hadn't occurred to me so far, and I had to admit, it did put a rosier glow on our new station in life. I would no longer have to squeeze into a corner of an overcrowded mansion, looking after my younger siblings, nephews and nieces. This was the common lot of a dependant, unmarried woman of my station in life. Good for nothing, trained for nothing but how to be a conformable wife. Independence would atone for many things I now stood to lose.

Lizzie must have seen my expression change. "There, now. I knew you'd see the advantages after you'd rested. Rose, I won't be hypocritical, not with you. We didn't know the last two earls and while I would never have wished such a terrible fate on them I cannot be sorry that the title has fallen to us."

Lizzie smiled encouragingly, the smile warming her face to enchantment. It was to her own merit that she set no store by such tricks.

I smiled back. "No one will look at me twice, next to you."

I was not being overly modest. Merely honest. Lizzie had everything required of a modern beauty—small stature, with clear skin, limpid blue eyes, hair like spun silk and a charming personality. I had always known that. From the moment of her come out, young men fell at her feet. She knew it, too.

"You have your qualities, Rose. You'll find someone."

"What? A widower wanting a comfortable partner?" I didn't want that. "Do you know such a man?"

In preparation for our next year's London visit, my sister read every newspaper and magazine she could lay her hands on. She rejected politics and news in favour of society gossip. She studied prints of society notables until she could recognise them on the street—not that any of them ever came to Exeter, the centre of our social world. She'd be well prepared to explode upon the London scene, and she would probably capture the heart of a duke in the first month. I wished I could be more like her, confident and charming, but her success didn't make me jealous. She was my sister and I loved her. She had always been generous with her expertise, helping me to choose the right fabrics for my clothes and showed me how to ply my fan flirtatiously, but it didn't help. I was too tall and plain for flirtation.

"Have you read anything about Lord Strang and his brother?" I asked her now.

"Oh yes," Lizzie said.

I sat up in bed, hugging my knees. "Tell me."

"Why the sudden interest? Can it be you feel a sudden interest in one of them? Has Mr. Gervase Kerre's charms reached even your stony heart?"

I managed a laugh, trying to keep our conversation light. "No, it's just that when one meets them face to face, it becomes more interesting."

"Yes, of course." A gleam in her eyes belied her docile agreement. She settled down in the chair and told me their story, or as much of it as could be gleaned from the papers she pored over. "Well, twelve years ago when they had both just turned eighteen, a terrible scandal erupted when the Honourable Gervase eloped with their neighbour, Lady Boughton. They ran away to France together. After six months, the families prevailed upon Lady Boughton to return. She lived apart from her husband for a year before he finally forgave her. Lord Southwood is a stickler for propriety, and he refused to let his son into his presence again, so Mr. Kerre took the Tour. He went first to Italy, then went on to India, where he engaged in various speculations. He returned to England at the beginning of last year, enormously rich." She looked at me, her eyes shining. "Still not interested? The family seemingly reconciled. But when he returned, he resurrected the scandal. Until Lord Strang offered for Miss Cartwright the papers were full of it."

"A beautiful summary."

Lizzie laughed. "Oh, I went and read it all when I knew they were to be here." She leaned back in her chair. "Lord Strang, meantime, has tried every extravagance he is capable of, but he didn't actually step over the line. He dresses beautifully and has affair after affair, but he never stays with any of the women for long. Wherever he is, trouble seems to follow. There have been scandals aplenty. Whenever you read about an elopement, a suspicious death, or a theft, he always seems to be there. I think he's more dangerous than his brother and now we've come into the title, I shan't look in their direction for my matchmaking."

"Lizzie."

"What? You want me to be less than honest with you?" She gazed at me, wide-eyed, lovely. "I thought we agreed a long time ago we would always be honest with each other."

She was right. Lizzie even knew about the mess with Steven. She'd implored me, for months, to sever all connections with him, but she'd told no one else, as she'd promised at the start of the flirtation. I knew I could trust her.

Therefore, I told her of my strange feeling. "After the accident, I felt something I've never experienced before for anyone. When I look at him, I feel weak, excited and very, very nervous."

I didn't look at her as she asked, "Who? Gervase Kerre?"

"No. His brother."

"Oh dear."

I met her gaze. "I've decided to do what I can to avoid him. I'm sure it's only the shock or something like that. I'll recover."

"I hope so. It's the only thing you can properly do. I know it's not incurable. Do you remember Mr. Jameson, last year?" The previous year Lizzie had been encouraged and then let down by a callow youth of our acquaintance. Martha had had hopes, but he dropped Lizzie in favour of a richer prospect. I wished him joy of it now, as only I knew how much Lizzie had suffered from this humiliation. She'd held her head high for months afterwards. I nodded, to show I remembered him. "Well, though I thought I would die of love for him, it passed in a month or two. I might be rather shallow, I suppose, but I'm not the only person this has happened to. Truly, Rose, life does go on afterwards. Now, all I want is to flaunt myself in front of him as Lord Hareton's sister and show him what he turned down. I will, you know."

I didn't doubt it. "He deserves it."

"Try to retain your own self in his presence. It will pass, I'm sure of it. Despite Lord Strang being contracted to someone else, he's trouble."

I had to agree with her. It sounded as if the brothers were trouble. I should fight to overcome my stupid weakness, keep it to myself. There would be plenty of opportunities to come, and this one was foolish, not to be thought of.

Chapter Six

I awoke early the next morning. I dressed, careful not to disturb Lizzie where she lay with her arm flung out on my pillow, the epitome of sweet disorder. I'd promised to help Martha after breakfast, but I needed some fresh air first. Mainly because it was the least overgrown part of the gardens, I took the path of least resistance to the stables.

The double doors to the coach house lay open, and the groom was about, busy about his duties in one of the loose boxes. I heard him singing softly, though I couldn't distinguish the song. I went to look in the coach house, at the end of the run of horse boxes, and there, in the dim light, was the ruin of the family coach.

My curiosity got the better of me as it so often did, and I went in to take a closer look. I examined the vehicle carefully, curious to know what had caused such a terrible accident. It was easily the worst carriage accident I'd ever seen. I walked slowly around it.

It had been put back on its wheels, but the rear end reeled back drunkenly on its chassis and tipped the front end high into the air. Clearly, the suspension had given way. Like the rest of the late earl's possessions, it had been allowed to deteriorate by simple neglect. The once proud monogram on the doors had been all but obscured by the passage of time; the leather seats inside were cracked and split in places, the discoloured stuffing protruding. The floorboards were scuffed and there were none of the usual items to help with comfort on a journey one would expect to find in any family vehicle, much less one which belonged to an earl.

A gaping hole in the roof showed where Mr. Kerre and the coachman had broken through to the casualties on the previous day. I peered inside, up through the hole to the roof of the coach house, and then at the ruin within. Bloodstains, splashed about the interior, added to the general dilapidation, adding a gruesome touch.

I moved to the rear of the coach, where the body sagged back on the chassis.

The heavy leather straps that had supported the body of the coach hung by its side, useless now. I assumed they had given way under the strain of the passengers. Four grown men, one of them overburdened with avoirdupois, must have been too much for the worn leather. It was neglectful of the late Earl not to have them checked properly before they used the coach. Then I bent to pick up the end of the strap nearest to me. I fingered the severed end and felt the sharp edges.

Dear God. The strap hadn't given way at all, it had been cut.

There was no mistake. I examined it closely, saw the clean break. It wasn't frayed or split; just that nice, fresh severance of one side from the other, nearly all the way through. The end was as an accidental break should be; thinned and jagged.

I held that strap, turned it over in my hand while my mind raced ahead, as I tried to work out what I should do. Should I tell James? He would be obliged to investigate the matter, or keep quiet, and I knew my brother's conscience wouldn't allow that. After all, I might be mistaken. I looked at the strap again. No, there was no mistake, I was sure of it. I decided to go back to the house and fetch Lizzie. She wouldn't rush off and tell someone straightaway, and a second opinion would be more than useful.

I heard a sound from behind me, a footstep in the yard outside, closer than the stable boy who still sang lustily in one of the horse boxes at the other end of the yard. Hastily dropping the strap, I stood, and brushed my skirts down with my hand in a nervous gesture. It must be the groom. He couldn't find me in this situation, mustn't guess my discovery.

Lord Strang walked into the coach house.

His held his injured arm in a sling fastened around his neck, and he was dressed simply in a country frock coat, slung around his shoulders against the cold. No makeup or expensive velvet today and a simple wig, fair hair close to what I now knew to be his natural colour, tied back. He looked comfortable, at ease, far more human than he had when he first stepped out of his coach the previous Monday and far more like his brother, but I would never have confused them.

He stopped when he saw me and slowly looked me over. I felt dowdy and provincial under his even gaze, and dropped my eyes. He came quickly towards me, and then stopped again, a few paces short of me. Regaining my courage I lifted my head and we stared at each other. "Good morning, ma'am." He bowed.

"Good morning, my lord. Do you feel better today?"

"A good deal better, thank you. Sleep and rest seem to have restored me almost to my old self. But not quite," he added in a quieter, more reflective tone.

I glanced at the sling, expertly tied, no doubt by his resourceful manservant. "You look much better, sir. I hope your arm does well now."

An easy, genuine smile transformed his grave features into something else, making him look like any other man—almost. It went right through me. "I hope so too. Carier certainly seems pleased with its progress."

I felt uncomfortable with just the two of us, and the unseen groom and I groped in my mind for something to say. "Your man is very capable with injuries." I tried hard to keep up a normal conversation. "I didn't think it was considered usual in a manservant. Not all military men are familiar with injuries, or how to deal with them."

"Carier joined me on the Grand Tour, direct from the army." He didn't seem aware of my awkwardness. I thanked the Lord for good manners that prevented him indicating any awareness. "He served a general for several years and took an interest in helping the wounded. He dealt with much worse during his service, or so he would have me believe."

I found it difficult to take my eyes off Lord Strang, but I knew I must do something to stop myself, or he might notice. I felt awkward and ungainly as I always did in difficult situations. My inner feelings intensified it, made it even worse. Partly to give myself an excuse to take my eyes away from him and partly on an impulse I turned away and picked up the cut strap. "Sir, I noticed the most dreadful thing, but I need someone's opinion."

His attention had gone to the strap in my hand, and he must have seen what I did. He took the step that brought him to my side. "Good God!" Taking the strap from me he turned it over so he could examine it from both sides.

We stood side by side and stared at the strap for a while in silence, for far too long. Then I found my voice at last; "It has been cut, hasn't it, sir?"

I smelled him now. An unidentifiable scent of manhood mixed with citrus, too agreeable for comfort. I wanted to move away, but thought he might realise something was wrong if I did. I would be deeply mortified if that were to happen. It was bad enough to have this crazy infatuation—much worse if he knew it.

"There's no doubt about it. Look, it's been cut nearly through. I'm surprised the coach got as far as it did."

He dropped the strap as though it had become suddenly hot, and went round to the other side of the coach to examine the strap on that side, but I didn't follow him. I needed time to get my breath back. His presence so close hit me like a blow to the stomach, especially in the way he had taken me by surprise by walking in so unexpectedly. I put my head back and took some deep, clear breaths of the chilly morning air, pulled it down into my lungs in an effort to clear my head. Slowly, I regained my self control.

Lord Strang walked round the coach carefully, examining it closely at several points, then he came back to where I stood. "This is very serious indeed."

"Shouldn't we tell someone?"

Impulsively, I turned towards him, but he was standing too close for me to avoid the power of his presence. I drew a breath and smelled him, the perfume he used and the unfamiliar scent of masculinity. I could feel the heat of his body. Then I let my eyes meet his in a careless second. Everything rushed in on me, in his blue gaze. I was lost.

His eyes widened in disbelief and the breath caught in his throat. "You too? Oh dear God." Without any more words, he drew me close with his good arm and kissed me.

Tiny tentative kisses at first, gentle, the kind one might give a friend at greeting, but they soon changed to passionate and demanding when, despite my good intentions, I responded and kissed him back.

This could not be happening. But I didn't pull away. I wrapped my arms around him instead, and touched him properly for the first time. His hard body tensed under the fine linen shirt and his warmth seeped through to my very heart.

I'd never known anything remotely like this before, this aching desire that betrayed all my self-control. Living in an overcrowded manor house had taught me powers of discretion no one had been able to break through before, not even Steven, although he had tried. While every sensible bone in my body screamed for me to pull away, to get away, my treacherous arms wouldn't push, and my legs seemed rooted to the spot. With those kisses, he unlocked something I had only been aware of dimly before.

Passion.

He bent his head to kiss my neck. Now I could call out, now I could say something, but I only sighed with longing. My throat arched, his kisses burned my skin. I wanted him to continue, but he pushed me away, gasping, "No!"

My astonishment reflected in his eyes as we stared at each other. All my good resolutions had gone, dissolved in the wake of passion. Only aware of him as he looked at me, I tried to think, stay calm, in control of myself, but had to fight for it like never before.

"Someone told me you were dangerous." My voice shook despite my best efforts to keep it steady.

"Then you have me at a disadvantage, for no one told me how dangerous you are." I stared at him uncomprehendingly, and a heavy silence fell between us.

I heard the groom outside singing; I heard the horses shifting in their boxes. I had better go. Finally regaining control of my body, I turned away, but he said abruptly, "Come and talk. I promise I'll behave." And I knew I too felt the need to talk about this, to see if it was real.

I followed him to the back of the coach house where to a couple of bales of hay, and we sat side by side, careful not to touch each other. I felt the shock of his arm around me, the desire in his kiss. I still trembled.

I dared not look at him again. Staring at my trembling hands, I tried to control them, gripping them tightly and watching the knuckles turn white. The dark red scab of the scrape split a little and oozed drops of bright blood.

"I'm sorry," he said in his soft, low voice. "I must have upset you. I had no intention of leaping on you like a rutting stag, and I apologise for it. I will, naturally, make arrangements to leave if you should wish it, but I would very much like to tell you something first."

I looked at him, startled by his warm tones. His eyes held something new. Did I imagine it? Of course, I did. He was just amusing himself, that had to be the case. Nevertheless, I still trembled at the sincerity and passion in his eyes, now held in check.

"I wanted you the moment I saw you step down from your carriage on Monday." He looked away and stared straight ahead, at the tilted back of the coach. He paused and the silence lay heavy between us. "This is beyond my understanding. I've never believed in such things before, but something passed between us and I feel as if we spent too much time apart. I've read the poets, the talk of twin souls, or one soul parted by some accident of fate and I thought it all fanciful, until that moment."

He turned his head to look at me. I felt dowdy, thoroughly countrified. I had nothing a connoisseur of women like Lord Strang could want. This couldn't be true. How could someone like him want me, a provincial nobody? He was trying to seduce me, to amuse himself with an inexperienced country girl. Nevertheless, that look in his eyes told me something special might be there for us, if I dared to reach out and take it.

"You have a bad reputation." Desperately, I tried to be cool. "How can I be sure of anything you say?"

He smiled, holding my gaze. My heart turned over. "You can't. Nothing in life is ever sure. And that reputation, I should tell you, is well earned." His smile turned wry. "How can I be certain you're the kind of woman I should allow into my life? I know very little about you and I'm used to fortune and title-hunters. How do I know you aren't one of those?" He startled me with his honesty, but he was right. My appearance wasn't calculated to fill him with confidence. The cynical smile disappeared. "I just know it. I'm not accustomed to following my impulses, not these days, but this one is too strong to deny. If I did, I'd regret it bitterly."

I'd begun to be sure this had all the hallmarks of a sordid seduction, a roll in the hay, but at that moment, in my foolish naiveté, part of me didn't care. I'd have done anything for him— his attention, his touch, was enough. I must have been stark raving mad.

He took my hand gently, still watching my face. He smiled at my look of disbelief. "My brother will tell you I'm quick to make up my mind and slow to change it. I know this can be disconcerting, but I beg you to believe I'm sincere. I fell in love with you at first sight, but that's my problem, not yours. If you can't return any of my feelings, you must say so, and think no more of it. I've lived with worse disappointments."

He waited, completely still, his hand linked with mine, but I said nothing. I didn't trust myself to speak just yet. He said 'love.' I had no idea what that was, or how it should make me feel, but if this uncomfortable, prickly feeling was love, then I had it. He squeezed my hand. "I didn't mean to speak to you just yet. I wanted this above all things to be right, with no scandal, no misunderstanding." He paused, and looked away. I didn't try to take my hand away. I felt the warmth, and knew it for a sort of comfort. "I wanted to arrange my affairs, and then come back, clear and open, to see if you would have me. Or at least consider it."

"How can this happen?"

"Dear God, how should I know? I want to wait and be sensible, but there's no time for that. If I want to take this chance, accept our feelings as real, then I have to take a few steps right away."

We looked at each other in silence, then he sighed. "I should tell you I've become aware in recent weeks I can't marry Julia Cartwright." The sensible part of me listened sceptically. He would say that, just to raise my hopes. "We simply wouldn't suit. This is nothing to do with you, but is the result of a growing conviction that I made a mistake. I've spoken to Julia before about breaking our betrothal. That is why she accompanied us here, I believe. She knows I'm about to bolt, but she won't give me the chance. I spoke to her yesterday, when she finally came to see me on my sick bed." A cold chill crept into his voice. "I told her I thought we wouldn't do after all, and I begged her to reconsider. Our union would make both of us unhappy. After furthering my acquaintance with her, I'm more sure of it than ever. I can't break it off. She must do it, or there'll be scandal, and it will attach itself to you. I won't have that. I've signed the contract. She, or her father, could take me to court if I break it."

He lifted my hand to his lips, kissing it softly and watching my reaction. His small gesture sent shivers through me. I said nothing while I frantically tried to bring myself back down to earth and collect my thoughts.

"Julia said I must be delirious from my injuries, but I insisted upon it, and she promised me she would think about it." There was no emotion at all in his voice when he referred to his affianced wife.

"Will you say the same to me in a few months?" Was this

the way his affair with Miss Cartwright had started?

I couldn't mistake the fierceness in his expression. "No. I swear it. I have no fond feelings for her." He gazed at me as if I held all he wanted. "I was a fool. Love is possible, you've already showed me that. I feel everything for you that I never felt for Julia. Or any other woman."

I found my voice at last in dealing with the practical. I needed time to think, to assess this terrifying, wonderful turn of events. "You shouldn't be out of your bed, sir. You lost a great deal of blood, you must be weak still."

He wouldn't let me change the subject. "I came to find you. I wanted to know if I should stay here any longer, if there was any hope for me. If you won't consider me, I'll take myself off to York. I spoiled it by kissing you. I had no intention of it, but you looked so vulnerable, so adorable I couldn't help myself. Please tell me, can I hope? Or should I leave you in peace?"

My words came with difficulty. "I'm sorry, sir. I must be very stupid, but I don't understand. You have the pick of society, you can have anyone you please. Unless you want to seduce me. I won't allow that." His physical closeness bemused me, didn't help me one bit.

"My poor love," he said, a warmth in his voice that previously I would never have imagined in him. "This is all very sudden isn't it? Do you think I'm in the habit of seducing respectable unmarried females?" He smiled at my expression, which betrayed my thoughts. That was exactly what I was thinking. A man of society seducing a relatively innocent country girl. My status might have changed in the last day, but my character had not. "My reputation is bad, but not that bad, I can assure you. I kept my philandering for those in a position to welcome it."

"Oh." I was uncertain what he meant. Perhaps I didn't want to understand. I sat quietly for a while, my hand in his, and he let me be. He must have known I needed time to absorb this. "To be frank, I approached women tired of their marriages, or women who sold their favours. At a very high price, but that kind of bargain was often more honest than the other. I never lost myself so thoroughly as to try to seduce young women of good family."

At least he was honest, but one thing still puzzled me. "I'm sorry to be so obtuse. I don't understand why you offered for Miss Cartwright in the first place."

He grimaced. "No more do I, now." I let my hand lie in his, luxuriating in his warmth, allowing myself this small indulgence. "At the time, it seemed the sensible thing to do. I found no sign of a woman I wanted to share my life with— I didn't look for love, you understand, but an agreement with a sensible, attractive woman with whom I could be friends. I'm the heir, and I have a duty, if not to my family, then to the estate and the prosperity of everyone working on it. I'm thirty, and my mother never ceases to remind me that it is time I began the tasks allotted to me by birth, so I settled on a woman who would make few demands of me, one who didn't repel me physically. One I thought would accept my way of life without asking too many questions." His expression was so sincere, it was hard to doubt him. "Then you came along and I saw what I had been looking for all this time. And more." He said it in such a matter-of-fact way that I almost believed him.

My heart lifted, despite my caution. "How could you know? You don't know me, knew even less of me two days ago. You said it yourself."

"I think it's something referred to as a *coup de foudre,* a clap of thunder. Love at first sight. The instant I saw you, I knew you were the person my lonely soul had been looking for. How it happened, why, is a complete mystery to me, but I knew. My brother knew, too."

"You don't mean..." I began, appalled.

"No, no. He knew how I felt, that's all." He grimaced, looking away. "After all these years apart, we still have the ability to read each others' thoughts." He turned his head to me again. "You suspected nothing? You saw *nothing* of how I felt about you?" He seemed incredulous.

"No, how could I? All I know of you is what I've read and been told. I still don't know what to believe. And I was too busy trying to cope with my own feelings." He had been honest with me, as far as I could tell, so I should take a turn now. However shy or reserved I was I owed him that much. "I've never felt anything like this before. I don't know where it came from, what it means. I don't know what to call it or what to do with it. At least—" I looked into his eyes again, and tried to be honest, "—I didn't. I think I love you too."

He drew me close and kissed me again. The desperate desire I had felt in him when first he held me was back in his control. We were sealing some sort of bargain now, having given ourselves a little time to recover from the shock. I could now return his kisses with a little more safety. In any case I couldn't think what else to do. Well bred young ladies were not supposed to think of love, at least, not until they were safely married, and I'd thought that particular fate had passed me by.

Completely content in his embrace, everything stopped for me. He pushed his fingers into my hair to cradle my scalp, murmured, "I knew I was right," and he kissed me again. His mouth was warm and gently demanding on mine. I could think of nothing I'd rather be doing. He pressed against my lips, encouraging me to open my mouth for him and when I did so, he slipped his tongue inside, tasted me as I absorbed his unique flavour, his passion and his need.

The sound of a horse as it walked past outside brought me back to my senses. "My lord, we should go."

He touched my mouth with another kiss, soft and gentle. "Never 'my lord.' Never again, when we are private. Richard, my name is Richard. Say it."

"Richard."

"How do you do that? It never sounded so sweet before." He kissed me again, another bargain sealed.

I smiled, saying, "My name is Rose. Rosalind, actually, but nobody calls me that."

"I can't imagine why. It suits you charmingly. Rose." His lips relaxed into a smile that threatened to melt me into a puddle at his feet.

When I saw the coach looming before us, hiding us from

onlookers but reminding us of the terrible events of the day before, I remembered why we were here and pulled away. "What about the coach strap? What should we do about that?"

His face settled into a serious expression again while he considered what I had asked, but he drew me back into his arms and I was too weak to pull away again. "It's been cut. Only on one side, so the coach would lurch when the strap gave way but the other was too worn to hold the weight on its own. It amounts to murder, but if it becomes known it could cause trouble for you and your family." He studied my face, frowning in concentration. "Will you leave it with me for now? I need a clear head to think and when I look at you, I have anything but a clear head."

I agreed at once. "Of course." I knew I could trust him in this matter. We gazed at each other, hands linked, his good arm around my shoulders, holding me close to his heat.

"We should go."

He agreed, his innate good manners coming to the fore. "Indeed we should. Though I'd prefer to stay here all day, with you. Getting to know you. Confirming what I already feel in my heart." He got to his feet and helped me up. "One more kiss, to take with me?" When I granted him that gladly, he released me.

He held out his good arm. I took it gratefully, needing support.

Passing by the ruined coach, I asked, "What will you do?"

He thought. "Nothing, for the present. There's too much for us to take in, now. We should give it a day or two. I'll have some enquiries put in hand, and we'll see what that turns up." He smiled at me. "And the investigation will give us more time to accustom ourselves to our new discovery."

I didn't flush when I met his gaze. It was almost as if we'd been fated to meet. Although fate had terrible timing.

Chapter Seven

We entered by the side door. Martha, passing by, saw us come in, and stopped, looking at us quizzically. I hoped my new feelings didn't show, but knew better than to take my hand hastily away from his arm.

Martha faced us squarely, disapproval clear on her face. "How are you today, my lord?"

"Much better, ma'am. My valet sent me out for some fresh air. My good nurse kindly offered to accompany me." He glanced at me and I smiled timorously back.

Martha gave me a look full of censure and warning. Lord Strang bowed and went upstairs, while I tried to assuage Martha's suspicions. "We didn't go out of sight of the house."

She pursed her lips, shaking her head. "You should be more careful. That man has a bad reputation."

"I know, Martha. I'll take care." Who would know better than I how well he'd earned his reputation?

We walked to the breakfast room.

I sat as far from Lord Strang—Richard—as I could during the meal, feeling stunned and unreal. Thoughts chased through my head, making no sense at all, but I couldn't bear to be near him in public in case I betrayed my feelings.

Fortunately, most of the household came in to eat so there were a lot of reasons not to look in his direction. Lizzie watched us surreptitiously, probably because of what I'd told her last night. Presently, she began to converse with Mr. Kerre, getting along famously with my lord's brother. I wondered why I wasn't more taken with him. They were so alike, and yet to me a world of difference existed behind those faces.

The crisp, white cloth on the large table complemented the clean cutlery and the fresh, hot food. The kitchen staff and the housekeeper had felt the presence of a competent manager, and had responded to the call.

When Steven arrived, he mentioned he'd been to see the vicar in the village. There would be a double funeral for the late earls the next day, Thursday. It would take place in the private chapel here in the Abbey, but all who wished to attend would be welcome.

James declared himself happy with the arrangements, asking Steven to inform Mr. Pritheroe.

Steven bowed. "Yes, my lord."

James looked at him, his eyes wide with startlement. Sir James had become Lord Hareton overnight, but it would take some time for him to grow used to the idea. I grinned at my brother, and he grinned back. The ten years difference in our ages made little difference to our closeness. "At least I'm still Miss Golightly."

"I thought you'd be a ladyship," James said, frowning.

"No, I'm the sister of an earl. Not the daughter of one. I don't understand it completely myself, but I daresay someone will explain it to us."

"Oh." James's brow cleared. He wasn't the quickest person on the uptake.

Lizzie shook out her napkin with a snap of well-starched linen. "We can be ladies if we wish. There are plenty of precedents for us to use the title."

"Not," Martha said firmly, "until we are certain. After all, Lady Hareton may still be enceinte."

Steven tried to catch my attention. I avoided him, but I knew he wouldn't give up. I would have to face him sooner or later, but not today. No, not today. I risked glancing across the table to Richard, currently engrossed in conversation with James, and took comfort from his presence, although he didn't look my way. Perhaps it was just as well, because I knew I would have given myself away if our eyes met. I looked away to see Steven watching me closely. I forced myself to smile at him.

"I've asked the housekeeper to take me round the house after breakfast," Martha said. "If anyone would care to accompany us, they would be more than welcome."

Most of us agreed to go. We were all very curious to see the state of the house, especially in the light of the recent revelations about the ready availability of money. It raised the question of why all this had happened even more starkly than before. I had agreed to help Martha, so I must go. It would give me something to chase out the thoughts rambling in my restless mind.

To my dismay, Miss Cartwright said, "I'd love to come. I feel so useless. Carier looks after Strang so well there is hardly any need for me to be here." She turned to her fiancé. "Have you the strength to come with us?"

"Of course." He regarded her with a level stare.

"You know, you must let us know if you feel too weak to continue," she said solicitously. "I can send for Carier in an instant." But not help him yourself, I thought, savagely. Whatever his feelings for me, he deserved better than Julia Cartwright.

Richard docilely agreed to accompany his betrothed. Why should she want him with us? I noticed he was paler than earlier, and after such severe blood loss, he needed to rest. "You lost a great deal of blood."

He looked at me, and everything else went away. It could have been the two of us alone in that room. I hated my weakness, marvelling that it should be so, but had enough control left to keep it hidden. I was concerned for him, else I'd have remained silent.

"My good nurse." I wouldn't have thought him capable of such soft tones on Monday. "I promise not to get overtired. I've already promised Carier."

I smiled, nodding. "You should rest until you've recovered your strength, sir."

"I know. Carier said that too."

"That man has too strong a hold on you," said Miss Cartwright. "After we're married, I shall ask you to dismiss him."

"I'm afraid you are doomed to disappointment in that respect." Richard's voice regained a chill. "No one shaves me as close as he does or has his way with a neckcloth. He has me hog-tied and I can no longer do without him."

At least he had looked away from me, but that chill in his voice reminded me that he was formidable, capable of great iciness. He possessed vast experience, much more than I had. I must be wary.

I pushed back my chair. "I should change." I could eat nothing more, though I'd had very little.

"Wear something old," Martha warned. "Whatever you wear is bound to become soiled. Those rooms haven't been touched in ten years or more."

I changed into my drab travelling gown with a heavy heart. I so wanted to show Richard that I could look attractive when in the right clothes, but I seemed to live exclusively in old clothes these days.

I stepped into a small hoop that wouldn't get in the way of the furniture. For formal wear and Court appearances side hoops were *de rigeur*, but thankfully, except for Court, much smaller than they'd been ten years ago. Briefly, I wondered if I would have to wear finery every day if I married a nobleman. Miss Cartwright certainly did.

Downstairs, I found quite a crowd in the Great Hall. Martha, James, the two Misses Cartwright, Lizzie, Steven, Richard, Mr. Kerre and a female servant. Quite a crowd.

"This is Mrs. Peters," Martha said. "She was promoted from head parlourmaid and retained as housekeeper after the third earl died."

The woman curtseyed. Like the manor's other inhabitants, she was half starved and thin. Her gaunt face showed unhappiness, stoicism, lines graven deeply, making it impossible to guess her age.

Mrs. Peters took a deep breath, turned to us in a businesslike manner, and began the tour, just as she might have done to visitors, had there been any. She pointed out the treasures of the Great Hall; the life sized statues that had been brought back by the third earl from the Grand Tour. We went upstairs and into the State Rooms.

They must have been magnificent once. "Goodness," Lizzie said.

The first room was a drawing room. Huge satin upholstered sofas stood against the tapestry hung walls, enormous gilded pier glasses set over half moon tables between the windows, silent portraits of ancestors hung on the walls.

Everything had been shockingly abandoned. This was the realisation of Sleeping Beauty's Palace, and it looked as though it had been abandoned for the legendary hundred years instead of the actual ten.

"It's been like this since the third earl's death, my lady," Mrs. Peters said.

"Ten years?" Martha dragged her gaze away from the murky magnificence before us to stare incredulously at the housekeeper.

I looked around, hardly daring to draw breath. Who would kill for all this, who would cut the traces of a battered old coach? Someone pained to see treasures like this left to rot, or someone who wanted to get their hands on it all? Even in this condition it was worth a lot of money and the contents of the house wouldn't be included in the entail, so didn't have to go to the heir. Perhaps it was for gain, after all. Or to cover something up. It would be easy to steal treasures from these rooms. I studied the rooms with more purpose, looking for where the dust was less thick, revealing the absence of a treasure, but I could see none.

Miss Cartwright repeatedly moved her gleaming lilac satin skirts away from the dust-encrusted furniture. Her supercilious expression showed what she thought of such a ramshackle place—she didn't bother to hide her disdain. The expression marred her pretty, round face. She would do well to hide it. I chided myself for ill wishing her. She had done me no wrong, not yet. I just didn't like her.

Her betrothed didn't look at me beyond an initial cold bow, but joined his brother. They walked around the room, and examined the treasures there. Mr. Kerre seemed very knowledgeable, and pointed out several items of distinction in the cold, unlived in room.

Martha carried a cloth, and from time to time, she wiped away a part of the dirt to see what lay underneath. She seemed satisfied with her investigations, and occasionally made a comment about the quality of the things on display, all of it fine. I joined her, glad of the opportunity to stay by her side.

Steven moved closer to me but I tried not to look at him. I wanted to hold my happy secret to myself, just for this day, and not face any problems until tomorrow.

The interior decoration in the room wasn't particularly distinguished, like a plain wooden box that held diamonds inside it. The treasures in the rooms indicated collectors of rare and beautiful things. "The third earl," Mrs. Peters told us, "always planned to decorate the interiors as elaborately as the outside of the Abbey but at his death everything changed, and the rooms were all closed." The curtains had been drawn and some of the great windows opened, but the fusty, unpleasant smell of disuse still permeated the air. Black mould encroached at the edges of the ceiling, and if left unchecked would destroy everything here.

The great Rooms of State were arranged in enfilade at the front of the house, so when the doors all lay open, the onlooker saw the end of the procession of rooms from the beginning. They were grand indeed, but in their heyday they would have intimidated, too. I understood why Martha had been so nervous at the prospect of another visit here, even when she assumed the house was being run properly.

"We'll come again in a day or two," Martha said to me. "Then we can bring a notebook and make our plans."

I saw Martha had already cast me in the same mould I had at home—that of dutiful spinster, a helpmeet to my sister-in-law. To help with the revival of such a great house had its appeal, but one way or another, I would have a life of my own, with or without my newfound love. I shot one or two looks at him, and Lizzie saw me once and frowned, but he seemed sublimely unaware of my presence. He didn't look at me once. I found his self control unnerving; I wondered if I could live with that.

At the end of the enfilade Miss Cartwright declared she would like to go back to her room and rest, so Richard offered to accompany her. I was glad to see him go, as I found his presence increasingly unsettling, afraid someone would notice. He didn't look at me, but his hand gently brushed mine, as though by accident, when they passed close by me.

With him gone, I felt entire once more, as though he had leeched me of my own self. Then I understood what Lizzie had meant last night, that I should keep myself intact in his presence. It would have been so easy to succumb without reserve, to do whatever he wanted me to do, but I would have to fight to retain my own independence of spirit.

Steven also left us, saying he had arrangements to make in the chapel. He had found the old vestments and sacred vessels locked in a cupboard, and commandeered all the maids he could find to clean and polish the chapel in readiness for the funeral the next day. "The maids won't work there on their own."

"Why ever not?" Martha asked.

"Because of the two earls lying in state there."

"Afraid they'll jump up and attack them?" Amusement coloured Mr. Kerre's voice.

Steven glared at him. "Just so. But I'd like to check on the progress and make certain everything is ready for the funeral."

Steven left, with a speaking glance at me. He wanted to meet me, perhaps to make good his hold over me. He must have known it had been weakening for weeks, but he couldn't know by how much.

To our surprise, the elder Miss Cartwright decided to stay. To our greater surprise, when on her own she proved to be a capable, practical woman, offering useful suggestions.

We went into the wing at the end of the enfilade, and found a dismal series of rooms. Before the Haretons had abandoned the greater part of the building, these had been the family rooms. An old piece of embroidery, still only half finished, sat in its frame by a window, and books lay on tables. Dust smothered everything.

"I'd like to restore this wing," said Martha. "We'll live in the west wing, for now, and move here if we stay. It's a shame to waste such potentially pleasant rooms."

"Do you plan to redecorate?" asked Mr. Kerre.

"I shall have to decorate some of the rooms. The upholstery is perished and there's mould creeping in. If only they had used dust covers." Martha sighed deeply, giving her ample bosom some exercise, her mind evidently on all the beautiful things that had been destroyed here by simple neglect.

We left the rest of the east wing for another day.

Martha took Lizzie to the kitchen, to direct the maids in a thorough scrub down. "For it's clear they need personal direction, and I won't eat out of the gutter any longer." That was Martha's way of indicating that the corners hadn't been swept in a long time.

✧

Martha had instituted the kind of meal we were used to at breakfast the next morning: a sideboard packed with dishes of hot food to which we helped ourselves. It was pleasing to have such a semblance of normality, almost as though we were at home again.

Richard still had his arm in a sling, but his colour was healthier and his posture better than on the previous day. He still wore a country coat. "Carier is fonder of my coats than of me, but that is what one looks for in a valet, after all." That drew a laugh from most of the company.

I had reason to believe this wasn't true, but he must wish to hide his valet's obvious devotion to him. Careful not to meet his look at all during the meal for fear I might give myself away, and deeply aware of my inexperience, I kept my head down. My night had been broken by fitful dreams that I couldn't remember properly after I'd woke up.

The door burst open, admitting two manservants carrying Mr. Pritheroe. In my agitation, I had forgotten his plight, and I felt guilty that I'd neglected him. The men struggled over to a vacant seat and installed him.

The self-proclaimed minister was dressed in aggressively simple homespun country clothes, and gave out his good mornings unsmilingly. "The doctor has instructed me to eat, to restore my strength. I do not indulge unduly in pleasures of the flesh, but I must think of my people." For a man who ate so little, he carried much excess weight. He had considerable presence. One must notice him, listen to him, though his words seemed to me to be nonsense when I thought them through properly. I began to see how he could attract people to his cause.

"I hope you will permit me to preach a short sermon this morning." He seemed to have only one pitch for his voice, and that was very loud, developed from years of preaching in the open, I presumed. Steven had to agree to his request, although he'd previously told us he planned only a small ceremony.

We'd barely known the late earls. It seemed hypocritical to mourn them with great ceremony, though the County would expect it, if only because of the consequence of the two dead men.

Lady Hareton had said her husband and his brother wouldn't have wished for any great ceremony, but they must be laid to rest in the family vault. It mattered little to me what they did. Ladies were not usually required to attend funerals, so I would spend the day helping Martha and Mrs. Peters. I wouldn't pretend grief for someone I'd met once, and disliked. Neither would I parade this, so I kept quiet.

"I was a Great Sinner until I found God." Now, we were forced to listen to Mr. Pritheroe's stentorian tones, as it would have been difficult to talk over them. "Then, one day, in the middle of a corn field, He made His desires known to me." I heard Lizzie suppress a snigger, and I too suppressed a giggle, just as though we were schoolroom misses.

Mr. Pritheroe didn't seem to notice. "He needed a valiant band of people to travel the world, spread His word, help His people see the light." So far, it sounded reasonable, if unusual. "I sold my property and took my wife and child to see the world. God said, unless I followed His word to the letter, He feared disaster." His voice rose at the end of his sentences, as though he preferred to make announcements, rather than conduct conversations.

The preacher began to hit his stride. He buttered toast while he spoke, and then took great bites and sprayed the assembled company with his half-masticated crumbs, showing all of us the tender morsel in his mouth as he spoke and ate. Fortunate to be at the other end of the table, I tried not to look. "I read the Bible from cover to cover and I strongly recommend you all to do the same," our lecturer announced. He looked round at his fascinated audience. "It will show you the error of your ways, the sin the rich are subject to, and the punishments which await the sinners in Death." He lowered his voice dramatically at that last word and paused for effect.

"What would they be?" Richard enquired, with no trace of irony detectable in his voice.

"They are eternal damnation for the rich who keep their riches to themselves and flaunt them in sinful ways," roared Mr. Pritheroe. "There are punishments for the immoral that will make you shudder in your skin. It is all there for anyone to read. Pestilence will visit the vain, and send them boils dripping pus and blood."

Martha tutted. Mr. Pritheroe glanced at her, and turned his speech a little. "The immoral will lose the offending parts and be made to suffer foul torment."

Martha went back to her breakfast. She would find foul

torment acceptable for the breakfast table, but not distasteful descriptions.

The Kerre brothers watched him with rapt attention. Their faces were grave, but their eyes betrayed their intense interest in this odd person.

"Divorce is a great sin." The minister applied yet another slice of toast to his ever-open orifice. "When a man cleaves to a woman he must do this for life. Only God can separate them."

"What if she commits adultery?" Richard leaned his chin on his good hand and turned a face of calm interest to our interlocutor.

"God does not permit carnal relations," Mr. Pritheroe said gravely. We all digested this statement in silence, but the sensation it made was almost audible, as its meaning slowly became clear to all of us.

"Then how are children made?" Mr. Kerre asked him, with every semblance of interest.

"In fifty years there will be no need for children. In the year 1800 Armageddon will come." Pritheroe threw his arms out wide and the remainder of his toast flew through the air in a dramatic gesture that took us all by surprise.

The toast hit me. Everyone turned to where I sat and I wanted the floor to swallow me up. Mr. Pritheroe begged my pardon in a voice no less booming than his lecture.

I smiled wanly and peeled the offending item off my skirt, wondering if I could use the opportunity to excuse myself. I wasn't sure the brothers would stop baiting the man before he had an apoplexy. Obviously deranged, Mr. Pritheroe's face had turned as red as a drunk's with the effort of his speech, but not with any embarrassment at flinging his breakfast in my direction. He subsided, but only for a time, until he had gathered his thoughts for another tirade.

James managed to take charge now, since a natural pause was reached. "I thought I might have the family part of the house to rights before I send for the others," he said, a little louder than usual, his ears probably numbed by Mr. Pritheroe's ringing tones, but otherwise he behaved as though this breakfast was quite normal. "I've sent them a letter, to inform them of the sad occurrences of the last few days, and I told them to get their mourning clothes out. Martha and I have decided six months would be appropriate, three in full mourning and three in half mourning." There were murmurs of agreement.

"I'll go into York next week and buy the necessary materials," Martha said. "We're unlikely to receive any mourning visits, so if the present company doesn't object, we will go about in our ordinary clothes until the rest of our things arrive."

"It would perhaps be better than no clothes at all." Lizzie's observation made everybody laugh and broke the tension in the room. The minister now seemed content to leave the rest of his sermon for the funeral oration, and the brothers ceased to bait him.

Then the door opened on our laughter, and it faded away in an instant as Lady Hareton came in. She had dressed in the deepest, unrelieved black, her small face pale, but composed. This was the first time anyone but Martha and her maid had seen her since the accident.

She had lost even more weight. She seemed so ethereal a good wind might have blown her away. "Good morning. Good morning, Father." She bowed to Pritheroe.

This stopped everybody, and the ordinary meal returned to the realms of the unusual. We'd had no idea the Dowager Countess and the minister were related. Nothing the man had said or done had informed us of any relationship. He'd not asked after the health of his daughter nor had he asked to see her, and the thought of such selfish callousness made me feel a little unwell.

Now he put his hand on her head, murmured a blessing and let her go to the end of the table.

Richard seated her next to me. I felt his hand on my shoulder for the smallest moment as he moved away, and I shivered at his touch. I despised my body for being so weak. He could so easily be playing with me; enjoying my reactions to his tiny gestures of affection, but I couldn't stop responding to him. I could, however, keep it to myself.

I asked Lady Hareton if she would like me to help her to anything on the sideboard. "You are very kind. Just a little, please."

I stood, picked up a clean plate and then found the best morsels for her. Thanks to Martha, who had discovered the chafing dishes the previous evening and pressed them into service this morning, the food was still hot, if a little dry by now.

"I should like to attend my husband's funeral." The lady looked straight at her father.

"I think you should do so." Her father's voice came relatively quieter, though it could still have been heard from one side of a field to the other. "You should show your respects to the man who fed and clothed you for the last ten years."

"Yes, Father." Lady Hareton began to eat. Idle chatter seemed intrusive with her quiet presence and the room fell silent. Lady Hareton put her knife down and addressed Martha. "I hope you are finding your way around. I always find it very difficult, I can never remember where things are kept."

"Don't you keep written records?" Martha asked gently.

"I cannot write," replied her ladyship.

After another stunned pause, the minister kindly explained, "Women's brains were created for obedience and housework, not ideas. They should know their place."

Well, that put paid to me joining his religion. I'd always taken great pleasure in reading and I found unquestioning obedience difficult at the best of times. Lady Hareton couldn't read or write, not because of any inability in herself, but because her father had deliberately kept her ignorant. What a horrible thought. I couldn't think of anything more cruel. That explained why she found it difficult to run the house. We had every reason to suspect her husband had kept her short of housekeeping money. Not knowing how to read recipes, wage bills, laundry lists and the like, it would be impossible for anyone not having a perfect memory.

I glanced at Martha who looked as incredulous as I felt. "I will help you to learn, if you would like." The lady cast a dark glance at her father. I interpreted it as hatred, but I must surely be wrong; I hadn't credited Lady Hareton with any spirit.

"I cannot allow it," her father replied. "It is not a woman's place to learn."

"Can the lady not make up her own mind?" Strang's face was calm, though the light tremor in his voice betrayed his anger.

"I will guide her in this," stated Mr. Pritheroe. "When her husband lived, he had a duty to instruct her. Now that he has sadly left us for a better place, I shall give her the guidance she needs."

"Lady Hareton is welcome to stay here as long as she wishes," James put in, angry and not bothering to hide it. He hated any form of bullying. He always had, even as a small boy. Only his good manners held him back from further comment.

"We appreciate the hospitality, but, when I have recovered, we will continue with the ministry." Pritheroe continued to eat. I watched him, concerned I might find myself the recipient of more unwanted bounty.

"Lady Hareton will, I hope, make up her own mind." By Martha's tone, I knew she'd decided to take the lady under her wing. Martha was born to be a mother, a caretaker, and she showed it in whatever she did. The minister shrugged, a gesture Martha might well consider a declaration of war. She would enjoy it.

"Another thing," Mr. Pritheroe said. "I know the Lord Hareton, of blessed memory did not have time to change his will in the way he would have wished. I thought I might speak to you about that, my lord."

James gave him a darkling glare. "Please come to my office after breakfast and we will discuss it all you like." Which meant, *No, over my dead body, I would rather give it to highwaymen than to you.* However, Mr. Pritheroe didn't know James as well as we did and appeared pleased with his progress, agreeing with alacrity.

Chapter Eight

The entertainment concluded, I excused myself. Martha had asked me to count and list the bed sheets upstairs, so I went straight upstairs and busied myself at the task. I heard the bell toll. I didn't know the chapel had a bell, but Steven had found it, and he made good use of it. In short order an echoing bell followed it from the church in the village. A figure hurried up the drive, on foot, his clothing indicating he was the village vicar. He had come alone.

I put my list down and watched from the window. Soon a gaggle of young women also came up the drive on foot. Unlike the solemn demeanour of the cleric, they laughed and nudged each other in some private joke. I assumed they must be the girls from the village. The men were due to come up later, when James had time to interview them.

A noise caused me to turn. Lizzie stood there, clad in a large apron much like the one I wore. My heart sank because I knew she wanted to speak to me. I'd avoided her since my encounter with Richard yesterday, pretending to be asleep when she came to bed the night before. Now that Martha had located sufficient bedding, we needn't share a room after tonight.

"How do you feel today?"

"I feel very well," I replied, in a useless attempt to fend her off.

Lizzie clicked her tongue in annoyance. "Don't try to put me off, you know quite well what I mean. Your foolish infatuation."

"Oh, that." I toyed with the idea of lying to her, but I

couldn't. I was very bad at lying, especially to my sister. I turned away and picked up a sheet to fold and add to the pile, avoiding her censorious eyes. "I saw him yesterday. I went to the stables and he saw me there. You'll never guess what we found."

"Do tell," said Lizzie flatly, with no enthusiasm at all. She lifted a pile of towels out of the cupboard and began to go through them, to look for damage or wear.

"You know the straps which hold a coach up?"

"The suspension, yes," said my sister absently.

"We're fairly sure the one at the back had been cut." I tried to make my voice as dramatic as I could; anything to keep her away from the other matter.

"It probably had been cut," Lizzie replied, "By the men when they righted the coach and brought it home."

"They had no reason to do that. In fact, it looks very much as if it had been cut deliberately."

I couldn't distract Lizzie from her original intention. "I'm sure there's a reasonable explanation. So what did you get up to, with your Lord Strang?"

I couldn't help but tell her, so I decided to get it over with. "He kissed me. And he said he loves me." I blushed at my own foolishness; it sounded so silly even to my own ears. I turned away and put some torn sheets on the relevant pile, so she wouldn't be able to see my confusion.

I heard her sharp intake of breath and the soft thump as she put the towels down. "I thought you were my *older* sister," she said, with all the emotion she had omitted from the previous subject. "But you have no more sense than a baby. Didn't I tell you how dangerous he is? Dear God, Rose, haven't you more sense than that?"

I regained some control over my complexion, and turned back to face her. "He says he's asked Miss Cartwright to break the betrothal contract."

"Please be careful, Rose, please. You mustn't ruin your chances now, and if you ruin yours, you go a long way towards ruining mine."

Lizzie was right. To enter society under a cloud after all those years of longing would be disastrous for her, but I hadn't remembered that until now.

"I'll be careful, Lizzie, I promise." I meant it, but I couldn't promise not to meet him again. When he'd touched me at breakfast the feeling had been delicious, even that casual, possibly accidental contact. I wanted to feel it again, my body yearned for it, but I wasn't so far gone that I couldn't see the risks.

"Shall I tell you what they say about Lord Strang?" Lizzie said in a small, hard voice. If I'd said no, she would have taken no notice, so I kept silent while she told me. "He has seduced more women and had more affairs than anyone else in society. Husbands keep their wives away from him if they want to keep them for themselves. When he visits a house party, it's frequently to carry on an intrigue, and he never seems to be there with the same woman twice."

She watched me closely. I met her look with equanimity. She sighed. "I know why it is, it's your lack of experience. You fell into his arms like a ripe plum." She could be right. Flushing, I looked down at the thin towels I had pulled out from the unlocked cupboard. Dry, crumbly herbs fell from the folds. "Well amuse yourself by all means, but he's strong meat, Rose. You're no match for him. Neither am I, come to that."

I tensed. "Has he approached you?"

"No," she admitted. "The first man in ages who hasn't. Perhaps he's saving me for later."

No. No, I couldn't believe that.

Lizzie remembered something. "But he's not the first, is he? There's Drury." She knew all about that particular problem. "You did the same with him, responded too strongly, too quickly. Back away, Rose, think."

She was right. "I know. And I promise I'll be careful. But the two cases don't compare at all. I was bored and desperate when Steven approached me. He seemed so desperate, so madly in love with me that I felt sorry for him. I've never felt for him what I felt yesterday."

"What was that?"

"Hard to describe, really. Complete contentment, a sense of rightness. I know it looks wrong, but I must see what it is, what he means by it. I think I have enough control to stop him seducing me. I don't think he means to. He says he doesn't seduce inexperienced maids."

A silence fell. Lizzie took her bottom lip between her teeth, thinking, while I sorted through more linen. "Yes. He might have a point, at that. Of all the accounts I've read of him, he doesn't go in for innocents."

I laughed. "I'm too old to be completely innocent."

"Don't be silly, Rose. I keep telling you, twenty-five isn't on the shelf."

"It is when you're here." I was sorry for my words when I saw her stricken look. "I didn't mean it like that, Lizzie, but no one pays any attention to me after they've seen you." I smiled. "I don't mind, really I don't." I was lying. My sister was a kind-hearted soul, and couldn't help the beaux's reactions to her stunning good looks but it did hurt when they constantly passed me by to get to her.

"Why don't you go home and marry Tom?" asked Lizzie.

"Tom?" Tom Skerrit was the son of the neighbouring squire at home. We had played together as children. "Tom doesn't think of me in those terms. He's just a friend. He likes vapid, blonde girls."

"Oh, I see." Lizzie didn't sound in the least convinced. "But I've seen him look at you sometimes, when he thinks no one is looking. I don't think he quite believes it himself, but I'm sure he thinks of you very warmly indeed."

I thought of Tom; tall, dark, gangling, my partner in all kinds of childhood mischief. I smiled. "It would be comfortable, a good arrangement. But I still don't believe you." In any case, I didn't feel the same lurch in my stomach for Tom as I did when I looked at Richard.

Lizzie sat on a rickety chair, the only seat on this narrow

landing. She'd made no attempt yet to help with the linen. I stood by the open door of a large linen cupboard, now almost empty of its contents. They lay in piles on the floor: sheets to keep, towels to keep and a rough pile of discards, to turn into rags and cloths. I took the last pile of towels from the cupboard.

I owed my sister my honesty. "I want him. If I can have him, I want him. It's the first time I've ever felt like that about anyone, the first time I've been so sure. If I can't have him, I'll live with it. I'll have to, but it won't come again. Not for me."

She looked at me without flinching. "I'm sorry you have chosen someone so dangerous. If you slip, if you let him seduce you, you could create a scandal that affects us all. Anything from our side would ruin any chances Ruth and I might have."

"Oh, Lizzie, of course I won't do anything foolish." What could I do but promise her I'd be careful?

"And another thing. If you should succeed, if he does want to marry you, he'll have to persuade Miss Cartwright to break the marriage contract. I've been watching her and I don't think she'll do that easily. Have you thought how much a breach of promise suit could cost? It could ruin us all."

The practicalities and the scandal associated with such a case would wipe out our newfound prosperity and status. His, too. I'd be prepared to face poverty with him, but I couldn't subject my family to the same fate. "I'll be careful. He's asked Miss Cartwright to break the contract, but she said no. I won't do anything foolish. I may be innocent, Lizzie, but I'm not stupid."

If he were to marry Miss Cartwright after all, I would die of anguish. I couldn't bear to think that he might touch someone else in that way when he should be touching me, even talking to her in that intimate, caressing style. I wanted him for myself. I shut the thought off. We had a long way to go before I could let myself think about that.

Lizzie watched me, her lower lip between her teeth, a habit she had when she was thinking. "Lord Strang's reckless behaviour has eased of late, by all accounts, ever since his brother returned from abroad. Maybe Mr. Kerre has a beneficial influence on him. But still, Rose, take care."

"I will."

There was no point continuing with that part of the conversation, so we went on to discuss Pritheroe's behaviour. "What sort of minister keeps half his congregation ignorant and passive?" Lizzie asked.

In this matter at least we were wholly in accord. "She has been kept ignorant. And maybe celibate."

"I can't see that. A man needs his pleasures, especially in marriage. The Church says in the marriage service that it's the duty of a married couple to procreate. Do you think they married properly?"

I looked at her curiously, a torn sheet in my hands. "I think it's immaterial. If she proves to be in the family way, James will be off to Devonshire faster than lightning. He'd be the last one to prefer a lawsuit."

"I suppose so," said Lizzie, with a sigh. She looked up at me brightly. "But everyone seems to think it's a done thing."

I agreed, and we went on with our work.

We finished the sorting and went downstairs to help Martha until it was time to dress for dinner. I wouldn't be able to wear colours for much longer. I did so want to show Richard I could wear clothes with style, so I fished out the best gown I had brought with me. Then I forced the maid Martha had sent up to pull my laces tight.

Unfortunately, the girl couldn't dress hair, so Lizzie and I did each other's. My rich brown locks had a mind of their own. They were dreadfully unruly, both a blessing and a curse. It did away with the need for curling papers, but was difficult to keep in any sort of style. Lizzie dressed it simply, and when I looked at my reflection the mirror showed gleaming red-brown highlights. I looked quite pretty, a miracle in the circumstances. Lizzie took extra time preparing for her entrance, so I decided to go down before her.

I was on my way downstairs when I saw Steven. My heart sank and I wished I'd waited for Lizzie now. He beckoned me into an empty room. With a heavy heart I followed, staying near the door. I wouldn't allow him to close it.

"Did the funeral go well?" I asked in an attempt to find some way to avoid personal conversation.

He grimaced. "Well enough. Mr. Pritheroe only preached for an hour, when I thought it might be closer to three." He waved the subject away carelessly. "Won't you kiss me?" He gave me that puppy dog look which used to make him look appealing, but I ignored it. I found it pathetic now, and wondered how I ever imagined myself attracted to him in the first place.

"I hope Lady Hareton didn't object to being the only lady there," I said coolly.

"I don't think so." He didn't seem interested. "Lord Hareton asked me if I would like to continue here as chaplain for the present, and in time I could take one of the livings within his gift. Several are vacant."

I wondered who he meant by "Lord Hareton," then remembered it was James.

Steven took a turn about the room. "It's what we always dreamed of." He threw his arms out in a dramatic gesture. "Remember those days in the orchard last year? I said I would offer for you, if only I had a decent living?" Unfortunately, I did, and could only be thankful I'd made no promises to him then.

As the younger scion of a respectable country family, he'd had to make his own way. While I sympathised with his lot in life, I couldn't approve of his way of trying to make his fortune. Tall, dark and classically featured, he charmed every eligible female in the district before he landed on me—the most desperate, and therefore the most promising. I saw now what my needy self had failed to see at the time. I also saw how difficult it would be to get rid of him now. He might be happy with one of the livings, but he must realise my dowry would be considerably more than I previously expected. That would undoubtedly weigh heavily with him. I remembered the rumours about him and the poorer girls in the district that I had previously discounted. They might very well be true.

My heart sank. Whatever happened, I wouldn't let Steven

trap me.

He took a step toward me. "Is there anything wrong?" He held out his arms but I indicated the open door, shaking my head.

"No, nothing, but it's not wise to meet like this." I despised myself for lacking the courage to tell him I wanted to break with him. I couldn't bring myself to do it and face the inevitable commotion he would be bound to make.

"Should I speak to Lord Hareton? Tell him how it is between us? We could meet more openly then, be truly a couple." His eagerness was frightening me with its intensity.

I nearly panicked, but I forced down my fright. I could deny it, if I had to. After all, I'd done nothing to be ashamed of. I'd made no promises, hadn't compromised myself. A few clandestine meetings were all, to listen to him, let him kiss me. My imagination had done the rest. I couldn't believe how stupid I'd been to let him cajole me in this way, but his looks and his address had flattered me into ignoring his more insalubrious habits.

"I don't think that would be appropriate. James has a lot to think about at the moment. We should let him settle matters first."

"You haven't forgotten your promises," he said gently.

I edged towards the door. "I made no promises. I wasn't in a position to make any, if you remember."

"Of course, of course," he said soothingly, but frowning in concern.

I didn't want him talking to anyone, so I said hurriedly, "We'll speak again," and left the room.

Martha had worked wonders in one afternoon. No longer were we confined to the one clean room in the house. While we had been upstairs sorting the linen, Martha had found some "perfectly serviceable" rooms in the bleak family wing and set her new army of servants to make them habitable. The upholstery had been taken outside, beaten to within an inch of

101

its life; the wooden furniture had been cleaned and polished. Fires had been set in the grates. Martha apologised for the lack of a fire in the dining room. She explained it smoked so badly she'd had it extinguished.

We complimented her on her cleverness. She said it had only needed hard work by more people than previously allowed on the premises, but the compliments pleased her.

His valet had allowed Richard a finer coat for his dinner, but he still held his arm in a sling. I cleared my throat and asked him how he did. "Tolerably well, madam" he replied coolly, but his eyes betrayed him when I dared to look at him directly. They held a new warmth for me. "Carier says I'll be able to discard this sling in a day or two, but he doubts I'll be fit enough to travel before the week's end. If that should inconvenience you, your ladyship," he said, turning to Martha, "please don't hesitate to mention it. I can easily find accommodation in York."

"My lord, I wouldn't dream of such a thing." Martha bridled at this insult to her hospitality, as he must have known such a hospitable woman would. "You must stay until you're perfectly well again."

He smiled and bowed, but Miss Cartwright looked dismayed. Perhaps this place bored her. Difficult to say, since she rarely ventured an opinion about anything. She appeared to be her usual immaculate, fashionable self, completely self-contained, betraying little except ennui.

The dinner was far superior to any we had consumed here, despite its simplicity. It consisted of only two courses, but that was one more than in the previous regime, verging on the respectable. Martha would soon have this place run as well as the manor at home. I guessed if she had inherited the Abbey as a fully functional country house, it would have intimidated her, but this way she'd settle in as countess before she fully realised it.

Lady Hareton had wanted to keep to the seclusion of her room. Her father had likewise refused to join us for dinner, though Martha assured us he wouldn't starve. He'd said he'd take dinner with his daughter in the small parlour, thus demanding her presence and snubbing us. I suspected this gave him pleasure. He seemed to enjoy upsetting people, but I can't say I cared overmuch.

In his absence, dinner was a convivial meal. There was tension, but I acquitted myself well. I sat next to Mr. Kerre who, whatever he suspected, treated me with consideration and kindness. He never once alluded in any way to his brother's feelings for me, and could even be said to show some interest himself. At least Lizzie seemed to think so, when the ladies withdrew for tea.

"You seem to have made a conquest there," she said in an undertone.

The Misses Cartwright and Martha sat apart from us, so we had a semblance of privacy. Miss Cartwright regaled my sister-in-law with tales of the conditions which prevailed in the other family estates of her acquaintance, especially that of Eyton, where she would soon be welcomed as a new bride. I tried not to listen, finding her descriptions of the house and her new position a raw wound.

"I think Gervase Kerre is taken with you," Lizzie said archly, behind her fan.

"Nonsense." I said. "He was only being polite."

"Do you like him as well as the other? That might be your solution, you know. Myself, I don't know how you can discriminate between them. They seem so alike."

"They are entirely different."

Lizzie frowned. "You should try. If Mr. Kerre shows an interest in you, it would prove an entirely possible match. I don't think you have any chances elsewhere. I would as leif avoid them both, but if you must have one, go for the younger."

"It's not like that. It's not something I *wish* for at all."

"Then you must suffer," Lizzie said. "I know these things pass."

I wasn't at all sure I wanted it to pass but arguing with her was fruitless and would only upset us both. I changed the subject and reminded Lizzie about our other discovery in the stables, the severed strap. "I think I'll go to see it for myself," she said. "If you're right about it, then James must be told. If you're not, you'll worry him for nothing."

"That had occurred to me, too," I said a trifle tartly. "Shall I take you in the morning?"

"Yes please." She might have an ulterior motive. If she went with me, I couldn't meet Richard again, if I'd planned to. I was grateful for her help, but annoyed with her for interfering. After all, she had shown no interest in the coach accident earlier in the day.

Chapter Nine

Lizzie was as good as her word. The next morning we went to the coach house together. After seeing the strap, she agreed with me the break looked too clean to be merely wear and tear. Someone had deliberately cut it.

A worried frown marred her perfect features. "We must tell James. But only when we can speak to him privately." At last, we were in total agreement, and it put me in better temper with her.

We decided to go back in to find our brother, but as we turned to leave the doorway darkened, and Richard came in. My heart sank. Perhaps he'd hoped to find me alone. Then I saw that James was close behind him. They bowed good morning while we returned the courtesy, giving me time to order my thoughts.

Richard glanced at me in warning. "I see someone else had the same idea as we did. It may serve to confirm my suspicions. Did you notice anything amiss, ma'am?" he said to Lizzie.

Lizzie indicated the bit of leather. "My sister noticed a problem with this strap yesterday. I wanted to see it for myself, before bothering James. You have so much on your mind at present." She smiled placatingly at James. "We didn't want to bother you with it if we had any doubt."

"I, on the other hand, have no doubts, about this." Richard took the strap from Lizzie's unresisting hands. "See for yourself, sir." He held it out to James. "The other side only confirms it. The strap has been severed nearly through, and left to finish the job for itself. The coach is in such a state of disrepair the perpetrator relied upon no one bothering to examine it. After all, you can't repair such a wreck, you can only have it destroyed."

James looked cynical, but he walked forward and examined the strap.

Eventually, he put a hand up to his mouth, rubbed his chin and sighed deeply. This problem settled on his shoulders. "There's no doubt about it. The strap has been cut. It's certainly the direct cause of the accident. I think this family owes you an apology, Strang. Someone in this household wanted someone on that coach dead. Whoever it was, he caused your injury."

Richard shook his head. "I need no apology, sir. After all, it was entirely my fault I was aboard the coach. My mother always said my curiosity would kill me, and this time she was very nearly right." He gave a wry smile. "I can't think, however, that the news would give her very much satisfaction."

A thought occurred to me, and without thinking first, I blurted it out. "Why use such an uncertain way of doing it? The accident might have injured people but not killed anyone at all. There was no glass in the windows to increase the danger, and coaches overturn every day with less serious results." Richard gazed at me steadily, an arresting expression on his face.

I looked away hastily, as he continued with my thought. "Then.... someone may have only wished to harm the occupants, or to give them a fright?"

We all paused, as we tried to work out the implications of this. "Who on earth could have wanted to do that?" James turned away from the coach, to face Lizzie and me, dropping the strap as if it burned him.

"With your permission, that's what I would like to try to find out," said Richard. "If you call in the authorities, the thing must reach the press, and I'm afraid the resulting publicity might do your family a great deal of harm."

"Oh God." Lizzie turned pale. With such a scandal, she would find things even more difficult in London. "So close. So close to everything I ever wanted. This could take it all away." She blushed in shame when she caught Richard's gaze. "I—I'm sorry, sir, it must seem so heartless to you. It's just that—that I've dreamed of a season for years, and when I realised it might be possible it drowned out everything else."

Richard patted her hand. "Society cannot be denied the opportunity of your company, ma'am. But if this thing should become known, I'm afraid the papers would make hay with it." He released her hand. "You're unknown to society, and if it becomes known that any suspicion exists about the deaths of the previous earls of Hareton, I'm afraid it will be the next *cause célèbre*. My reassurance that you had nothing to do with it won't count for much, I'm afraid, unless we can find out more about it."

"So we need to keep this to ourselves," James said grimly. "Do you think I should destroy the coach?"

Richard held up a restraining hand. "No. It's your only proof. If I can find who did this, and it was, as I believe, nothing to do with you or your family, it might be as well to bring the attention to the authorities to it, and have it cleared up. You'll still carry a certain amount of notoriety, but it won't do you any harm in the long run. Especially once people get to know you."

"But—we can't appear like that." The thought of appearing in society frightened me enough, without this complication.

He smiled reassuringly and met my eyes. I tried not to catch my breath. "Everything will be fine, but we must be careful."

I took comfort from his words, but it seemed Lizzie did not. "Fine for you to say. We'll never be accepted now."

Richard smiled reassuringly. "I'm sure it won't come to that," he said in soothing tones, as he might to a child thwarted of a toy. "I've been of some service in matters like this before, and I've seen far worse than this. Polite society prefers to keep its dirty linen away from the public eye."

I understood my sister better than he did. She would think first of others, but in this case the only people who stood to lose were us. And she had longed, year after year, for a society presentation, a life at the centre of affairs. To receive it, only to have it cruelly snatched away would devastate her.

James rubbed his chin again; his habitual gesture when he thought hard. We waited for him. He sighed again. "I don't like to put you to such trouble, my lord. Our sorry business is hardly your concern."

"Please don't think of it like that," Richard answered. "Such problems divert me."

James's brow cleared. "In that case, my lord, name your terms."

"I wouldn't dream of it. Although," he continued quietly, "I may ask a favour of you some time."

He didn't look at me, but I prayed that the favour would include me.

"I'm glad we're to keep this private," James said. "Apart from the public implications, it would worry my wife very much, and she already has too much to do."

"Of course," Richard answered. "I'm afraid I've already told my brother and one other, but I can vouch for their discretion. I'll tell no one else until we can get to the bottom of this problem."

We all agreed to keep this conference quiet, then James thanked him again and said we had better get back to the house before we were missed.

Only one half of the double door to the coach house stood open, so we had to pass through it singly. Richard somehow contrived to be between Lizzie and me, and walked a little slower, so by the time James and Lizzie had reached the house, we had dropped a little way behind. Having manufactured the slight distance, he took my arm and steered me in another direction. By the time Lizzie realised I had gone there would be nothing she could do about it.

Richard took me to a door near the room we'd been received in when we first arrived. "This corridor leads to the chapel. I found it yesterday when I explored this wing a little. I like to know my way around."

He opened the door on the left, which led into a small,

sparsely furnished, but clean room. "I think Lady Hareton used this as a morning room."

Indeed, with a little more comfort it would be a pleasant room in the mornings. It must face east, for the sun streamed in through the windows, and gleamed on the polished floors and hard surfaces.

He looked at me. My heart rose to my throat, and I found it hard to breathe. I didn't find the feeling entirely pleasant, although it was undoubtedly exciting. His presence made me respond so rapidly, it unnerved me.

I turned away from him to stare out of the window in an effort to regain my composure, but he put his good arm on my shoulder and turned me firmly back to face him. He drew me closer and bent his head to kiss me. He gave me a gentle, closed-mouth kiss, but one full of fondness and longing.

"Good morning, my love." His smile turned my heart over.

I found my voice with difficulty. "Good morning,"

He kissed me again, outlining my lips with his tongue until I opened for him so he could dip his tongue inside and taste me.

But he drew back after one, brief taste. "Yesterday I promised myself I'd do my best to avoid your company until I can speak to you openly, without censure. But much to my dismay, I find I can't. I can't be close to you without wanting to touch you."

"Lizzie knows," I said unhappily. "She thinks I must be mad."

"I agree with her. We must both be mad. This whole affair is madness. I don't know you, you don't know me, but I'm as sure as I've been about anything in my life that I don't want to let you go."

I stumbled, unsure on my feet. It was most unlike me. Richard put his arm around my shoulders and led me to an oak settle by the wall opposite the fire. We sat close together, his arm still around my shoulders. I leaned against him, enjoying his steadying presence until I felt a little better. The soft cloth of his coat lay under my cheek; I smelled the faint scent of citrus and knew I had come home. It would be so easy to relax, let him take control, but while I knew I loved him, I didn't know if I could trust him.

I took a deep breath. "You have a great advantage over me, sir. I've never felt anything remotely like this before in my life. I don't know how long it will last, why I feel like this, or even what it is, for sure. It frightens me, it excites me, and it gives me thoughts I don't know what to do with."

I lifted my head to meet his perceptive gaze. He stared back at me, no artifice left. Just a man, listening. "You must have felt this before," I said, imploringly, despairingly, "You might even be trifling with me for all I know."

He protested, "No—" but I carried on. I had to have my say before I lost my nerve.

"On the one hand, my sister says you're an unreformed rake, and I shouldn't listen to a word you say, and on the other, when I look at you I can't imagine you doing anything wrong, but—" In my agitation, my inability to express myself, a lump formed in my throat. Angrily, I dashed away a tear from the corner of my eye before he could see it.

He recognised the gesture. Taking his arm away from my shoulders he took my hand instead. "Look at me." I sniffed, and fought to control my wayward emotions before I looked up to meet those icy blue eyes.

"Do you think I wanted any of this?" His quiet tones sounded very much like anger. "I don't know you any better than you know me. When I first set eyes on you last Monday, you could have been as cold and stupid as Julia, but I wanted you just the same. Now I know you a little better I want you more. Yes, I want you, desire you, and yes I've felt that way before, but I've never felt such a foolish desire to let someone into my life the way I want you to share mine. Please trust me, and I promise I'll do my best to get us out of this mess, and into the light."

"I have to trust you, I can't do anything else, can I?" I hated feeling so helpless.

He kissed me again, gently. It felt like a promise. "All I can say for certain is I'm falling in love with you. Now, today. I don't seduce innocent, respectable females, though I know many who do. My prior philandering mainly involved married ladies looking for a change, or high flyers. I thought that would be my lot for the rest of my days." He shrugged. "It has been that way for most of my acquaintances. Now I'm not so sure. Believe me, if I wanted a little light relief, I wouldn't be here now. I would have gone to my parents' house. A large country house and a multitude of guests masks any amount of frivolity. We could have turned around and left, that first day. But I stayed here because of you. I planned to let you know of my interest, see if you might one day return my regard, extricate myself from Julia and then return to court you properly. But that's changed. You're in trouble now and I have to help."

"Is it bad?"

"It could be. Your family arrived and the next day the earl and his brother die in an accident which is no accident. If we don't discover who is responsible, your family will enter society under a cloud. Suspicion will always lie over you, rumours and innuendo follow you, until we can determine the truth."

"Will it really put paid to Lizzie's ambitions?"

"What about yours?" he asked, smiling.

"I have none. I've been on the shelf since Lizzie made her come-out."

He lost the smile and his brows lifted. "How so? I can see something in you that should draw suitors to you. You have grace, you're beautiful—"

"No." I looked away, ashamed at his teasing.

He put his hand under my chin and turned me back to look at him. "Yes. You just won't let yourself be as beautiful as you are. Stand up straight and be proud of your height and your figure. Your hair will be glorious, with the right attention—" I grimaced and put my hand up to my unruly locks, already tousled and coming loose although still early in the day, "—and your eyes, your eyes..." He looked at me in silence for a heartbeat. "Your eyes hold everything I need." He leaned forward to kiss me again, a reverent gesture of affection.

111

He drew back, gazing at me. "Whatever happens, I want you, scandal or no."

"You've signed your marriage contract. You're to be married in a few weeks."

It was his turn to grimace. "That was true madness. I just didn't think properly, didn't work it out, what it would mean. I can't go through with something so heartless. Most couples have a small degree of liking for each other, but Julia doesn't think of me in that way. Do you know, I've kissed you more often than I've kissed her? Once, I think, when I proposed to her. But if I break the contract, the consequences for my family and for yours could be dire. You know that, don't you?"

I swallowed. "Yes."

"They will put the greatest pressure on me to go through with it, but I've never been more grateful that I inherited the family temper." He grinned. "It's a vile thing. It's led me into more scrapes than I care to remember, but at least I'll be able to stand up to my father. His wrath, like the Lord's, is terrible."

"I thought you cold." I still did, when I saw him with others present, but I was beginning to understand the attitude he told me about, his society face that kept him aloof and aristocratically disdainful. "I don't like to be on show. I never have. Certain things...I assume you know about Gervase's troubles?" I nodded. "Certain things enhance my disguise. The maquillage, the clothes, all help to keep me private." He paused, smiling self-deprecatingly. "There's proof, if you require it. You're the first person to whom I've explained myself. I don't care what other people think of me, but your opinion is very important. I want you to know you can trust me, that I'll care for you, always put your needs first."

This open statement took my breath away. No one could say such things and not be sincere. It would be easier to take the path of least resistance, and let Richard move away, marry the woman he was betrothed to, and look for a different suitor but I knew that my life would lose meaning if I allowed that to happen.

We watched one another. I wanted to learn every line of his

face, every shade of blue in his eyes, so if he left me alone, I could remember it whenever I wanted to.

"My first stepmother used to say love had little to do with marriage." He let me talk. Perhaps he realised I needed the time. "That is, the lady who brought me up. She said it was based on respect and friendship. But after her death, my father married again. A woman his own age, whom he told us he'd loved since boyhood, but had not been allowed to marry. When my stepmother died, she was also a widow. They married, this time to suit themselves. Smallpox carried them off eventually, both of them in a week. I'm not sure he would have cared to live without her. Sometimes we children felt like interlopers in our own house, they were so happy together."

"We'll be luckier than that." He sighed, looking at the polished floor, as though discovering answers there. "But it won't come without a struggle. I spoke to Julia again. I assured her I was of the same mind and I thought we would not suit. When she asked why, I said I'd been considering it for some time. When I found myself near to death—forgive me the exaggeration—thanks to your prompt help, I was nowhere near it—I felt I should speak. I told her she could pretend a quarrel, or say she had found me *in flagrante* with a parlourmaid. I don't care what she says, as long as it does the trick, as long as you're not compromised from my side." His next words made my mood plummet. "She still refuses to consider it. She said I must be mad to think she would do such a thing. I said I'd help her find the proper man, but I wasn't that man. She laughed at me, and said I would do." He gathered my hands, held them warmly between his. "If Julia brings a breach of promise suit, it will ruin us, my family and everybody associated with me. Do you understand?" Concern etched his features.

I thought of what that would mean. Not to me, but to all the other people. Richard's younger sister, making her debut in society. My sisters, making theirs, too. There'd be no money for them after such a court case. Julia Cartwright would win, hands down. Richard had signed the marriage contract, as binding a contract as any other under law. "It's hard."

He nodded.

"I can do it, but I'd hate to see those I love compromised. I can't see any other way. We must face it, and hope it's not too bad. Are you sure she'll take you to court?"

"She's vengeful. She won't let such an insult pass. I can try to persuade her that such an act would hold her up to public ridicule, but that is our only chance."

I couldn't think of any way to avoid the scandal. "I'll face it with you."

His response was prompt, unhesitating. "No. I'll face it on my own, so you're not compromised. Any scandal is mine." When I opened my mouth, he gripped my hands harder to stop me protesting. "After this matter is cleared up and when you're out of black, I'll come a-courting properly, and prove to you I mean what I say. I will not marry Julia now, whatever pressure people bring to bear on me."

My heart raced. To spend time with him, have it as my right, was more than I hoped for. He tried to shrug, wincing at pain in his injured arm. I put my hand up to it in an instinctive gesture of concern, and he caught it, and held it with his uninjured one. He didn't appear to feel the pain any more. "I should have told Julia I've lost my position in society, that I was ruined. She might have reacted to that." He smiled sardonically. I looked at our linked hands, now resting on his leg.

"We may have to give up." I met his gaze. With the threatening scandal, I didn't know if we could weather it. "You might have to marry Miss Cartwright." I didn't want to use her name, didn't want any indication at familiarity so I kept my reference to her the more distant, formal term.

He drew a sharp breath. "No, I'll never do that. Julia accepted my offer because she wanted a man with a certain position in society. It could have been any man. This is her first season, my twelfth. When she ensnared me, she dined out for weeks on the triumph. Even if I hadn't found you, I would have come to this in the end. I can't stand much more of her vacuity, her vanity, her selfishness. I decided to offer for her out of respect for my parents." He laughed. "I don't care if they hate you. I will have you."

He released my hand to draw me closer. I went to him willingly. I couldn't believe he could say all these things and not mean them, though I had very little experience of men and what they could say or do. Perhaps that naïveté saved me, the lack of cynicism that steers people away from the truth. I made my mind up. "I will trust you, I do."

We kissed again, this time so deep and longing, I never wanted it to end. He opened my mouth with a flick of his tongue and explored me deeply, invited me to taste him. Delicious, addictive. His hands, until now merely holding me for his kisses, became more adventurous, caressing my back, lifting my fichu in search of the bare skin underneath. I shivered, wanting more.

He pulled away, begging my forgiveness. "I should leave such loving until a more appropriate time. You are very desirable, my sweet, but that's something I will not do. Not to you." When I shook my head and pulled him closer, he gently pushed me away and stood.

He held out his hand to help me to my feet.

"That was wrong, but I promise, it won't always be."

I blushed, ashamed at my sudden surge of passion. He kissed my hand. "This will be more difficult than I thought. I suspect you of something of which proper single ladies should be innocent. It makes me all the more eager to claim you for my own."

This only made me blush deeper than ever, tongue-tied. I couldn't think of anything to say which seemed appropriate. He held me, as well as he could with only one good arm. I leaned against his shoulder. I loved to feel his warmth. "And we'll have to keep this secret," he reminded me. "If Julia gets an inkling how I feel about you, she'll slam the door on any negotiations and ensure the gossip that will spread about you. There'll be scandal and the courts. If she won't break it off, I will, but I don't want you involved in that part. I want the public to see us meet formally after I've dealt with the nastiness. I don't want to see you hurt."

I smiled to reassure him. "I won't be hurt, not if I'm with you."

"I'm very much afraid you will. This isn't the first scandal my family has been involved in recently and this might be one too many. Your family, too, is vulnerable. You're new to society. The old cats will look for something. The coach accident, then my involvement with you will give them all the ammunition they need. That's another reason why we must keep the other matter secret." He paused. "No. *Nil desperandum.* We'll see this through." He gave me a quizzical look. "And you thought I wanted all this?" He laughed.

"Not exactly. But I thought you might be trying to seduce me, especially after the reports I read about you, and what Lizzie told me about you."

"Don't believe everything you read." He took me to the door. "I fear we must go now, or we'll be missed."

"Richard—" He met my gaze. It had its usual effect and I lost myself in him once more.

"Rose," he said and kissed me. "Now we really must go. You leave first, and I'll follow in a few moments."

I opened the door and peered out, before I stepped out of the room. Catching my hand again, he pulled me back. "Once more," he whispered, and gave me one more kiss, sweet and long. Then I went back to reality, back up the corridor to my breakfast, feeling lighter at heart than I could ever remember.

I had, once and for all, made my mind up. I would have him.

Chapter Ten

Martha had asked me to help her after breakfast, but Richard waylaid me before I reached my room. "Pritheroe wants to see us."

I blinked, startled, but he shook his head. "I don't know what he wants, but we'd better go and find out. The man's a nuisance, but it can't be helped. Don't worry." He smiled warmly. "There's little he can do. Perhaps he wants to tell us something about the accident."

"Perhaps he's seen us together—" I gasped out, but he smiled and shook his head.

"With his leg in that condition? I doubt he's nimble enough to spy. He might just want to sermonise us. He's in the small parlour." He took my hand. "Don't worry. If anyone does see us, I'll make it clear there's nothing wrong in it." He kissed my hand and dropped it, after a warm smile.

We went to the parlour, and found James and Lizzie already there. Mr. Pritheroe sat in state in a hard, wooden chair, and the man Ellis stood beside him. The fire was still cold and the room stark, a contrast to the comforts Martha had introduced to the other rooms we used. A crude crutch was propped up by his chair. He sat completely still.

Richard saw me to a chair, remaining on his feet, close by. I felt better for his presence. Mr. Pritheroe made me feel as though I had done something wrong, and was now about to face retribution.

Pritheroe rubbed his large hands together. "Earlier today,

this good man, Ellis, took an early morning constitutional." He paused so we could take in the implications of his words. So perhaps he had seen us through the window, and reported us. But why were James and Lizzie here? The tension rose in my stomach.

Pritheroe cleared his throat, never taking his gaze from us where we stood or sat, waiting, in front of him. He would read nothing in Richard's face, and I tried to school my features into something resembling calm interest.

"He came back, and saw something he thought unusual. He saw you leave the coach house." I silently breathed out in relief. "When you'd gone, he went to look himself. You know what he found, do you not?"

"Do tell," his lordship drawled. He had stationed himself so I could see him. He had his hand on the back of my chair, but he withdrew it, and took his snuffbox out of his pocket. It gave us a pause, broke Pritheroe's impetus.

Pritheroe cleared his throat again, but Richard merely took his time, restored the box to his pocket when he had done, and looked up questioningly. "Do go on. You had no need to stop."

"I require your full attention," Pritheroe said.

Richard's brows snapped together in a frown. "The last person to say that to me was my last tutor. He never saw me again after that."

Pritheroe looked down, then rallied. He didn't apologise for his cutting remark. "Tell them what you saw, Ellis."

The manservant strutted forward. "I inspected the coach. You appeared concerned when you left the stables, so I thought there must be something there. I found it. That strap, the one at the back. It's been cut, hasn't it?"

"Are you sure?" asked Strang after the horrified silence that followed the servant's revelations.

"Completely, my lord. The cut is fresh and clean."

His lordship sighed. "That's what I thought. And perhaps you could explain what business it is of yours?"

"That's rich, since I see no reason why you should be

involved." Pritheroe answered.

James took a breath and looked around. "I've asked Lord Strang to use his influence to discover who might have done this."

Richard looked down at the sling on his injured arm. "Besides, I didn't come out of this unmarked myself."

"So what have you discovered?" demanded the obnoxious man.

"In the few hours that have elapsed since your creature saw us?" Richard received a daggers look from Ellis for his pains. He ignored the servant.

"I expect," Pritheroe continued doggedly, "to be informed of any developments that occur."

"Expect all you like," said James, truly riled now. He shifted uncomfortably in his hard, wooden chair. "I'll tell you what I see fit."

Pritheroe turned his great head, his jowls following the movement shortly after. James met his stare blandly. "Then I should tell you that I see this as a sign from God that he means me to fight for this inheritance. Lord Hareton promised it to me, and it should be mine."

I glanced at Lizzie and saw, by the tight line of her jaw, that she felt the same tension I did. More complications, more delay, more scandal.

"I think someone did this to deprive me of my rights in this case. I think there must be a more recent will than the one Fogg used, and this makes clear the intentions of the last two earls of Hareton."

"Whatever their intentions," James said, thoroughly agitated, "there are a few things you can't change. The entail cannot now be signed away, and that stands apart from any private will. Whether you like it, or whether I like it, the estate comes to me. I signed nothing before they died, and if I'd known the true circumstances, I would never have done so."

"It was God's will," Pritheroe repeated.

"I don't think so," James went on. "All the income from the

estate comes to me, and the land, and the houses. Moreover, I don't intend to give you a penny. Your daughter will receive what is due to her as the widow of Lord Hareton, and perhaps more, but you have no claims on the estate and you won't get any."

"My claim is a moral one." There was no doubt in Pritheroe, only certainty that his cause was just. I restrained myself from asking him how often he had conversations with God. He would probably tell me.

James turned red, showing signs of his anger, and in a moment, he would say something he might come to regret. "There's nothing moral about it."

Richard interrupted my brother, his voice a cool chill in the heat of the room. "Nevertheless, the matter remains. If you wish to take Lord Hareton to court, that's your concern, though it might bankrupt you, leaving little time for your other— activities." The delicate pause before the last word showed what he thought about those activities. "You wouldn't win, anyway. It might inconvenience him, but little else. Leave it alone."

Pritheroe stared at Richard for a full minute in silence. "That may be. But if the last two earls were murdered for that inheritance—"

"That," Richard said smoothly, before James could speak again, "would be another matter, but you still wouldn't inherit. It would be seen as an action of mere spite on your part."

"It would give me a platform," Pritheroe pointed out. "All I want is the opportunity to preach and bring more people to God's word."

"You'll find lawyers impervious to your charms, but you're welcome to try. For my part, I intend to try to find the culprit and why he or she did it. When I have that information, a course of action may occur." When Richard turned, the skirts of his blue cloth coat followed his action gently. "You may rest assured, that if I find the present Lord Hareton has done this thing, he won't go unpunished."

Lizzie and I gasped. How could he do that? All my doubts resurfaced. He'd never want a criminal's sister, whatever he said privately, and I wouldn't consider anyone who had brought that kind of misery to my family.

"I don't think he did do it," Richard said, glancing at James, who was still red faced, but had the sense to remain silent. "He believed the estate bankrupt, and he has a tidy property of his own back in Devonshire. Why should he want to exchange that for this? His wife is distressed rather than delighted."

The reasoned tones brought Pritheroe around. I stared at his quivering jowls as he moved his chair, and nodded.

Richard continued, his reasoned tones adding soothing balm to what could have been an explosive situation. "This is the last thing most right thinking people would want. What's the use of a title, when there's nothing to back it up? There are viscomtes in France in charge of nothing but a farm. No one seeks them out, no one is interested in them." He gave Pritheroe his full attention as if they were the only two people in the room. "No, let it be. If you leave this with me, I can promise to let you know what I find out. Not because you have any rights in the matter, but because you suffered as I did." *Not until he fell off the coach he didn't.* "And I will also promise to bring the perpetrators to justice. If we bring the authorities in now, this place will shut up as tight as a drum. There are enough resentments and petty infighting here to fill the House of Commons, and they'll all join together to fight a different adversary, if strangers come in. We'll never discover anything."

A heavy silence fell and Pritheroe harumphed again. "You promise me, your word as a gentleman, you will tell me, whatever you find?"

"My word as a man who keeps his word."

Richard crossed the room and offered his hand to Pritheroe, who, after one look at him, grasped the slim hand in his own meaty paw, shaking it thoroughly. "Very well. But if I find you hiding anything, I'll go straight to the magistrate."

"Anything?" A note of amusement crept into Richard's voice.

"About this matter," Mr. Pritheroe finished as Richard

121

smiled, briefly.

"Very well," he said.

Richard bowed to Lizzie and me. "I'll take my leave. I've given myself a lot to do."

I didn't meet his gaze, not trusting myself. We took his cue, and left the room. I wanted to consider what I could do to help my brother.

◇

After breakfast, Martha asked me to help her. I joined her growing train of followers and, clad in the same kind of sacking apron as everyone else, enjoyed myself hugely helping to clean the Great Hall. The life-sized statues ranged around the first floor glared at us balefully as we scrubbed, dusted and polished. Even the oil paintings were thoroughly soaped, but they turned out to be unremarkable daubs when clean. Lord Hareton had concentrated on his classical acquisitions, it seemed. I had another reason to be glad Martha had decided on this thorough cleaning. Anything we discovered—any clue, would be easier if we discovered it in the natural process of cleaning. And if society knew about the condition of the Abbey as it is now—the scandal would be even more juicy. Who could resist the story of the mysterious death of two brothers, who had lived in the ruins of a once great house?

Early afternoon found us ascending the stairs to give the statues a much needed scrub. These were classical statues, and their unashamed nakedness made the younger maids giggle. Looking at a fine reproduction of the Apollo Belvedere, I wondered if naked men really looked like this. My cheeks burned at the thought, now I had a specific person in mind. However, when I examined at the female statues, I supposed not because none of them looked the least like me.

The work gave me a much needed outlet for my overstrained thoughts. Two things circled each other in my head; Richard and the murder of my cousins, and hard physical work gave me something else, something innocent to do.

Several people came to view our efforts that day. Gervase, Richard and Miss Cartwright came up and laughed at the sight of us all.

"Like so many ants around a queen," his lordship commented, watching Martha direct operations. They toured the first floor, trying to identify the various statues. They did well. Though the figures were nude, most of them wore or held the item with which they were associated. Martha said they must write it down for her.

I was scrubbing Aphrodite's feet, on my hands and knees in front of the goddess, appropriate and deeply embarrassing. I looked up at their approach, gratified to see a brief flash of shock in Richard's eyes. He had not noticed who the nondescript cleaner was.

Pushing back a stray curl, I wished them good day. I must have been very grubby. A sneer rather than a smile spread over Miss Cartwright's pretty round features. She moved her heavy skirts aside to avoid the puddle of dirty water which swam around the feet of the goddess.

"Good afternoon, Miss Golightly," Richard said coldly, but when I looked up to meet his eyes, I saw the same warm message in them I'd seen earlier in the day.

"Good afternoon, my lord." I nodded to Mr. Kerre and Miss Cartwright. "I apologise for my appearance. Martha needs all the help she can get, and to be truthful, ever since I saw this hall I've longed to sluice it down."

"How does Lady Hareton feel about this upheaval?" Miss Cartwright asked maliciously. "We must be forbearing with her in her grief."

"Martha spends some time with her every day. The widow said it was time the Abbey was restored and used properly, and she's given this project her blessing." Lady Hareton had been very glad to relinquish the keys of the Abbey into Martha's hands, even though her father had demurred, loath to let any symbol of control go.

I must have protested too vehemently, for Miss Cartwright

smiled coldly. "I must say, you have more strength than me, Miss Golightly. I've never scrubbed a thing in my life."

"Yes, ma'am, you have all the appearance of it." Her carping annoyed me, and I felt at a distinct disadvantage.

Before the situation grew worse, Mr. Kerre intervened. His brother watched us, an amused light in his eyes. "It's most admirable of Miss Golightly." To my surprise, he stripped off his coat, "You seem to be having a great deal more amusement than me. I didn't think to offer my services before, for you must know I hate to be idle. I'm sure my brother would offer as well, were he able."

Richard laughed. "I thought you knew me, Gervase. The woman who persuades me to scrub would be a remarkable woman indeed."

He didn't look at me, but at Miss Cartwright, who had the grace to blush, the first time I had seen her superiority dented or even the least abashed since she had arrived at the Abbey. "I would never ask such a thing of you. There are, after all, servants for that kind of thing."

Mr. Kerre had by this time rolled up his sleeves, picked up a cloth and wetted it. He rubbed vigorously at Aphrodite's arm. "Your servant, ma'am." He bowed deeply, much too deeply, to Miss Cartwright.

This time the lady blushed. "I beg your pardon, sir. I meant no offence."

"And I took none, I assure you," said Mr. Kerre. "I would like to help here. I'm used to a more active life, I never know what to do with myself in these long afternoons at country houses and this will answer splendidly. I hope it will give Lady Martha some small assistance."

"Very well. I'll restore Julia to her duenna, and then I'm sure I'll find some trifling occupation." Richard smiled, bowing, and left. Julia picked her way carefully around the pools of dirty water, which accumulated on the floor around all the statues. I watched them go with mixed emotions.

I turned back to Mr. Kerre "How many statues do you think there are?" He glanced at me and smiled briefly. The smile echoed his brother's, but without that pull I felt so strongly when Richard smiled at me. "We counted twenty-two."

"I didn't know there were so many. How did they ever keep track of them all in Roman times?"

"I believe you selected the ones you had most sympathy with," Mr. Kerre replied, smiling. "And then gave obeisance to the greatest ones when required."

"They were shockingly depraved, weren't they?" I attended to Aphrodite's ample breasts. It might be better if I did that part of her.

"Shockingly. The explosion of fine art that attended such depravity is even more shocking, in a different way."

"I'm sorry, sir, I don't understand."

He took a deep breath, and by his rapt expression I could see this was something dear to his heart. "Well, as you know, most well-born Englishmen end up at one time or another in Rome. And, sadly, circumstances meant I saw it alone. However, when I stepped into the Pantheon, I was so taken aback by the sheer beauty of it I forgot my troubles. It was the only thing that consoled me at that time. I spent months exploring the classical beauties of Italy. Rome in particular, of course, but there are miracles everywhere in Italy, if one looks for them."

How hard it must have been for him to give up the woman he loved, especially if they had felt for each other what his brother and I felt. I began to understand why a man would court ostracism from his family and his world for one person and I grew afraid.

I tried to push my fears to the back of my mind, to think of something else instead. "My brother Ian would love to meet you, sir. He's long dreamed of going to Rome himself. He's at Oxford at present—" I broke off as a thought dawned on me. "Now he can." I sat back on my haunches. I remembered all the books Ian had read during his many childhood illnesses, how much he longed to see more of the world, and I was glad this change in our fortunes should bring one person at least nothing but good. Ian had grown out of most of his sicknesses, although he still had a tendency to breathlessness, so there was absolutely no reason now why he should not undertake a full Grand Tour if he wished it. I smiled. "He'll be so pleased."

"If you let me know when he plans to go. I can give him several introductions." Mr. Kerre applied the cloth to Aphrodite with great vigour.

"That is most kind, but I don't imagine it will be for some time yet."

We finished Aphrodite in companionable silence and turned to the smaller statue of Cupid, which appropriately stood by her. Mr. Kerre stayed with us until the time came to dress for dinner, and by then we had made a difference to the Great Hall.

We stood back and examined it from all angles. The black and white tiled floor gleamed. Columns supporting the roof were made of a green stone that hadn't been apparent under the layers of grime. Resplendent white marble statues stood between them, counterpointing the green with white.

When we had admired our handiwork, Mr. Kerre excused himself to clean up. His fine clothes were begrimed, but he assured us it didn't matter in the least. "It was worth it, to see such a result."

Martha and I stood aside while the long ladders were collapsed and taken away. "Well, Rose, my dear, I never thought it would scrub up so well." She echoed my own thoughts exactly. When she turned to me she laughed. "Look in the mirror."

Reflected in the gilded pier glass was an urchin, face grubby, hair atumble in long, untamed curls. I smiled at the figure and it grinned saucily back at me. "Should I go to dinner like this? Then what would the odious Miss Cartwright say?"

"Rose. You mustn't talk of her in that way!" Martha said, scandalised.

"What? You don't think she is?"

"That's beside the point," Martha said, trying to draw shreds of dignity about her neat person. "You shouldn't talk about people in that way."

"You mean you never have? What about Mrs. Terry, last year, when—"

She interrupted me. "Well, in the heat of the moment, I might have said something. But my impression of Miss Cartwright doesn't matter a jot. We might be invited to the wedding, but I don't suppose we'll ever be anything but acquaintances in the future."

"That's as good as saying you would rather not further the acquaintance," I pointed out.

"Maybe. You are an abominable person. Go and change, immediately."

I went off to my room, laughing.

Three quarters of an hour later I left my room once more, washed and dressed as becomingly as I could manage in the circumstances. Steven waylaid me again. He pulled me into the same room as before. I kept him from embracing me by putting a chair between us. "I wish you wouldn't do this, Steven, it isn't at all proper."

"It seemed all right this morning."

My mind raced back to that snatched half hour earlier in the day. He couldn't have seen, surely. Oh, God, that last kiss.

"I couldn't believe my eyes when I saw you." He acted the curate, appalled by a sinful parishioner. "The man's a known libertine and he treated you like a chambermaid. You're making a fool of yourself."

I hoped not. "We had to discuss a problem we discovered earlier. If you don't believe me, ask James and Lizzie."

He frowned, glaring at me sceptically. "This problem. Would that include kissing Lord Strang?"

I frowned, and gripped the back of the chair for support. "A mistake. Innocent flirtation." Not the kiss, I thought, but letting ourselves be seen. "It won't happen again."

He seemed to accept it. I'd been leaving the room when Richard pulled me back. It could easily have been the action of a rake, seizing his opportunity.

"I shall try to ensure it doesn't happen again," Steven said, the pomposity of the minor cleric still with him.

This alarmed me. "What do you mean to do?"

"I shall speak to your brother. Not about your slip, since you assure me no harm will come of it, but about our intentions for each other. I can see you need some firm guidance, my dear." He smiled. I think he meant it to reassure me, but I could only see it as sinister.

"No, I forbid it." I groped at the only straw I could think of. "We're in mourning. It's not the right time for this."

He stood still, frowning, and then he nodded. Since he was determined to be the outraged cleric, I would use it to advantage. He couldn't avoid the proprieties. I was so glad I'd thought of that subterfuge. "We don't have to make any public announcements. Not yet, at any rate."

The very thought of such a thing appalled me. I wouldn't be immured as a country parson's wife, not even if circumstances forced me to say goodbye to Richard forever. I'd been insane to think I could have done so. "You're going too fast, and I would prefer to be courted properly, in public."

He smiled, indulgently. Maybe he thought he had the upper hand again. "Women are so foolish. Very well, my dear, the world shall see me court you. When you're out of mourning, we can do it properly."

So sure of himself, he saw no opposition in me. It must have been a mixed blessing, to be born with such spectacular good looks, but it had given him the confidence he had dearly needed in his straitened circumstances. I suppose he thought I now had money for us both, and if I had loved him truly, it would have been enough. But I didn't, and now it was too late.

A new light dawned in his dark eyes. "What problem did you discuss?"

"I can't say. I promised James I wouldn't tell. If you ask him, he may tell you." I was glad I'd made that promise. The fewer people who knew about that little problem the better.

Shrugging, Steven seemed to accept this. He let me go,

kissing my hand briefly as I left. I felt a tug, as he tried to pull me to him, but I slipped my hand out of his and left the room with a great deal of relief. The situation with Steven was getting increasingly difficult.

Chapter Eleven

An hour before dinner on the following day, I found Richard alone in the drawing room, reading a newspaper. I hadn't seen him all day, after Carier informed me that his master was exhausted, and he'd given him a sleeping draught so he could rest. That meant, he'd added meaningfully, that Miss Cartwright couldn't go bothering him again. If that was so, I agreed heartily with his valet's competent actions.

Richard rose when he saw me, throwing the paper aside before he raised my hand to his lips. "I missed you today. Couldn't you come and see me?"

"Of course not. Besides, your valet said you must be left alone to rest."

He gave a heavy sigh. "Julia was with me most of the time. I think she wants to convince me of her charms. She read to me, conversed with me, and generally ruffled me, until Carier managed to eject her." So Carier's scheme hadn't worked.

Then I noticed something about him. He wore a beautiful lilac brocade coat. I couldn't imagine how I'd missed it. "I didn't know you were so much better. I'm so glad to see your arm out of the sling."

"When Carier changed the dressing, I persuaded him to leave off the sling. See—" he swung his arm gently, "—there seems to be no infection, and Carier says he will take out the stitches in a few days. If I hadn't offered to help your brother discover exactly what happened to the coach, I'd have no reason to stay here any longer."

I looked at him in dismay. "You must stay as long as you like."

"Julia is anxious to leave. When I'm better, I'll escort her home, speak to her people, then go to my parents. After we've sorted out the other matter, of course." He lowered his voice. "I hope to fetch you for a visit shortly after that. I'm convinced my parents will love you, as I do."

I cast my eyes down, but I felt a rush of delight. However, at the back of my mind I still knew this might all be an elaborate masquerade, or the threat of ruin might eventually deter him. But surely, he wouldn't go this far if all he wanted was a quick seduction. "I'll be in mourning until March."

"You'll meet them after Christmas, when you're out of deep black. Then we can be married in April."

It was the first time he'd mentioned marriage. This, together with his careful attention to me, went some way towards convincing my cynical self. "Aren't you forgetting something?"

"Someone." His disdainful expression reminded me how he appeared to other people and I didn't like what I saw. He might turn that look on me one day. "We'll come about, never fear." I wished I could feel as optimistic.

He still held my hand. I asked about the coach accident. "Some interesting facts have emerged about the servants' hall, but nothing we can act on yet. We must tread carefully, the whole thing is a nest of vipers. But now Pritheroe knows, we must try to sort it out. If he hadn't discovered it, we could have kept it to ourselves, but if we can't discover the culprit, he'll spread damaging rumours—even go to the press."

"I know. He'll tell anyone who listens that Lord Hareton came by his estate and fortune by nefarious means."

His grave expression indicated how serious this could be. "He could cause your brother a great deal of trouble. We have to find out who cut that strap now, before anything can spread." I wondered if he would still have me if I was disgraced—or if he would be allowed to.

"Richard—Steven Drury saw us together."

He sighed. "Does he know?"

I shook my head. "He thinks you were stealing a kiss. But we have to be careful because he'll be watching us now."

Richard drew me closer and I felt his warmth. My instinct was to nestle against him, but I couldn't allow myself to do so for long. "If he importunes you again, come to me directly. The man's a nuisance, no more." He touched his lips to mine in a gentle kiss and I savoured his taste, his closeness.

He dropped my hand and moved away at the sound of approaching footsteps. The door opened to admit Mr. Kerre, and Lizzie. She looked charming in pale blue.

We bowed. Richard made an elaborate leg to Lizzie with such finesse it made her previous swains look like clodhoppers. She was delighted. I promised myself that one day, if things worked out, I would take him back to Devonshire. The pretty girls who had despised me for being too tall, clever and plain should see what I could do in Society. Then I stopped my train of thought, deliberately choked it off. I could count on nothing, yet.

Lizzie laughed, saying, "Thank you, sir. You have left off your sling. Does this mean your arm is getting better?"

"It improves daily, ma'am." Richard led her to a sofa. She wore her widest hoop tonight, so there was hardly room for anyone else on the sofa, especially as his coat skirts rivalled hers in width. I sat on the other sofa, and Mr. Kerre next to me, giving Richard no chance to join me. Our siblings knew of our attraction for each other, but we couldn't be demonstrative in front of them. I wouldn't have known how. I longed to touch him, to hold him, feel his warmth but the thought of doing it in front of anyone else made my flesh heat.

Richard sat and watched me until Mr. Kerre frowned at him. Richard looked back at his brother with such an untroubled, enquiring expression it nearly made me laugh.

Mr. Kerre didn't respond to his brother's unspoken challenge. "We have to consider who could have cut that strap on the coach. Hareton can't keep the matter private for too much longer."

"Especially now that odious minister knows," his brother added, frowning. "He is such a despicable man. I'm convinced he wants as much money as he can squeeze out of the estate, not for his vaunted religion, but for his own use."

"Blackmail?" I found the implication startling.

"Oh yes," Richard said softly. "He'll never leave Hareton alone, once he's been paid. He'll be back for more. Another reason why we must clear up this matter, face the consequences. It mustn't be allowed to drag on."

"Contemptible." Disgust filled Mr. Kerre's soft voice.

Richard leaned back in his chair, stretching his foot to the fire. Dispassionately, he examined the glittering paste buckles on his red-heeled shoes. "He knew there was money to be had. He may have persuaded the last Lord Hareton to start converting his assets to cash. Easier to transfer, you see. He couldn't break the entail, but he could render it worthless. Thanks to the probity of the present Lord Hareton, that won't happen. But we must find out what happened, find the culprit, bring it into the open. If we never find out, it will be a constant thorn in the side, a topic for scandal and discussion." He looked at Lizzie, who appeared to be distinctly worried. "It will be difficult, but not impossible."

"So who do you think did it?" Lizzie asked. "Have you any idea yet, sir?"

Richard frowned. "It can't have been the fourth Lord Hareton, because he had no reason to do it. He was planning for his future, so why should he want to do such a suicidal thing? It can't have been the minister because he was with us the whole time. He had too much to lose, too." He thought, frowning. "It could have been the unfortunate fifth Earl. He may not have fancied a connection to our family—"

"Or he may have fallen in love with Maria, or rather, the idea of her, and done the deed out of despair when you refused to allow her to come." Mr. Kerre's eyes twinkled with sudden mirth.

His brother nodded, serious. "Stranger things have happened, but it seems a very roundabout way of committing

133

suicide. No, I think someone cut that strap to commit murder, or to injure someone in that coach. We should look for the intended victim. I have my enemies, but I doubt they'd have followed me here, or taken such an uncertain way to dispatch me." I wondered what enemies he meant, and decided I didn't want to know. Things were complicated enough as they were. He continued. "I doubt I was the intended victim. It must have been Lord Hareton, his brother, the minister or Lady Hareton, for she should have gone, you know. Only when I expressed a desire to accompany them did Lord Hareton order her to stay behind. The deed might already have been done by then."

I hadn't thought of that. The rest of my reckoning had been much the same as his. I hadn't spent the whole day mooning. This problem was too serious to be eclipsed by my selfish troubles.

"Carier has made himself busy below stairs," Richard informed us. "And Bennett has kept his ears open in the stables. The late earl ran this establishment with a staff of six, keeping them busy from noon until night. Two of the staff were outsiders, recruits to this cult Mr. Pritheroe leads. The others hated them, but they're still here. I've asked that they remain here for the present because they may have had a motive. The only stable groom is a simple lad who, Bennett thinks, is incapable of doing such a thing. I think we may discount him for the moment. But I haven't yet discovered what I've been looking for—a witness, someone who might have seen someone in the stables the night we arrived, the night before the murder."

A noise heralded a flood of silk as most of the other guests arrived. We could discuss it no further.

The rest of the evening passed pleasantly enough, but not memorably, except for Richard's obvious coldness to Miss Cartwright. He didn't bother to hide it now. He wasn't impolite, merely indifferent. She didn't seem to notice, but tried to pay him flattering attentions, which he politely declined. Perhaps she really did care for him, and if this was the case, his coldness to her was cruel. It troubled me to see such cruelty in a man I was about to give all my hopes to. I hoped he was right about Julia, that she only cared for the position in society that he could bring her.

Chapter Twelve

Our mourning dress arrived, standard sizes, standard designs. A maid quickly fitted me into one of the gowns allotted to me, and took my measurements for the other. Martha was annoyed that maids neglected their housework to sew, but it had to be done.

After the fitting, I changed into my old gown, and went upstairs with Mrs. Peters. Our task was to assess the work yet to be done, and make a list for Martha.

Only the servants' quarters and the leads lay above us. The roof, James informed us, seemed to be in fair order, so we hadn't expected to find the devastation damp could wreak. But we did find it.

The rooms had been used by the family, and contained the nurseries, schoolroom and several bedrooms. Everything had been abandoned where it had been left ten years before, just like downstairs. I opened a door. "Do you think we'll find her in here?"

"Who would that be, madam?" Mrs. Peters asked.

"Sleeping Beauty." Richard's conceit never appeared so apposite as it did now.

I don't think she understood. "There's been nobody up here for years, madam."

We began to make a list of the rooms, their contents and what needed to be done to restore them. Up here on the second floor, the pervading odour of damp and neglect was overpowering, so the first thing would be to light fires in all the fireplaces, once they were clear of soot. We couldn't get the depressing odour out of our nostrils. For hours after I went back downstairs, I could smell it. The upper walls and ceilings of the rooms were fringed with the creeping black stains of untreated damp. At the far end of the building, it seemed to get better. Then we opened the door to the nursery.

I have rarely, if ever, seen such a shocking sight. Toys lay strewn about randomly, as though the children had only just left the room, but they were mildewed and black with damp. A baby house lay open in the corner, its delicate contents poured out on the floor in front of it, as if the house had vomited them.

A doll I would have loved to own when I was a child sat on a table, its beautiful silk gown torn and rotted. I picked it up. It had a vacant look because it hadn't been loved for such a very long time. It wore a fontanges, one of those high headresses fashionable fifty or so years before, and as I placed the doll back down again the head-dress slid off. It took the wig with it, leaving the doll obscenely bald.

I shuddered. "I don't want to stay here too long, Mrs. Peters. This nursery isn't pleasant." Mrs. Peters didn't seem to feel it, but she nodded. We wrote down what we needed to, and hastily left.

The night nursery was next to it, and on the other side the little room once occupied by the night nurse, or the nursemaid. To our surprise, we found this much neater than the other rooms. Someone had neatly folded the bedding away, the drawers and cupboard were bare—all much more normal in appearance.

"Perhaps this room was discontinued for use before the rest of the house was abandoned."

"Very likely, ma'am." Mrs. Peters didn't venture any theory of her own.

We passed on to a dark and grimy series of bedrooms, children's for the most part, which contained small beds and nightlights. The room allotted to the governess was much like the others, except for a bigger bed, but we found some clothes in the drawers, which we pulled out and examined. They were all plain, serviceable clothes, full of moth holes.

I made a note for the maids to empty the drawers here. "Why didn't she take her clothes with her?"

"The last governess never left, ma'am. She died of a lingering illness. It began with a lump in her breast and ended with a stick thin woman sitting in the servants' quarters, crying with the pain that laudanum could no longer touch." Mrs. Peters related this terrible narrative with little emotion. "I wasn't working here then. I heard about it in the village when the poor lady was buried."

"She was buried here?"

"She had no family."

I dropped the clothing hastily, noting down that they be burned, for fear of infection. Poor woman. When I reckoned it up, I realised this must have been the governess of the last two earls. There had been no children in the house since. How had it had affected them, what had the painful death of someone so close to them done to their spirits?

I wanted to discuss this with Richard. This was passing strange, since I hardly knew him, but I wanted to tell him how sad it was up here, perhaps even show him if he wished me to.

"Mrs. Peters, do you know anyone who had a grudge against the last two Lord Haretons?"

"In what way, madam?"

She wasn't stupid, only acting so. "Did anyone dislike them?"

She shrugged. "Most of the village. They took away jobs and custom. The landlord at the inn was very bitter." The list of suspects had widened, but I thought we'd best forget the village for now or the search would become impossible. Later, it might prove necessary to enquire there.

"There's always Ellis." Mrs. Peters straightened from her task of looking through the drawers.

"Ellis?" Anything I could find out about that man would help.

Mrs. Peters lowered her voice. I had to assume she did this

for effect since no one else was within earshot. "He came back with Lord Hareton after visiting Mr. Pritheroe. He never mixed with the other servants. They resented him. Then, the day before you arrived, he went into Lord Hareton's room and we heard a terrible sound of raised voices." She paused. I kept silent, waiting for her next words. "We couldn't hear a word anyone said, however hard we tried." I'll wager you tried hard enough, I thought, but kept it to myself. "He's still here, but Lord Hareton isn't. He stays in the kitchen now."

"Do the other servants get on with him?"

"No. The extra servants her ladyship has employed are from the village. He only speaks to tell us we're doing wrong."

"I'll speak to Lady Hareton. I think it might be better if he goes home with Mr. Pritheroe, once he's recovered."

"Thank you, my lady," she replied, with considerably more warmth.

I meant to repeat the gist of the conversation to Richard that afternoon. Carier had surprised me, asking if I would assist in taking out Richard's stitches. I'd been there at their inception, so to speak. I was more surprised to find we were the only three people in the room, as when he'd made the request Carier had led Martha to believe Miss Cartwright would be present.

Richard met me at the door. He kissed my hand and led me to a seat. Carier had made the room very comfortable with a warm fire, cushions, books and other comforts. Richard's considerable collection of toiletries were neatly ranged on the dressing table, crystal bottles glittering among the panoply of silver-backed brushes and pounce boxes.

There were two chairs placed either side of the fire. We sat and smiled at each other. He wasn't wearing his coat, just shirt and waistcoat. I loved to look at him, but I had to stop thinking about what he looked without the shirt and waistcoat, how he'd feel. That way lay madness.

I told them what Mrs. Peters had said about the servants.

139

"It tallies with what we've discovered," Richard said. "What do you think, Carier?"

Carier looked grave. "Yes, ma'am. Those two servants Mr. Pritheroe sent are hated by the others. The only books they read are the Bible and Mr. Pritheroe's sermons, and they don't join in. Now there are more servants they've been pushed aside. They only attend their master now."

"The argument sounds interesting," Richard added.

"I heard something of that in the servants' quarters, my lord," Carier said. "But either no one knows what they discussed, or won't say. I'll talk to Mrs. Peters, to find out more. She was in a place of advantage during the argument."

"She stood right behind the door," I said.

"Precisely, madam," the manservant agreed.

Richard looked up at him. "You'll have to use your seductive charms on her, Carier."

Carier's face was expressionless. "A bottle or two of good red wine should do it, my lord."

"Let's hope so."

No twitch marred the manservant's stern features. He busied himself about the task for which I had supposedly come here.

Carier proceeded to roll the sleeve of Richard's shirt out of the way, tenderly resting his lordship's arm on a small table covered by a towel. Another table held a decanter of red wine, one of brandy, and three glasses. Carier poured some brandy into a glass, handing it to Richard. "There shouldn't be too much discomfort, my lord, but this will help to ease any you might feel." Richard obediently drank, and leaned back in his chair.

I went over to where Carier was unrolling the bandage, both of us anxious to see the wound. I'd seen such injuries before, swollen to twice their size with pus and bad liquid. These often killed the unfortunate person who had sustained them, so I hoped with all my heart I saw no signs of this on my lord.

We were lucky. The wound looked clean, probably the result of the gin that Carier had poured so liberally over it that first day, and they way he'd changed the dressings twice a day. I breathed out in relief, but I hadn't realised until then that I was holding my breath.

The ten brown stitches Carier had put there held the edges of the long gash together, but the flesh was beginning to grow over them. When I mentioned this to him, Carier nodded. "That's why they must come out now. They could grow right into the skin."

I nodded.

"You're a wonderful woman." Richard looked down at the wound. "Any other lady would have fainted or thrown a fit of the vapours or the like."

I made a scornful noise. "I've always been interested in healing. There were accidents aplenty around the village where I grew up. After I stood by helpless when a man bled to death from a scythe cut, I promised myself I would learn more. It will never happen again when I'm there to help."

Richard smiled. The brandy had been a generous dose. While not drunk, I think he felt a trifle relaxed. "A wonderful woman." He smiled and leaned back, closing his eyes.

"Hush, sir," I scolded sharply.

He lifted his head, looking at me through half-closed eyes. "Don't mind Carier. He knows all my business. He guessed how it is between us, but he knows how to hold his tongue. Besides, he would infinitely prefer you to Julia. Wouldn't you, Carier?"

The manservant glanced at him. "It's not for me to say, my lord," he replied primly, busy now at his work. He picked up a small pair of scissors which lay on the table, and with those, and a pair of tweezers, he snipped and pulled out the stitches. Richard fell silent.

I decided to distract him, telling him about our discoveries in the governess's room and the nursery that morning.

His first comment was a brief, "Poor woman." But after a few moments he added, "From what I've heard of their father, the boys were given little familial affection." He glanced at Carier, who continued stoically with his work.

I saw his point. "You mean they would have looked for that attention elsewhere?"

My heart turned over at his smile. "Just so. What a perceptive woman you are! Now if the governess died in pain in front of her charges, without anyone to love her, it must have had an effect on them."

"If their father had ignored her illness. They might have resented his indifference."

A pause followed, broken by the crackling fire and snipping scissors. Richard said, "I don't suppose we'll ever know for sure, but I would be very surprised if this house isn't haunted."

Carier was halfway done. "Would you try to flex the arm just a little, my lord?" Richard obediently bent the arm. We were relieved to see the reddened edges of the wound held together. Carier smiled in satisfaction, and gently pulled out the last five stitches. Richard sat back in his chair, his eyes closed for the most part while Carier worked on him.

When all the stitches were removed, Carier examined the wound closely for any gaps. Then he sighed contentedly. "That will do very well, my lord." He picked up a fresh bandage, lighter than the original one, and I returned to my chair while he bound the arm.

Carier rolled the shirtsleeve back down, fastening it. He took the operation's debris into the dressing room, returning with the most beautiful dressing gown I'd ever seen. Richard refused it. "I'm quite warm enough." Carier poured wine for us, and left the room.

Richard flexed his arm once or twice, grimacing, and then picked up his wine and took a sip. "Carier does like you, but he never took to Julia, so I must be right this time, don't you think?" He looked at me, and lost the smile. "And there's another thing—I haven't yet toasted you in any form." He raised his glass. "To your beautiful brown eyes. May I drown in them forever." He drank.

I laughed. "You're the first person to notice them."

"They hold everything I need. You'll be a great hit in London, you know." He sat back. He must be more comfortable now the stitches had gone. I could only hope so.

I shook my head, troubled. "I don't think so. No one noticed me in Exeter, next to Lizzie. Well, only one person."

He opened his eyes more fully now, looked at me with that clear blue stare that missed nothing. "Who? That Drury fellow? I thought it a tryst. It dismayed me, but I didn't think you entirely welcomed his presence, and from what you told me later I was right."

I bit my lip. "I didn't. I suppose I'll have to tell you the whole." I looked down to avoid his eyes. I'd been so foolish. I couldn't bear the thought of Richard's disapprobation, but I couldn't let Steven hold me to ransom over it. Richard sat perfectly still. He let me take my time telling him, giving no clue how he would feel about the business.

I took a deep breath "I never took when I made my come-out. I don't know how it happened. Perhaps I'm too tall, or blondes were all the rage that year." I wouldn't let him comment, desiring no sympathy. "The following year I was just part of the scenery. I wasn't unhappy ever, I had a loving family and friends, but I just never took." He made a sound, but I carried on, still not looking at him. "Then word got around about my sister, Elizabeth. She's very beautiful, everything a young man could hope for, pretty, clever but not too clever, and amusing. No young man wanted me after that. I didn't realise I was on the shelf until a couple of years ago. Martha's remark about wanting an extension because the manor house was too small for all of us made me realise I was probably there for good." I cleared my throat, remembering my unhappiness. It might be an old wound, but it still hurt.

"Then, the year after that, Steven Drury arrived; tall, handsome, and penniless. He had excellent manners, and he came from a good family, so he was made welcome. At first, he charmed everyone. Then someone told him about our fine relations, and this must have tipped the balance in our favour. He sought us out, and paid us a great deal of flattering

143

attention. When Lizzie made it clear she had no interest in him, he concentrated on me."

I stopped to take another sip of my wine, and Richard quietly came over and refilled my glass. Afterwards he sat and listened, his fingers curled around the stem of his own glass, his feet crossed before him. The pattern card of peaceful repose.

"I foolishly let myself think I loved Steven. Of course, I didn't. Infatuation might be more like it or desperation, but it filled long hours and provided me with some excitement. Oh, I did nothing to be ashamed of, but accidental meetings in the village, which were not so accidental, little notes, foolish things, which I should really have got out of my system at sixteen. All this made me think I could be loved and wanted."

"What made you realise what his true motives were?"

I frowned, and tried to think back, tried to be as honest as I could. "Nothing in particular. Just a gradual realisation. He never seemed interested in my personal problems—he'd never have listened to my nonsense as you're listening now. And he asked me about my illustrious relations rather too much. When we received the invitation to come here, and my brother Ian hurt his foot—he should have been our other escort, you know—Steven quickly volunteered his services, even before he had asked permission from our vicar, his superior. He abandoned his duties without a second glance, although some people depended on him."

I took a deep breath. I had never told anyone this much before, and I found it hard. I tried to think of him as someone else, anyone else so I wouldn't falter in my confession. "I knew by the time we reached here I wished to break off my connection with him. To tell the truth, he irritated me with his solicitous attentions and attempts at lovemaking."

I looked up, startled. I'd forgotten to whom I was speaking. I'd never told the full story to anyone like this, and now I had started, I found it such a relief to talk, I could almost be talking to myself.

Richard gave me no clue what he was thinking, his face serious. He gestured for me to continue.

"Now he's waylaying me, asking me about the promises I made to him—"

"Did you make any promises?" he interrupted, his eyes intent on me.

"Never. I took care not to. He assumed I did, but I never promised him anything, I swear it. But I'm so worried he'll make trouble. The prize is so much greater for him now, you see, and oh, I wish none of this had ever happened!" The dam within broke as my stupidity and unhappiness broke through. I twisted my fingers around the stem of my glass, and very nearly snapped it.

Richard looked startled at my last outburst, but since I had by then burst into tears, the least he could do was come across to comfort me. Without any hesitation at all he knelt before me and took me into his arms and I rid myself of a great deal of my anxiety in a long bout of crying. I hadn't cried like that for years.

After a time, he lifted my chin and dried my tears with his own handkerchief. "Poor sweetheart. To be so distressed by your first fortune hunter. That's all he is, my love, and easily disposed of. They crawl all over London in the Season. My sister's been approached time out of mind, and these days she deals with them herself instead of asking us to help."

I glanced at him through tear-blurred eyes, shyly. "You're not disgusted with me? You don't think I'm a hussy, or too forward?"

"No, why should I?" he said, laughing a little. "I've had my fair share of fortune hunters too. They come in female form as well, you know."

"I feel so stupid, for allowing him to take me in."

"Not at all." He kissed me, very gently. "No wonder you doubted my approaches. To be taken in by a fortune hunter, and then to meet a libertine... Shall I let you into my secret? Yes?" I nodded. "Perhaps it's my turn to confess." He leant back on his haunches and took my hand. "I can't deny I've known many women. I used to collect them like butterflies, and they had about as much meaning for me. Last year, about the time

145

my brother returned from his travels, I realised I was bored with it all. There's nothing in such encounters, nothing at all, except some amusement and a little experience. No real links, no communication, no fondness. Other vices have no appeal for me. I've never seen the appeal of gambling to excess, though, of course, I do play. Everyone plays, but I've never been too excited about the turn of a piece of pasteboard. So, that leaves my interest in my little problems—and you." He looked directly at me. "I was ready for you, but I didn't know it until I saw you."

He'd made me smile again. Sharing my problem did seem to halve it, like the proverb says.

"Now." He kissed the tip of my nose. "I want you to promise me you'll go to your brother and ask him to give this curate a living."

His solution startled me. "But that's just what he wants."

"Not in East Anglia. Or perhaps Northumberland might be better. Then you can send your would-be lover away happy, never see him again and keep him out of the way."

I laughed shakily. "You make it seem so simple."

"Nothing is simple when it worries you night and day."

He stood and looked down at me. His amused expression changed to something that evoked a response I couldn't remember experiencing before I met him. Warmth, intimacy and a connection that astounded me.

He watched me with such a heated expression I might have melted. "Every day—everything you say makes me want you more. I want to share my life with you, to have you for myself. I want everyone to know and love you as mine." He pulled me to my feet and kissed me, not at all gently this time, exploring my mouth thoroughly, returning for more when I held him as tightly as he was holding me. Then he drew back.

"It occurs to me I've taken a lot for granted here. You must tell me truly." He released me and left me to stand alone. His face grew colder, as though he cut himself off from me, and I remembered with a little shiver how coldly he behaved with Julia Cartwright. His self control chilled me, made me afraid of him until I recognised that this was his way of hiding his emotions.

"Do you want me in this way? I'm sure that when you appear in London you will undoubtedly take there. You have a grace and a poise which squires' sons may not appreciate but which will be in great demand with many of my contemporaries. Believe me, Rose, you have no need to worry on that score." He paused and looked at me to see if I understood. I did, but I still didn't believe him. "When I tear up that wretched contract, will you receive me? May I, in short, pay my addresses to you? I want no scandal to touch you because of me, and I want you to choose me of your own free will, not because I'm pushing you into anything."

I knew what I wanted, and I knew it for sure. "Oh yes please."

He let his face relax again, and lost the cold look, took me in his arms once more, and kissed me, long and slow. "You may have caused chaos in my life, but chaos can never have been so welcome before."

Chapter Thirteen

Martha kept her army of servants, and me, very busy for the next few days. The State Rooms were filled with the sounds of chatter, scrubbing and shouts of "mind your head" as great paintings and chandeliers were lowered for cleaning. We began to unlock the beauty under all that decay.

Richard came to watch, and would occasionally take a hand with the more delicate treasures. From time to time, he caught me looking at him, and the warmth would always be there for me. If Lizzie saw him, she deliberately walked across our line of vision to break the contact. I decided to hold on to what I had and take action to resolve other matters. I would take Richard's advice and speak to James about Steven.

I found him in the little office he'd set up as his temporary base. While Martha attended to the house, he rode around the estate visiting the tenants and noted what needed doing. When I closed the door firmly behind me he looked up, smiling in welcome.

He picked up a paper. "I want to get the Dower House put in order. I want it for Lady Hareton to use as long as she wishes it. It's her right, as the dowager countess, and it might give her a sanctuary against her dreadful father."

"Rich—Lord Strang says he's trying to blackmail you over the coach." I hoped he wouldn't notice the slip.

He didn't seem to. "Yes, I know. I agree with him—the man's a worm. Look at the way he's treating his daughter." His voice warmed with rising emotion. "He'll not get a penny from me. I couldn't trust him, so what's the point?" He glanced at me. "If I thought this might affect you, or Martha or the others, if I could stop it by paying him, I'd give him everything he wanted."

I was touched by his concern. "Oh James, I'm sure we'll come about. What about his servant, that Ellis man?"

James grimaced. "Another worm. I don't trust him, either. If Strang doesn't discover the culprit, we must face it. There'll be rumours, but it should be all right, in the long run." We exchanged reassuring smiles.

James picked up another of the papers and made a scribbled note in the margin. A small pile of the ones he'd already dealt with lay on the corner of the desk, about the only order in that untidy little room. I sat in the chair on the other side of the large desk, its surface completely covered with more of the papers he was trying to make sense of. "His daughter has her rights, though he has none. I'll give them to her. She will decide what to do with them. She has a jointure and the use of the Dower House until she dies or remarries. I'm afraid her dreadful father will get it all."

"Might he move there and convert the villagers?"

James laughed. "He'll not have much luck there."

"Martha doesn't want to turn her out of doors too soon. She's trying to befriend her. Poor Lady Hareton is terribly upset, and her father is no use at all in comforting her."

"I wish he would concentrate on comforting her, instead of pestering me," said James, exasperated. "He came to see me again yesterday, says it's his moral right to have the entail broken. He said Lord Hareton's stated intentions on the night before he died amounted to a living will. I reminded him that it would be impossible to break the entail now. There aren't enough signatories for it, and in any case, I didn't consider myself bound in any way to follow the ravings of a poor unfortunate madman."

I burst into laughter at James's righteous indignation when I imagined the scene, but he had reached the end of his tether with the putative minister. "I'm tired of arguing with him. Every day the man visits me. He wants the riches transferred to him and to his ministry, hints he will go to the authorities if I don't comply. Do you think I'd let him have a hold over me and my family?"

"No."

"As if I haven't enough to do." He riffled his hand through the layers of papers on his desk.

I felt so sorry for Lady Hareton. Her father would, no doubt, make her give up her jointure to his cause. He might force her to marry another fanatic. I didn't think her heart was in it any more, if it ever had been in the first place. From the few times I had noticed her glance at him when she thought it had gone unnoticed, I knew for sure she disliked him, maybe even hated him.

I put the thought aside and tried to broach my own problem. "I'm sorry to add to your troubles, my dear, but I must talk to you. Things are becoming a little uncomfortable for me here."

He put the document down at once, and looked at me in surprise. "You, Rose? This must be serious. You don't usually complain."

I folded my hands carefully in my lap. "The truth is that I've been pestered too much recently, and it's getting worse."

Puzzled, he asked, "Has someone upset you, or is it the situation here? You can always go home to Devonshire, if you like."

"Oh no." I managed to curb my passion, afraid James might divine my true meaning. "I enjoy helping Martha here, unwrapping this house, so to speak." Remembering my duty I added, "If you wish it, of course I'll go to Devonshire, but I'd like someone else sent away as well."

"Who is it? One of our visitors? If they've upset you, they can leave tomorrow." My best of brothers.

I took a deep breath. "It's Steven Drury."

James sat back in his chair and pursed his lips. "Drury? Well. He's the one who's pestering you? I'll send him home at once." He didn't doubt me.

"No, don't do that," I amended the facts a little to protect the innocent. "He pulled me into an empty room, wanting to kiss me. He's always fancied himself in love with me, and this recent turn of fortune has increased his eagerness. Lord Strang and his brother came along at the right moment. They rescued me, but they saw my upset." I paused. "They called Mr. Drury a fortune hunter, James. Do you think he is?"

"Undoubtedly, now I come to think about it," James said, promptly. "I should have sent him back as soon as we knew we were to stay here. Well, I'm sorry for your distress, Rose. I'll deal with it today, and see what can be done."

I gave him a grateful look, every inch the dutiful sister. "Thank you, James. Lord Strang—and Mr. Kerre told me that they've come across a lot of these types. They advised us not to send him home. They said he could be bitter about it, and spread unpleasant gossip." James raised his eyebrows, nodding thoughtfully. "Lord Strang said we should send him far away, where he knows nobody. Give him a living, promote and exile him."

James thought, pen to mouth. He sucked the end of the quill. "A capital idea. I'm sure there must be something here." Waving his hand, he indicated the papers. His expansive gesture wafted several to the floor. "Mr. Fogg might have a more orderly list. I'll ask when I see him tomorrow. I never did trust Drury. Much too handsome for a cleric."

"Thank you, James." I tried to rise, but James waved me back, something else on his mind. "Martha isn't happy she can't chaperone you properly, especially with those two young men around. They don't pester you in any way, do they?"

I assured him they didn't. In my opinion it couldn't be called pestering.

"I like them, despite their reputations," my brother confessed. "But we hardly know them, and you've been left to yourselves pretty much. We'll have them back when we've put the place to rights, if they'll come. Do you think they will?"

Embarrassment heated my face. "I think so." I hated having

secrets from James. We were very close, and he had always been the best of brothers to me.

I excused myself, going to help Martha, feeling guilty. I would tell him, I resolved, as soon as possible.

The following day, Martha and James set off in their new blacks for a short visit to York to see Mr. Fogg. It would also give Martha an opportunity to shop for the many items the Abbey was crying out for. She could have summoned shopkeepers to us, but this trip would give her a break from the hard work at the Abbey. James confided in me that he wanted her to take it a little easier for a few days. Lizzie and I were to supervise the work in her absence, as Martha didn't wholly trust Mrs. Peters.

Lizzie ordered the meals, and I kept an eye on the progress of the maids in the State Rooms. I made sure they did the work properly and none of the treasures we were uncovering took a walk. I found it easier to avoid Steven with all the extra servants about, which was a blessing. I noticed Richard and Gervase were careful to locate him, heading him off whenever he came to close to me.

When the gentlemen joined us after dinner, Mr. Kerre, who had bidden us call him Gervase in private, said he had tried very hard to engage the curate in a discussion of his experiences in Rome, but Steven had been uninterested. "He knows I don't like him," Gervase complained, "and he won't be drawn. He won't bother you again, ma'am." Steven had excused himself early. He was tired, he said.

"Lord Strang told you, then?" I asked, wondering just how much the unnerving Gervase Kerre knew.

"Lord, yes," he replied, cheerfully. "We were never able to keep secrets from each other. Worse, when we're together." I looked into his startling blue eyes, so much like Richard's. "He's very fond of you, ma'am."

Lizzie had taken Richard to the harpsichord that stood in a corner. They amused themselves trying to see which notes were off and by how much.

Miss Cartwright stood by, trying to make herself agreeable to her betrothed. The elder Miss Cartwright sat by the fire, engaged in some stitchery. She had been of signal help around the house. She showed a practical turn of mind, entirely absent in her niece, and we were quite in charity with her. She looked up from her work. Her stern face relaxed into a small smile as she saw me look in her direction. That might have been me, I thought, overlooked and only asked to parties for convenience. I smiled back.

"I'm very fond of him," I confessed to Gervase. "But I should like to know him better."

"He's made up his mind." Gervase gazed at his brother. "He wants, and damn the scandal. I don't know how he's to do it without uproar and gossip, but who am I to comment on that?" He grinned disarmingly. I sighed, and he leaned forward and patted my hand, making the elder Miss Cartwright, the good duenna, glare at us sharply. Gervase raised an amused eyebrow and leaned back.

"I don't know him, you see."

Gervase smiled reassuringly. "He's much better than anyone knows. And his attachment to you is most sincere. Do you know, when he felt that first jolt, I felt it too? That's how I guessed, though I thought he was drawn to your charming sister."

His face became more serious, and he lowered his voice. "Miss Golightly, I've never seen Richard like this before. He's consumed with a violent desire to *care* for you. It's even difficult for him to think about the problem of the coach, and usually these matters fascinate him beyond everything."

I was so happy to hear this, but I didn't want to show too much outwardly, for fear I might give myself away. "Has he come to any conclusions about the coach?"

"Ask him yourself." I looked up to see Richard walking toward us, Miss Cartwright leaning on his arm and Lizzie behind them. "One more thing," added Gervase. "I wouldn't mention anything about the coach in front of Julia. She's one of the biggest gossips in London." I nodded, and they were upon us.

"Miss Cartwright finds herself fatigued," said Richard in a bored drawl. "She wishes to retire."

The aunt immediately stood, and put down her sewing. "Come, my dear." She led away her charge. She frowned over her shoulder at Richard as they left. His blatant indifference to her niece was clear now, and Julia had probably told her aunt about Richard's efforts to break the marriage contract. A man should pay more attention to his affianced bride than Richard was doing, although he couldn't be said to be discourteous.

I turned back to look at Richard. He looked at me with an expression I couldn't quite fathom, serious, studying. I wished I knew him better.

"Have you found anything out about the cut strap?" I asked.

"Nothing too important. However some interesting snippets have come my way, thanks to Carier and Bennett." He sat opposite me, while Lizzie sat by his side on the couch. They made a handsome couple, I reflected, wondering why he hadn't taken to my sister.

"Carier has been making himself pleasant downstairs," said Richard. "And there is some gossip about the late Lord Hareton's private servant."

"Ellis?"

He smiled in acknowledgement. "The man was a libertine, a very unskilled and unscrupulous one. Not only did he get a village girl in the family way, he denied it afterwards. Someone saw him." He took out his snuffbox. Lizzie and I watched in fascination took snuff, then Richard shut the box with a sharp snap and restored it to his pocket. "Now another girl claims his fatherhood for her coming child. And from her description it seems there's some truth in it."

"James thought he would send him away with Mr. Pritheroe," I said.

"After he has fulfilled his obligations. It seems he goes in for some unpleasant and unusual practices. The two girls described almost identical experiences."

"Oh, what were they, pray?" Lizzie eyes shone.

He turned to her, frowning, but not altogether serious in his tone. "Dear, ma'am, I couldn't possibly assail the ears of a gently nurtured lady with such scandalous gossip."

"Oh, *please*, sir." He flinched when she touched his sleeve. His arm must still be sore. Lizzie didn't notice, but leaned forward and spread her fan coaxingly. "Just between us two?" She held up her fan to hide their faces.

I heard his throaty laugh. "Madam, I predict you will be a sensation in your first season." He put one hand on her fan, lowering it. "Since you are so insistent, I must find a way to convey indelicate information without offence. So." He looked around at us all. "It seems the man likes to recall the sin when he indulges in the pastime itself. He reprimands the other party in the most lurid language, using physical force. Both girls suffered this no more than—three or four times?"

We laughed at the inference, but the reference to something I'd thought about a great deal recently made me blush. I hoped they hadn't noticed. "There was an argument, the day before we arrived, though the servants didn't hear what they discussed."

"It must have been about this matter," Richard said. "Perhaps Lord Hareton tried to persuade Ellis to do the right thing by one of the girls. There's something else, however. Did Mrs. Peters tell you about the argument?"

"Yes," I said.

"Did she tell you what was said?"

"No, she said she couldn't hear, and she couldn't find out."

"Then she lied to you. She knew all about the pregnancies, because one of the girls is her cousin."

There was a short pause. "She may have been trying to protect the girl," I said.

"Possibly. Or she may have her own reasons." He crossed one elegant leg over the other. "Say she cut the traces. She had the opportunity, she had many reasons to do it. Lord Hareton's servant used her cousin badly, the village had been depleted and impoverished by Lord Hareton's refusal to use it as he should have done." He leaned back again, his face serious.

"One more thing," Lizzie added. "There's a girl who helps us to dress in the mornings. This morning I found her in tears and she confessed she was upset about Lord Hareton's death. Not the fourth earl," she added, "but the fifth."

We were suitably surprised, as she had intended, and Richard raised his brows. "We have been busy."

"She was having an affair with him." Lizzie's eyes gleamed with triumph when she saw the impact this had on us. Gervase forgot himself so far as to whistle.

"This business is more complicated than I'd supposed," said Richard. "But if the girl was upset, I don't think she wanted him dead."

"It could have been guilt," I said. "Or perhaps she meant to kill the elder, while keeping the younger."

He frowned, nodding. "I'll ask her. What's her name?"

"Grey," Lizzie replied.

"Thank you," Richard said. "I haven't found a witness yet. Carier has done his best in the servants' hall, making friends with both factions, but he's sure nobody there saw anything, or knows who did this. I'm very much afraid this affair may remain a mystery, though now that wretched Pritheroe knows, not a private one."

Lizzie looked afraid, her eyes wide, her mouth turned down at the corners.

"Face them down," he told her. "Only the undeserving will give the rumours any credit."

Strangers, new faces, with a place to make. When I thought about it I felt quite sick.

"I must make myself busy," Richard said. "I promised your brother I would look into this, but my own affairs are becoming urgent too. I fear I must take my leave soon."

His statement hit me with the power of a fallen oak tree,

although I knew he would have to go eventually. In a daze, thoughts passed through my mind, that Lizzie was right about him all along, that he had only amused himself with me. I would become an anecdote at dinner parties, no more.

All this shot through my head in my panic, as he continued to speak, but his next information mitigated his previous statement. "I do not scruple to say in present company I have found my betrothal to Miss Cartwright unsupportable." I nearly sighed with relief, catching it back just in time. "I have to extricate myself from the contract before I pursue anything else. I'll escort the two ladies to their home, then speak to Miss Cartwright's father. Then I must face our own father." Gervase grimaced. "I'll burn the damned papers. Then I hope to return here. It may be some time," he said addressing me directly, "but we will come about." When he looked at me like that I believed him. Doubts assaulted me when I wasn't in his presence.

"Miss Cartwright may prefer a breach of promise suit," said Gervase. "It could prove very expensive."

"I know. But I see no alternative."

There seemed to be little else to say. On that gloomy note, we retired.

Lizzie came into my room later and sat on the edge of the bed. "You're determined to have him."

"Yes." I sat up and pulled the covers around me.

"You know what this will do? Not just to you, but to the rest of us?"

"Yes. I'm sorry. We'll do our best to mitigate it, but some of it will get through, I know. You can face it out. And if we discover who cut the strap on the coach, that can be sorted out and the perpetrator brought to justice."

"Yes." She leaned forward and took my hand. "But what will you do, Rose? You can't manage Strang. I've watched him. He knows his place in the world, and what he wants. He'll drag you behind him, might even leave you after a while. Rose, I'm dreadfully afraid for you."

I bit my lip. "I'm afraid for myself, but I can't stop now. I'd regret it for the rest of my life if I didn't give this a chance. I know what he is and has been, but I must trust him, not all the stories about him." I met her worried gaze. "I have to, Lizzie."

"Oh, Rose." I felt her hand, warm in mine and saw the anxiety she was feeling.

"I know this will resurrect all the old scandals associated with him and his brother. It may mark us as *personae non grata* forever. But we'll go away and live quietly somewhere."

"Run away." Lizzie grimaced.

"No, Lizzie, go away. Give you and the others a chance to be accepted into society before we return, to drag scandals behind us. You can refuse us—turn your backs if you want to, if it saves you from the mire."

She shook her head. "You know we'll never do that. We love you, Rose. We'll never forget that, whatever trouble you find yourself in."

"Thanks for that. I love you, too."

"It seems you love someone else now."

After she had gone, I sat for a long while, thinking, before I finally went to sleep.

Chapter Fourteen

Richard's statement made me act the next day. There was a strong possibility he would leave and never come back. His father was a formidable opponent, by all accounts. Perhaps Richard could stand firm against him, but there was no guarantee of it. His family might persuade him to take the sensible course. If he did, the next time I saw him, he'd be a married man. It had to be now, I was sure of it. Thinking of my plans mind knotted my stomach so badly I couldn't eat, but I determined on my course and I would know him, if only once. I had spent my life thinking about the right thing to do, but this time I wanted something for myself alone.

I'd avoided Richard's company in private while I thought things through, but after I'd made my preparations, I sought him out. I found him in the small drawing room shortly after breakfast, reading. As I entered, he cast his book aside and stood to greet me. Since we were alone, he gave me a kiss, but then released me. Someone might come in the room at any moment.

"Will you walk with me?" I asked.

"With pleasure, my delight." I laid my hand on his proffered arm and we walked through the State Rooms, looking at all the improvements that had taken place there in so short a time.

The servants were still hard at work there, supervised by Lizzie, busily and noisily industrious. I'd asked her to take over for me and she'd reluctantly agreed. I said there were things I wanted to discuss with Richard before he left. "But don't be too long, and don't go out of my sight," she told me. I docilely agreed, then went my own way. The smell of beeswax pervaded the rooms, together with the sharper smell of ammonia, used to clean the porcelain, the windows and the mirrors. It was much more pleasant, but it reminded me of my home in Devonshire. After this visit, nothing would ever be the same again.

Richard opened a door for me and we passed through into the old house. Here it remained the same as it had been for the last ten years—gloomy, damp, filthy and cold. He looked around, frowning. "Shall we go back?"

I shook my head. "There's something I'd like to show you first." I took him through the wrecked rooms, upstairs, and into the old nursery.

He saw the pathos at once. "All these things just abandoned." He stopped short when he saw the old baby house. "Wait—" He examined the house, and the shattered remains of the contents strewn before it. "This house was purposely tipped over." Upon further investigation, it seemed the other toys had been purposely hurled around the room, deliberately destroyed.

I hadn't noticed that before. "Someone very disturbed has been here. We can't know who it was, but from the age of the things it must have been one of the last two Lord Haretons. Or both of them."

He stood amongst the shattered, damp ruin. "It's grotesque. I'm not sure I want to stay here any longer. Is this what you wished to show me?"

"Just one more room." I opened the door to the nursemaid's room and we went through.

In stark contrast to the nursery, here all was in order. The sparse furniture, chest of drawers, cupboard and made-up bed were clean and tidy. Richard surveyed the room. "Now who could have done this?"

"I did," I said. "Yesterday."

He was silent, his face serious. He stood apart from me, and waited, watching me.

"I wanted to give you something before you left," I rushed

what I wanted to say, too nervous to remember the speech I'd rehearsed. "Something you can remember me by, but all my dearest possessions are still in Devonshire. I have nothing worthy of you, nothing you would want." I took a breath. Now or never. "Except, perhaps, one thing." I waited for him, my gaze never leaving his face.

He stared at me for several minutes before understanding my meaning. Then shock registered on his face, eyes widened, holding a numbness I could interpret as horror, shock, repugnance or all three. He looked as though I'd shot him. "Oh, no."

I couldn't tell whether I disgusted or dismayed him and I felt the familiar sensation of deep embarrassment and the desire for the earth to swallow me up. By my reckless plan I had destroyed any hope of happiness. He'd think I was like all the other women who'd offered themselves to him for an afternoon's amusement.

The possibility of this reaction frightened me very much, but I knew I had to try, for my own peace of mind. I needed to come to terms with the longing I felt every night since I'd fallen in love with him. I knew only this way to do it, and I didn't know if it would help, or if it would make matters worse, but I couldn't go on like this. If he went away and never returned, I'd always wonder, never move on with my life. I had to know for sure if this was real, or if he was playing with me. He said he wanted me, but how did I know if he didn't say that to anyone? Deep down I felt the truth of what he told me, but I didn't trust myself enough to believe it. And I wanted him. Just once, I wanted this for myself. If he left, I might never know what it was like to give myself to a man in love if I didn't persuade him now.

Richard's presence made me yearn for his touch, but I didn't understand why. Not yet.

Richard strode quickly to the other door, which led to the hall outside and my heart sank. He was rejecting me. He paused, and turned around to face me with an abruptness that was so unlike his usual grace that I knew he was deeply troubled.

"What made you think I would consent? Did you think I had so little consideration for you, I could do such a thing to *you*?" Hurt and anger suffused his voice. "Did I give you any sign that I wanted this? Did I, Rose?"

How could he think that? After those first, passionate kisses in the stables he'd kept a rigid hold of his physical response to me. I shook my head. "The fault is all mine." He might see me as a hoyden, someone unfit to be his wife. But for now, I would settle for mistress. It was an answer—of a sort.

"No. I should have remained more circumspect. I knew it." His face twisted with hurt as he regarded me. "I have consorted with the more promiscuous woman for too long now. I no longer know how to behave with someone like you. You thought I wanted this, didn't you? That's why you've taken these steps."

"No, no!" I tried to assure him from where I stood, as I didn't have the courage to go any closer to him yet. I tried to explain. "It's only—this is all I have to give you, and if you never return, or you come back married to—someone else, I can never offer it again." I swallowed, but said it all. I might never have another chance. "I want you, Richard, in every way. Just this once."

"And what if someone found us? What then?"

I was more sure of this part. I'd made my plans carefully. "Lizzie is supervising downstairs. Steven is in the chapel, the Misses Cartwright are in their rooms, resting. None of the servants come up here because they think it's haunted. There's no one to find us."

I crossed the room to him, but I didn't touch him, so nervous I could hardly breathe. "It's such a little thing. My virginity means nothing to me, once you're gone." With this statement and my offer I was betraying everything I'd been brought up to believe and hold dear, but none of it mattered to me now. I'd have said anything to persuade him. I leaned forward and kissed him, and he didn't resist or break away, but circled me with both arms, returning my kiss softly, but his lips trembled when they left mine. "What are you thinking of?" He gazed down at my tense face.

"You've done it before."

"Many times. But never with a—an inexperienced woman. A virgin. You can't know what this means, my love, you can't allow this. Whatever you say, you know this is precious, that you're expected to keep your maidenhead safe."

But I wanted this. I wasn't entirely unaware of the passionate urges felt by a man for a woman. I didn't know I could feel so strongly, could betray all my better judgement so thoroughly. I knew if I didn't persuade him to make love to me just once, even if it led to disgrace, something inside me would die, never to be rekindled. Rather than lose that, I would do this now.

"I've thought about little else since I met you. I want to know why I feel like this, what it's all for, why I feel so tormented. I can stand anything if once, just once, I knew."

"My precious love!" He kissed me. I think he meant it to be gentle, but I wouldn't let him stop. After the first, tender caress, I pulled him closer, opened my mouth to him and he took possession, stroking his tongue against mine in the most intimate caress I had ever known—until now.

His kisses became increasingly deep and longing. I tried to make him see how much I needed this, since I couldn't explain in words. His body hardened against mine, heated me to fever pitch and he held me tightly against him, so I felt all his body's responses.

He had been celibate for some time now, according to his brother and his confession to me earlier in the week. This must have taken its toll on him, and I hoped this too would help to persuade him. He stopped once, drawing back to look at me, seriously. "Are you sure? Oh, my love, you must be sure, we can't go back once we've done this."

Triumph surged through me when I knew I'd won. "Yes, oh yes,"

They were the last coherent words I spoke for some time.

He kissed me again, harder, more passionately than I'd known him to do before, and I began to realise how much he'd held back before. His tongue took possession of my mouth, owned it. He unhooked the front of my gown with practiced fingers. I helped him out of his coat, not as expertly but with the same intent. Feverishly shedding clothes, we made our way to the little bed. We kissed, caressed, and exchanged murmured words of love as we went.

I pushed my hand up and felt his strong, muscled back beneath the fine lawn shirt. Impatiently, he pulled the garment up and drew it over his head. I thought he looked beautiful, but it was he who said, "Rose, Rose, you're lovely," when he stripped me out of my chemise and drew back to look at me. I felt no shame as his gaze heated me as much as his body had. "Dear God, I've never felt this about another woman. I didn't know I could burn like this."

I barely had time to pull the covers back before he lifted me off my feet and laid me down on the pure white sheets. He looked at me as I waited for him, and let me look at him. Strongly muscled but lithe, if I'd thought I knew what a nude male body looked like, I was wrong. Marble statues and small children held no resemblance to the aroused, strong body before me now.

I felt no shame, no reticence under his loving gaze. He lay down beside me and took me into his arms; the very place I longed to be.

Consumed by passion, hot with it, he couldn't have stopped now if I'd asked him to. For the first time, I experienced the power a woman has over a man, and began to understand these mysteries.

I arched my throat for his kisses. This time he didn't stop when he came to the base of my throat, he didn't pull away as he had before in the coach house, but continued down, all the while murmuring endearments I could hardly hear. He kissed my nipples, roused them into unbearable centres of sensation. I wanted him to stop, I wanted him to carry on until I exploded, I wanted more. He seemed to sear my skin where he touched me with his hands and his mouth, as he made sure I was ready for him. No one had ever touched me in those places before. It was as though they had been asleep, waiting for his touch to awaken them. I gasped when I felt his fingers gently probe me, but I wasn't afraid. I moved into his touch, pressing against him. He kissed me. "You're so beautiful. I want you so much." He lifted his body over me, kissing me again, passionate and loving. His legs rested inside mine, the rough hair abrading the sensitive skin of my inner thighs. I bent my knees, the better to accommodate him and his shaft met the opening to my body.

He pushed, gently at first, then gave one hard thrust.

Pain shot through me and I cried out into his mouth. He broke away, gazing down at me with concern. "Never again. I'll never hurt you again, my sweet love, my angel. I swear it." He soothed me with words and hands, stroking my hair, softly kissing my face.

He shifted to let me know he was still inside me, but didn't try to move any deeper until I kissed him back, in an attempt to let him know my desire for him had grown again. "Richard. Love me."

"I do. I will." Smiling, he did as I asked, and thrust deeper, until he was fully seated inside me, then withdrew, only to push inside again. The heat that suffused my body became more focused on the place where we met, where his body invaded mine and radiated out once more, sending shivers through me. I braced my body against the bed, used my feet to gain purchase to push up as he drove into me, until we achieved a rhythm.

His movements became stronger, more urgent as my body dampened and made his passage easier. I rejoiced in his power, his control. The waves of warm ecstasy, strengthened, grew and spread until they racked my whole body with agonising joy. I could only feel, gasp and arch my body under him. He watched me as I laughed in delight before the thrills cascading through my body escalated to one hard wrench and my body convulsed in response to his thrusts.

He seemed relentless. He caressed and kissed me, pushed me to greater and greater heights until I thought I would die of pleasure, but I didn't care.

All at once, with a great cry, he closed his eyes and gripped me tightly as he sank down over my body, engrossed in his own little death. His shaft pulsed inside me, urging me to another climax of sensation.

It was as well we were alone on this floor, or someone would have heard us for sure.

We lay still, panting, then he moved to one side and, took his weight off me. He gathered me back into his arms and kissed me lovingly, murmuring endearments I heard properly now. "My heart's treasure, oh my dearest love."

I felt warm, wanted, feelings entirely fresh to me. I lay against him, and luxuriated in the newness of my body.

I shivered when the sweat chilled on me, and Richard drew the covers over us, returning to hold me. He kissed me again, slowly, then opened his eyes and gazed at me. We stared at each other.

I smiled. "And this is it?" I knew full well it was.

"Yes. This is it. This is why I'll never let you go, why I'll love you until I die. If you planned to capture me completely, you've achieved it now."

"No, that wasn't my plan, I only wished to know why I felt like I did. Now I know. I understand some other things too. My whole world has changed." Wonder filled me when I realised that was no more than the truth. I understood him, understood myself and I would no longer doubt his intentions. He gave himself to me just as much as I did to him. Naked and open to each other, I knew what he'd told me was nothing less than the bare truth.

He laughed then, a long slow chuckle of sheer pleasure. "I adore you. Leaving will only be bearable if I'm sure you'll welcome me back."

I studied his dear face; short, fair hair tousled, nothing but love in his eyes, he seemed much younger than his thirty years—very different from the creature who had amazed and intimidated me on our first day here. "How can you say such a thing?" I was sure of him now as never before. "Wherever I am I'll always welcome you, in my heart and in my bed."

"That's more generosity than I've any right to expect."

I laughed. "Pooh! Many women opened their beds to you before. This isn't new to you." But my words were more in the nature of a tease than a demonstration of the doubts I'd had before we'd made love.

He kissed me tenderly. "No one with as much to lose, no one who showed me such trust before. But you won't lose, my sweet life. I promise you now—in six months we'll be married. We'll spend every night together, if you wish it."

I caught my breath, sure something would go wrong, to stop this pure delight we found in each other. This couldn't possibly be for me. The obstacles waiting outside this little room might defeat us yet, but I would always have this. I was so glad I'd had the courage to go through with it.

"I didn't know. I didn't know if you wanted me forever, but it didn't seem important any more."

"It's important. I'll write it down for you, if you like. Would that help you? Give you some proof of my intentions while I'm away, something to be sure of?"

I shook my head. "I don't need proof, other than this." I meant it, too. I was as sure of him now as I was of myself.

He touched his lips to mine in a gentle kiss, passion assuaged for the present. "We might cause scandal, but I don't care any more. My family will have to look to themselves. God knows, I owe them nothing. Except, perhaps, for my sister, Maria. I'll be sorry if she suffers because of anything I might do."

I, too, would be sorry to bring his younger sister trouble. But when I looked at him, relaxed and happy, I couldn't regret what we'd done.

He smiled. "I haven't been this out of control for years, if I ever was. We shouldn't be here, should never have done this. But I needed you so much. You took all my senses with your first kiss, and after that, I was yours. Could you bear this, in the years to come?"

"Oh yes."

He kissed me deeply in response, his tongue caressing every part of my mouth.

"I won't believe it until it happens," I said then.

"Should you mind *where* it happens?"

I didn't understand. "What do you mean?"

"If we cause unpleasant gossip, if scandal erupts, we might be better going away, for a while. Then I'll be the disgraced brother. I don't want you to enter the bear pit in London without some experience behind you and I won't subject you to that kind of attention. If Julia still won't cry off, but makes me break the contract, would you come to Venice with me after a quiet ceremony somewhere?"

"Venice? I always wanted to see Venice," I said happily.

"I've a small apartment there. It's mine, bought with money I earned. I've never taken anyone else there before. It's always been my sanctuary and I'd like to share it with you."

"It sounds wonderful."

He drew me to him, punctuating his words with small kisses, on my mouth and throat. "I have a great desire to make love to you in the bedroom there, with the windows open to the sound of the water, and the church bells, and the light." I blushed, a different kind of heat suffusing me. He laughed softly. "How can you blush? Not a stitch on, and still you can blush!" He lay back on the bed, drawing me closer into his arms, one arm behind my head, the other softly caressing my body, as if he couldn't stop touching me. I knew how he felt. I traced an imaginary line on his chest. Touching him was a joy, everything I'd thought it would be when I'd lain awake during those lonely nights since we arrived at the Abbey.

He looked around at the sparse little room. "'For love, all love of other sights controls; And makes one little room an everywhere.' I never knew what he meant before, but it makes sense now."

"Who?"

"John Donne. I'll read the whole poem to you one day."

I was relaxed and happy, ready to explain something to

him. I took a breath. "I wanted to do this now because I wanted to give you my maidenhead. I didn't want you to take it as your right, as a husband does, I wanted it to be a gift."

He turned his head to look me in the eyes. "The most precious possession you have."

"Had," I corrected him.

"It will most likely take me a lifetime to pay it back. Have you thought of that?"

I laughed. "Then you mustn't try. I give it to you freely."

His caresses became less gentle as the answering tingle rose within me. His skill meant I could enjoy his loving more than once—even now, my first time. I lay against him, enjoying the sensations, trying to remember them for when I was alone, though now I knew for certain he would come back for me. I watched his tender smile when he saw my reaction to his loving, and reached my hand up to him, touching the slight roughness of his cheek. He moved his head to kiss my palm.

Desire rose again within me when I felt his shaft harden against my body. I had never known anything so exciting in my life before. He leaned over to kiss me and love me again and I seemed to know what to do in return, as if it had always been there inside me and he released it all. I touched him and felt triumph when his soft groan told me just how much my touch affected him. His hands released all the sensuality I never suspected I owned.

Smiling, he paused, his hand resting on my stomach. "Can you do this? I love you so much, want you so badly but I'm afraid I'm forgetting your well-being. I'm not so far gone I can't think of your welfare first."

I smiled back at him, taking his hand and placing it on my breast. "I can do this."

This time, we were not so frenzied. He had more time to love me and I him. I touched him, felt his eager response, knowing it was all for me. He kissed me, slowly, lingeringly. He kissed a nipple, suckled until it stood hard for him, leaving me gasping with desire. His hands, his graceful, mobile hands moved over me, caressing, exploring, making me feel complete.

Lifting over me, he entered me again, laughing softly when he heard my contented sigh. I opened my eyes and watched him loving me, felt his hands on my body, reached my hands up to touch him. He helped me to heights more sustained than last time, but just as wonderful. I could mark the climb, instead of plunging straight into mindless pressure. I was glad he had so much experience, so he could bring this confidence as his gift to me. Even then, I guessed it must be rare for a woman to achieve so much joy during her first encounter. I couldn't have loved him more.

Curling my legs around his, I pulled him close when I felt his body tremble, invited him to thrust as deeply, as hard as he needed to. I had never felt so at one with anyone before. He rolled to one side, taking me with him, settling the covers over us.

Overwhelmed by ecstasy and exhaustion, I fell asleep, safe in his arms as he murmured words of love.

It was a singularly foolish thing to do.

I awoke with his hand pressing my face against his shoulder. I knew a moment of panic before I heard what he had—footsteps coming up the corridor outside towards us, the occasional opening of a door, as though someone was exploring. Then I panicked even more.

Richard prevented me from lifting my head and being recognised by whoever approached the door. He put his mouth by my ear. "Stay still, say nothing." I rolled on to my stomach, and he pulled the covers up around me. He drew my loose hair over my face, and we waited.

I heard the door to the corridor open, and I knew someone stood there, looking at us. A breathed, "My God," told me who it was. I moved involuntarily, but Richard's hand pressed into my shoulder in warning.

Richard turned his face to the door. "Good afternoon." I nearly laughed at the formality of his greeting.

"Good afternoon, my lord," said Steven.

Chapter Fifteen

I heard Steven breathing heavily, recovering from the shock of discovering us like this. "As you can see," Richard said calmly, once Steven had regained some self control, "your presence here is rather *de trop*."

"I cannot believe you would do such a thing, my lord," Steven gasped. Agitation coloured his voice.

"Believe it," Richard said firmly, but without heat.

"Who is it? Tell me which girl, my lord." Typical of Steven not to forget Richard's title.

"No. You will most likely get her into trouble with her mother or Lady Hareton. She's mortally afraid of either eventuality. Aren't you, my dear?" He was lucky I didn't giggle. Shock had given me that strange impulse to laugh that comes over people sometimes. I said nothing.

"This is abominable!"

"I fail to see your reasoning, sir. True, I have taken a girl from her proper work for the day, but she didn't object. I'll see her well rewarded for it."

"My lord, you have abused her ladyship's hospitality."

"Really? I shall apologise to her then. But I think that may cause more embarrassment than if we kept silent, don't you think?"

I knew that Steven, having got over his initial shock, would try to make something of the situation. "As a man of God, I do not feel equal to that proposal."

Richard laughed. "If you were a true man of God, I doubt you would chase after quite so many skirts yourself." He had given Steven a facer, a deliberate provocation to put him on the defensive, to block further questions. It didn't matter if it were true or not, only that Steven responded.

Steven rose to the bait. "I beg your pardon, sir, you can have no such information." The very air bristled with his indignation.

"I'm not blind, Drury. And neither is my brother. You seem to have designs on half the females in this house. And don't tell me you've not made a play for at least one of the maids, because I won't believe it. However, I've beaten you to it this time, so kindly take yourself off and close the door behind you."

"His lordship shall hear of this immediately upon his return."

Steven left, but closed the door behind him as Richard had asked him. We heard his hurrying footsteps retreat down the corridor and the stairs at the end.

"My guess is that he'll lay in wait for us below. Is there any other way out of here, my sweet love?"

I lifted my head, pale with shock. I thought Steven would insist on seeing me, and I couldn't believe he hadn't recognised me, but Richard's accusations distracted him.

"There are the back stairs," I offered, almost whispering.

He smiled to reassure me. "This whole thing is so outrageous, he'll never guess it was you. Whatever made me insane enough to do this I can't possibly imagine." He paused, his gaze growing more intent. "Oh yes I can," he corrected himself, and he drew me back into his arms and kissed me, long and lingering. "I will return as soon as I can. Just wait until the scandal over Julia has passed and then I'll return. I don't know how I'll wait until I have you in my bed once more." He gave a self-deprecating laugh. "Of course, my reputation is already so bad your brother might well take it into his head to keep you away from me for good."

Nobody would do that, not now. "I'm my own person. I'll have whoever I choose."

"Well said." He took my face in his hands and kissed me one more time. "Don't fear—we'll see them all off. But, Rose...now we've committed ourselves thus far, I have to ask you something."

"Yes?" My stomach muscles tightened.

His gaze remained loving, but gained a graver cast. "Will you take me with nothing? Julia's father loves her very much. He may seek such revenge in the courts that I'll be left with nothing. I have a personal fortune, but I could lose that in any breach of promise case. My father may well cast me off and disown me, as much as he can. He's threatened it before. He might actually do it this time, if things go badly for me. He can't take the title or the entail away, but the Southwood title has very little entailed property, so he could will them away from me. I have the means of making my own way in the world, and I'm not afraid of working for a living. I don't care, for myself, but for you. You deserve better. We can avoid the worst of the scandal if we go abroad, but no one will receive us. We'll be outcasts. It might seem trivial to you now, but we may be thrown on each other's company with no distractions and no comforts. We won't starve but we won't have any spare income for a while. Can you bear all that?"

I relaxed, smiled. "You're all I want. Nothing else." I meant it. If doing without him meant facing society on my own, going back to a life of comfortable spinsterhood, then I knew I couldn't do it. Not now.

He kissed me for a long time. "I'll make you happy. I swear it."

We gazed at each other, totally content, then he smiled. "I fear we must face the world again, sweetheart, so—" He sat up and flung back the covers, swung his legs out of the bed, then turned to help me out. "By the way about these sheets. I would have thought after ten years they would have been in a worse condition than they are—"

I bit my lower lip. Time to tell the truth. "I put them on the bed yesterday. I took them from the discard pile and I shall take them to be burned now. No one will miss them."

To my surprise, after an astonished, "You little schemer!" he burst into laughter, finding it difficult to stop. "I...I only thought," he gasped after a good minute of trying hard to get his breath back, "how my friends in town wouldn't believe it. I allowed myself to be seduced by an inexperienced country girl." That sent him off again. I saw the funny side, though I'd begun to think it wasn't that funny, when he controlled his mirth.

He put an arm around me, drawing me to his side. "You're so good for me. I can't remember when I've laughed so much. There seemed precious little reason to laugh in recent months." He kissed me soundly, and then bent to pick up my shift, the last article of clothing he had removed from me. "I make an excellent lady's maid."

He was right. He knew just where every lace and pin should go, and he even made a reasonable job of taming my unruly hair. He needed no help himself, except with his heavy coat, which was too much for the stiffness in his arm.

Properly dressed, we were ourselves again, and I felt shy, foolish even. "I'll follow Drury on my own. If he's waiting, I'll keep him busy. Can you find another way out without anyone seeing you?"

I nodded.

"One more thing." He took my face in his hands, looking directly into my eyes. I saw no amusement there now, no laughter. He looked at me steadily. "Everything I said to you today, I meant. I love you more than I can say. While we both know this shouldn't have happened, I'll never regret it. I will marry you, and I'll do it after a proper courtship. I'll take Julia home, and come back for you. This I promise, whatever it costs."

I knew this was a solemn oath, and he meant what he said.

I leaned forward to kiss him but he drew back after one, tender exchange. "And if you quicken, you must promise to tell me at once. What other plans we have will be as nothing. We'll marry at once, and damn the scandal."

I promised and he kissed me once more, his lips lingering on mine as if he couldn't bear to part with me. Then he left, quickly, before, as he said, I undid all his resolve. God knows I wanted to.

I stripped the sheets off the bed, leaving the blankets neatly folded on top, and then I knelt to check the floor. Unfortunately in our haste, we had torn off several of his waistcoat buttons, and Richard being Richard, they were fine, distinctive ones. I scrabbled about, locating as many as I could, then I pocketed them and left the room—not by the corridor, but by a small door in the corner. This looked as though it should be a cupboard, but opened on stairs leading down to the servants' corridors. I had discovered it the day before, when I cleaned the room and made the bed.

I went down to the basement. I'd screwed the sheets into as tight a bundle as I could make them, the secret of my lost virginity tucked inside.

Servants filled the kitchen, so dinner must be well under way. I threw my bundle on the fire, pushing it to the back with a poker, making certain sure the fire caught it. "Rags," I explained to the one maid who lifted her head. Then I went up the backstairs to the outside of the house, coming in again through the side door.

I went up to my room, noticing it was half past two. I must hurry, to dress in time for dinner. A maid entered—Grey—and I looked at her with new understanding, wondering how she'd felt having her lover taken from her.

If she noticed the knot that tied my stays was not the same one she'd tied that morning, she said nothing. "Is it true," I asked her, "that you loved the last earl, the younger brother?"

Her hands faltered at the back of my gown, and then she continued. "Yes, ma'am."

"Would you have done anything for him?"

"Anything."

She fetched the black gown from York from the bed, and held it open. I slipped my arms into the sleeves and she busied herself hooking it up at the front. "I understood he knew a few of the village maids."

She snorted. "They didn't understand him, ma'am. He needed care and understanding, but they didn't notice that. His brother kept him short of money all the time." I looked up and met her sorrowful gaze. "He needed looking after, ma'am. He was so sad, so afraid of everyone and everything."

I nodded. "Thank you." From what she had said, I doubted the fifth earl was in complete command of all his faculties, though whether by birth or the abuse heaped on him from childhood could never be discerned now. His father's draconian treatment, then his brother's deprivations would be enough to turn anyone's mind.

I had eliminated another suspect. I met Lizzie on the way down to dinner and told her my news. She sighed. "I talked to her, too. She seems to have had real affection for the poor man. I'm glad he had someone." She glanced at me, sharply. "So where did you get to this afternoon? I couldn't go and find you without causing comment, but I would have done if I could."

"Oh, we toured the top corridor and then we walked in the gardens for a while." I marvelled how easy I found it to lie to her, when I'd never kept secrets from her before. "Then he went in to rest, and I stayed outside. Do you know how much work there is to do in the gardens?"

"Oh, I can guess." Lizzie seemed satisfied with my explanation. "Ten years' growth must amount to a forest."

"You can just discern flower beds from hedge," I said, improvising wildly. "I think it would be best razed to the ground and done all over again."

"You're probably right," she agreed, and we went to dinner.

Steven behaved towards Richard with increasing insolence, perhaps thinking they shared a secret when he'd discovered us *in flagrante*. Richard took no more notice of him than he did of Miss Cartwright, treating them both with the same rigid politeness.

That first night, I dared not catch Richard's attention, but after that, I felt easier in his company. In public, he was careful not to touch me or look at me more than needed to. From that I knew our encounter had affected him as much as it had affected me. For the next few days, I was happy just to feel the warmth of his presence. Lizzie watched me so closely it became impossible to have any private time with him, but now I was content to wait. I was sure of him as I had never been before and I realised that it was at the moment of complete vulnerability, complete surrender, that I'd won everything I wanted, and more.

I hugged my secret to myself, dreaming of it in private moments. I couldn't believe that people like Martha and James had a similar secret, because I was so self-centred in my own happiness. The knowledge that they'd had ten happy years of marriage and three children of their own didn't seem to coincide with what I had experienced that wonderful day. I was sure he wanted me. I was sure I wanted him.

Martha and James returned from York. Behind them followed a hired coach full of Martha's purchases, with more to follow. James reported that probate of the will was passing through the court smoothly, though, since it was a Church court, it might take a little more time. Wills usually passed through Church courts, due to some archaic law. He would use the title and have power of attorney on the estate until it formally passed to him. If Lady Hareton proved with child, James would be guardian in the baby's minority, so his care of the estate seemed certain, either way.

Mr. Pritheroe hadn't yet made any formal objection in the courts, though he continued to protest to James personally. He got about a little better now and the joiner James had engaged for the estate made him a crutch. His approach, heralded by a stumping noise, usually caused a general exodus from whichever room he headed for, but he showed no signs of leaving the Abbey. In a way, that was a good thing, for he intended to take Lady Hareton with him when he left. Martha wanted to prevent him from doing so, if she could.

Mr. Pritheroe tried hard to keep his daughter apart from us. They took their dinner in the little parlour and he made her stay with him afterwards. He read his choice of passages from the Bible to her. In his stentorian tones, we could hear it all over our part of the house. She didn't offer to help Martha, but that was probably because he didn't allow her to. She seemed totally cowed by her father, and it was sad to witness such capitulation. She could have been pretty if she had worn her hair in a looser style, if her caps—now black—had sported more lace than linen, but since she had never been taught self worth, it had never entered her life. I had chosen to be careless of dress, not been forced into it, and these days, I found I was more attentive and took more care over my appearance. I knew exactly why.

Chapter Sixteen

I'd volunteered to help Martha, so I put on the dress that I'd worn on that memorable afternoon—old but respectable and not too worn, sighing at the necessity. I had found a vanity I'd never been aware of in myself before. I found my pocket on its string, and felt a clinking weight when I tied it around my waist. Upon investigation, it proved to be the buttons I'd picked up. I'd forgotten all about them, but resolved to return them before a maid found them and reported it to Martha.

I wrapped them in a little parcel and walked to Richard's room.

Carier opened the door to me, and after a swift, conspiratorial look around that amused me more than a little, let me into the room. My lord was attired in the magnificent dressing gown I'd seen the other day, all dragons and crescent moons, and small Chinese figures going about their business. He laughed at my frank admiration of it after he'd kissed my hand. "They were all the rage last season so, much to my mother's despair I set about obtaining the finest one I could find. My father said he hoped my mistresses would be pleased with it. And you do seem to be pleased," he added in a low tone, making me blush. I hadn't thought of myself as his mistress, but there seemed no other relationship to be had, and so I supposed that must be what I was. I looked behind me, but the estimable Carier was busy brushing down a blue cloth coat. I put the little parcel into Richard's hand. He looked at it, quizzically. "Another gift?"

"No, merely your own again." He opened the parcel, letting the contents fall on the dressing table as he laughed at them. "How considerate of you, my sweet." Carier glanced up at the endearment and smiled grimly, but said nothing.

"I must go. I only came to return the buttons."

The manservant forestalled me at the door. "You'll allow me to look first, madam." He put his hand upon the door, just as a knock fell on it. I started back in shock. Richard stood quickly, gesturing toward the dressing room door. Carier took me there. Unfortunately, the outer door proved to be locked, so the manservant went back for the key as Richard opened the door to his visitor.

"Good morning, my lord."

"Good morning, Julia. You shouldn't be here, you know."

"I wish to discuss something with you, sir, in private," came the cultured, chilly voice. It drifted languidly into the room where I stood trapped. Carier couldn't rescue me now. I sat quietly on the small couch amongst coats, waistcoat and other male paraphernalia which hung there. I smelled his scent on some of them. I breathed it in, loving the reminder of him and waited.

The outer door opened and closed again. Carier had gone. If he'd managed to get the key, he might come to let me out now, but he didn't come. The door to the bedroom was slightly ajar, but I dared not close it in case Miss Cartwright faced that way. I could just see Richard where he stood by the fire. I couldn't read the expression on his face, but his clenched hand, rested on the mantelpiece, the knuckles white.

Miss Cartwright's clear, cultured voice drifted over the room. "I wanted to discuss your desire to break our contract."

His grip on the mantelpiece relaxed a little. "Yes?"

"It has come to my notice that you have been—taking your amusements with the maids of this house. I do not believe it."

"Believe it," he said steadily, as he had to Steven. "Did Drury tell you?"

"Mr. Drury believed it his sad duty to communicate the fact

to me. I didn't believe him. I said as much, then he said he had proof." She extended her hand to him. I guessed what lay on the palm—a button.

Richard took it. "Thank you. I should be sorry to lose the complete set."

"Is that all you can say, sir?" She raised her voice for the first time I had known in our short acquaintance. "Don't you think you owe me an apology, at the very least?"

He sighed. "Julia, you know what I am, what I've been and what I told you I would become if we married. I never hid anything from you when I made you that infamous proposal. If you can't put up with it, then it's better you know now that I'm not the man for you. You could never tolerate my behaviour if I married you." He paused. "Let me go. Let's do this in a civilised manner and part friends. You know what your father will do when I break the contract. And if you won't release me, I *will* break it, have no doubts on that score."

"What will my father do?"

"He'll bring a suit in the courts. Everyone will know our business. Everyone will read about us. Do you know what that will do to your prospects? Do you want that?"

There was silence. I heard her breathing hard. I felt distinctly uncomfortable, listening to something I shouldn't be hearing.

"But I want you." Hearing only her voice, I didn't think she meant it in a loving way. It sounded more like the way a spoilt girl might demand a new plaything. "I've set my heart on it."

"That can't be helped. You cannot have me." He hadn't moved.

She burst into a sudden flood of tears. "Richard."

He waited until it was clear this ruse had failed, too. "I'm sorry, but this can't go on. We simply would not suit, we would only make each other unhappy. If you won't break the contract, then I will. By far the best way would be to make a quiet statement to the press. You can go back to London with no fuss at all next season. But if you make me, I will break it, and that will lead to the scandal which both of our families must be anxious to avoid."

"What's wrong with me?" she cried, dramatically, deaf to reason. "Do you prefer a common maid to *me*?" I saw her hand move and heard the tearing sound of fabric giving way.

"Oh, my God." His hand moved, and the skirts of his robe swirled as he turned around. "For God's sake, madam, cover yourself."

The outer door opened. Julia's purpose became clear to me, as it must have done to him—this was an attempt to entrap him. I saw her now she had moved closer to him. Her torn bodice gaped obscenely against the otherwise perfectly groomed figure, and her bosom heaved with agitation as she thrust her breasts at him, challenging him to take hold.

The door opened. "Really, Richard, you should make certain you close your door if you insist on torrid encounters." The key turned in the lock.

I saw Richard breathe out once, heavily, then, without touching her he picked something up from the dressing table and crossed to the room where I stood, hardly able to breathe. He walked around Julia, giving her a wide berth. "See to the lady, will you, Gervase? She's as safe with you as she is with me."

"Safer," came the amused reply.

By the time he reached the room I had risen to my feet, so I wouldn't be seen when he entered. I moved in my old gown without a rustle. If I'd been wearing good quality silk, it would have been impossible.

He closed the door behind him and put his finger to his lips. Then he took one of the coats from the peg, stripped off his dressing gown and threw it across the couch where I had so lately sat. He needed my help with the coat, as his arm was still a little stiff, and then he opened his hand to show me he had the key from the dressing table. He unlocked the dressing room door, looking out before we stepped out. We couldn't hear Julia's noisy sobbing out here, now Gervase had closed the door.

Richard stepped into the corridor, gave the lace at his neck a final hitch and held out a hand to me. We hurried down the hall, to the stairs and the family rooms.

"She wanted to trap me or seduce me. If that is so, she'll need a witness, so her duenna can't be far behind."

"I thought it was the older Miss Cartwright when your brother came in."

"Thank God it wasn't."

He opened the door of the small parlour for me. The minister and his daughter looked up at us, their brows lifted in surprise. She was sewing straight seams on a coarse man's shirt, while he read aloud.

"Miss Golightly wondered if she could listen for a while," Richard said, with a completely grave face. "I, too, would appreciate a quiet half hour."

The minister could only agree, but he examined us closely through suspicious, beady eyes.

Richard led me to a hard wooden chair. He sat in a similar one himself, since they were all that was available. We sat for half an hour, nodding appreciatively. Richard in all his finery looked like a Turk in the New World. The rest of us were plainly dressed, and could have belonged to the same congregation. Not for the first time, I felt apprehensive of the future lying ahead of me. I might be sure of him, but what of his world? I would have nobody I knew to support me, no one but him. He was giving up much more for me. I hoped he would continue to think I was worth it.

We had our witnesses, in case Miss Cartwright should try to pursue her claim, and Gervase would do his best to restore her equanimity. Why, he might even succumb to her charms, I thought, but then I recollected that he'd never given her more than the usual courtesies.

After "Judges", I made an excuse and left, smiling at my particular Samson as I went out. He stood and bowed, remaining there while I went to find Martha to help her, as I'd promised.

Lizzie was her usual tardy self getting ready for dinner. Even though we were in black now, she spent a long time curling her hair. She primped and posed in front of the mirror, trying to get the right effect. I recollected, ruefully, how good blondes look in black caps. Mine made me look dowdy. It was different when mourning someone for whom you truly cared, I thought, sadly. I recalled the last time I was in black, grieving for my father. What I wore mattered little to me then.

"I'll see you down there." I went on ahead.

It surprised me to find only Richard and Gervase in the parlour. Richard at once came to me and kissed my hand, retaining it to draw me across to the sofa next to the fire. He sat, still holding my hand. Gervase regarded us solemnly, not pretending to ignore this indication of his brother's partiality. "Are you set on this course, Richard?"

"Completely. It's my turn to make trouble in paradise."

"If you're referring to society, your usual epithet of bear pit would be more appropriate," said Gervase acidly.

I said nothing, overwhelmed by Richard's first public act of affection towards me.

"Very well, Richard. God knows you've paid your dues. I'll do what I can to help. Does Miss Golightly know about this morning?"

Richard pressed my hand encouragingly. "She was in the dressing room."

Gervase paled. "Dear heaven, Richard, you can't carry on like this."

"I know it," Richard said ruefully. "Rose was merely returning something to me when Julia arrived. I didn't know the dressing room door was locked. I was trying to conclude matters with Julia when the lady made her move. By the way, did the elder Miss Cartwright arrive?"

"Right on cue." Gervase gave a wry grin. "Julia's gown had only come loose at the fastenings, so I could put her back together without too much trouble."

"You mean you didn't succumb to Miss Cartwright's ample charms?" Richard asked, with a gleam in his eye I didn't quite understand.

"Hardly." The brothers regarded at each other levelly. "I told her aunt she'd slipped. Though she must have known better, she had enough sense to accept it. She took the girl away. For all I know, Julia's crying still. If Carier hadn't fetched me, you'd have been well and truly caught, Richard."

"No." His grip on my hand increased slightly. "Not now. The only choice left to her is whether to make it a public matter or a private one."

"She seems determined to have you," Gervase said.

"I'm one expensive toy she must learn to do without."

Gervase nodded. "Where did you go this morning? I looked for you everywhere but I couldn't find you."

"Ah, but you didn't go into the small parlour." Richard watched his brother, who first looked surprised, then laughed.

"Then there is some justice in the world. How long did you listen to the inestimable minister?"

"Too long," sighed his twin.

Gervase laughed again. "It serves you right. But it's a good alibi."

"I thought so," agreed Richard urbanely.

"Julia is taking dinner in her room today. She says she has the headache." Gervase turned to me. "I'm sorry, this must be very confusing for you."

"Not at all. I've never been so sure of anything in my life."

Gervase looked from one to the other of us. "So it's like that, is it? Well I can't deny I'd rather welcome you as my sister-in-law than Julia, but there'll be a hell of a stink about it."

"I plan to take her to Venice after we're married," Richard told him.

"Really? Never known you to take anyone there before. Still, it would probably be the best place. He lives as a private citizen there," he informed me. "Even calls himself something else, so no one will reach you there unless you want them to. Our

185

parents won't be happy, but they'll have to cope with it the best they can. I'm sure you'll come about."

It sounded wonderful to me. Time enough to get used to being a viscountess after I'd become used to being his wife. If I ever did.

"I hope, for Rose's sake, you're right. I'm sure you will be." I felt the warmth of Richard's hand and I didn't care. I suppose I might, one day, but not for the foreseeable future.

Gervase tapped his lower lip with one finger. "So how are the investigations into the coach accident going?"

Richard sighed. "I've discovered nothing. All my enquiries, and Carier's have led nowhere. No one saw anything and everyone protests their innocence. It's impossible to know who cut the strap. It must have happened the evening before, when the brothers announced they were going to fetch the preacher. Apparently, the last time the coach was used was six months before." He shook his head. "Nobody knows anything about it. We've tried bribery, drink, simple asking, and it's got us nowhere." He looked at me then. "I'm sorry, my sweet. Your family will have to enter society under a cloud, after all."

The door opened to admit Steven. The brothers looked at him, but didn't stand. Richard didn't release my hand quickly enough. Steven's look travelled to it, and then to my face. I didn't blush before his amazed stare, but held my head up, meeting his gaze steadily, daring him to say something. Then Martha and James came in, closely followed by Lizzie, so he couldn't say anything after all. I still had the uncomfortable task of breaking with Steven, which meant I would have to meet him in private. I knew he wouldn't go quietly, but I was determined to make it clear where we stood.

When the ladies retired after dinner, I realised I'd lost my necessaire. I remembered having it last in Richard's dressing room earlier that day. I had felt it when I put a hand in my pocket to retrieve the parcel of buttons, but I couldn't recall having it after that. I decided to retrace my steps as far as I could, so I went to the small parlour first. I put my head cautiously around the door before going in, not wanting the minister to trap me for another sermon. There was no one there, so I went in and set my candle on a small table by the door.

The fire glowed dully, banked down for the night. Martha had overruled Mr. Pritheroe's request not to light the fire. She'd said Lady Hareton might easily make herself ill if she were not warm enough, and had the fire lit anyway. I found two more candles and lit them. The autumn afternoon darkened into evening, and I needed the light. I took one of them with me to search closer.

Near a chair, I found the silver chain that secured the necessaire to my waist. It must have broken under my skirt. Items lay scattered beneath the chair. I put down the candlestick, picked up the pieces and put them in my pocket. I only had to secure the chain again. I put out the candle, then turned to the mantelpiece to put out the one I had left there.

In the heavy carving above the old mantelpiece, by the raking light of the single candle, I saw what looked like a gap. I investigated. I took the little pair of scissors from my pocket, and inserted one of the blades carefully into the slit. I heard the snap as a secret door flew open.

These little cupboards were often fitted into mantels as a place to store valuables, but I found no treasure there. I felt inside, and then felt something sharp, and pulled my hand out precipitately. It bled from a new cut. I cursed myself for a fool, sucking angrily at the wound, and felt in my pocket for a handkerchief. Thankfully, the cut wasn't a bad one, and it only took a moment to bind.

I cautiously reached my hand up again, and this time I held the candle high so I could see inside properly.

What I pulled out of that cupboard made my breath catch. A knife, a large hunting knife, and as I had discovered, very sharp. It couldn't have been there very long, because it was shiny and clean.

Why would anyone want to put a knife in a secret cupboard? I could only think of one reason. Someone hadn't wanted to be caught with it on their person, and had hidden it quickly. The presence of the minister and his daughter in here every day must have made retrieval difficult, so it was still here. The parlour was near the back door, making it easy for someone to come in here and conceal it after they used it to cut the traces on the old coach.

This was a murder weapon.

At the realisation, I nearly dropped the thing. I gripped the hilt tighter, fearing that if I dropped it, the noise would attract attention. I couldn't replace it in its erstwhile resting place, for someone might come and take it away. Then any hope we might find the culprit would be lost for good. I'd have to take it away, and seek out Richard, James and Lizzie in the morning.

My pocket wouldn't hold so large a knife, and, since it had no sheath and was so sharp, I didn't want to hide it about my person. I closed the cupboard, blew out the candle on the mantelpiece, and took the one by the door out with me into the passage beyond. I was in luck: no one about to see I concealed the gleaming blade behind my black sleeve, hurrying to my room. I sighed in relief as I closed the door. They would miss me downstairs if I was away too long, so I had to be quick. I looked about and hid the knife in a drawer, tucking it under a large pile of stockings.

Downstairs, I was welcomed by calls to make a fourth at whist, but I'm afraid I didn't play very well that evening.

Chapter Seventeen

Before breakfast, there was only time to inform Lizzie I had something important to tell her. A maid accompanied her, helping her to dress, so I went back to my room.

The maid came to me and brushed my hair, drawing it back into a simple knot. I was wondering how to get a message to Richard and Gervase without compromising myself even further when a knock fell on the door. It was Carier. The maid let him in, leaving the door open for propriety's sake. The maid, the one with the broken heart, looked at him curiously. "From my master," the man said, woodenly. I thanked him. He bowed and left the room. I put the note away, until I should be alone. The maid finished and when she had gone, I opened the note.

"My courtship of you will begin in earnest, in a few weeks. Meanwhile, my only love, my future wife, this is what I referred to when you honoured me with your gift."

Then followed, in his own handwriting, a transcript of John Donne's "The Good Morrow," the one that begins:

"I wonder, by my troth, what thou and I
Did, till we loved? Were we not weaned till then?"

My memory flew back to that little room. I glowed with remembrance while I read. He had written this, knowing it gave me power over him. I could produce this as proof of his love and intention to make me his wife, should I need it, as clear proof as any signed contract. He'd signed it at the bottom, with a bold flourish.

I hid the note and went to breakfast. I gave Martha a beaming welcome that made her look twice at me. "Why, Rose, you're in good spirits today."

I agreed with her.

In the end, it was much later in the day before I managed to convey my information about the knife. Gervase helped Martha while Richard sat nearby, watching his brother scrubbing china shepherdesses with a beatific smile upon his face. Servants were, as usual, milling about, performing the many duties involved in restoring the Abbey, or at least, making it habitable. I said that I hoped Richard and Gervase would join Lizzie and me for tea in a little while, and they accepted. To my relief, Martha refused my offer, saying she preferred to work through. I promised to have some refreshment brought to her.

I had tea served in the sunny little room where I had seen Richard once before. He evidently recalled it too, for he smiled when he came in and his eyes met mine, burning with remembrance. He took my hand in his and Lizzie's eyes widened when he retained it, although she said nothing. I let my hand rest in his, and we sat together on the oak settle, which Martha had by now found cushions for. I took my hand away, poured the tea, and told them my story with no preamble.

"I think I found the knife used to cut the traces."

The result was everything I'd hoped for. Tea dishes were replaced. Quietly, by Richard and Gervase, and with a clatter by my less careful sister. I stood and went over to a small table by the door, and took the knife out of the drawer. Savouring my triumph, I crossed to the tea table and put the knife down in the middle of it, right in front of the teapot. The blade gleamed in resonance with the carefully polished silver pot, winking balefully at us.

I sat again. Richard picked up the weapon and balanced it on one finger where it swayed slightly like a lethal seesaw. He watched the gentle movement thoughtfully. "Where did you find this?"

"I went to look for something I'd lost in the little parlour when I noticed one of those secret cupboards you often get above fireplaces. I forced the lock, and that's where I found this." I waited for them to digest that piece of information before I continued. "So what do we do now?"

Everybody watched the knife as it swayed on Richard's finger, and nobody spoke for a while. Then he looked at me warmly. "Clever girl. There's little doubt this is the knife which cut the strap." He turned his attention to the knife. "Why else would anyone want to hide it? It's a perfectly ordinary knife. There's no hidden mechanism, it's not made of a precious metal, so I think we can conclude it has been deliberately concealed for another reason." He thought, frowning, never taking his gaze off the weapon, until he replaced it on the table. "It's not been hidden long, it's too shiny for that."

"Should we put it back?" asked Lizzie.

"Most certainly not. If it disappears, we have nothing." He paused again while he thought. "Perhaps we should see what bait rises when we announce what we know. My love, would you consider taking part in a stratagem?"

"Richard," Gervase warned

He looked at me, deaf to the protests of his brother. I think the endearment slipped out because he was concentrating on another matter, and it had come naturally to him now.

It would be foolish for him to apologise for the slip. He'd said it now, and it would be equally foolish for me to behave in a missish way and protest. "Yes, if it would help." He squeezed my hand and smiled before he turned away to address his brother.

"I'm sorry, Gervase, you were saying?"

"Could you be a little more careful, Strang?"

"What?" He really couldn't seem to remember using the endearment. Gervase threw up his hands in a gesture of submission. "I beg your pardon, Miss Elizabeth, I'm sure he meant nothing by it."

Richard replaced the knife on the table. "Yes, I did. I meant what I said and I'm tired of concealment. Soon there'll be no need."

"How soon?" his brother said.

"I've written to our father, requesting an interview with him and his man of business when I return home after taking Julia and her aunt back to her father's house. I will inform him that I am no longer bound to Julia Cartwright and I intend to court Rose Golightly."

Gervase paled. "Then I think, with Lady Hareton's permission, I'll remain here. Or even return to India. Even that might not be far enough."

Lizzie had gone white. "I had no idea it had gone this far."

I met her accusatory stare without blushing. I had nothing to be ashamed of. "Yes, it's gone this far."

"But the scandal. What will Miss Cartwright do?"

Richard gave my hand another squeeze. "It's true she's proving a trifle difficult, but when I've spoken with her family, I hope they'll bring her around. I will not marry her, and if she brings a breach of promise suit, she'll make herself a laughing stock in society. Better if she cries off, and we agree to part. Besides, I plan to take Rose away, as soon as we're married. Bride visits and such can wait, I want her to myself first. She won't have to face anything without me, and it would probably be best to give society time to accustom itself to the idea. It will leave the way clear for you, although, I'm afraid it might add to your burden of scandal."

Lizzie turned a pretty shade of pink, while I, surprisingly, stayed calm. To hear him talk about it like this made it almost real. He must have seen my hesitation, for he tugged at my hand, making me give him my full attention. "Never doubt it."

I nodded, feeling safe. I'd come to harbour with this man.

Lizzie looked from one to the other of us and sighed in defeat. "I only hope I do as well."

"Madam, you will be a sensation," Gervase said.

"You will, indeed." Richard's charming smile did the trick, and Lizzie smiled timorously in return. "Now, may we return to the subject in hand? It would be very gratifying if we cleared the matter up before I left." He released my hand. "This is a long shot, but I think it's the only hope we have. I want to try to flush the culprit out into the open." He paused. "If Rose announced loudly over dinner that she found the strap, it may happen. The culprit could panic, and make a dash for the knife's hiding place."

"It's possible," Gervase agreed. "Would you object, ma'am?"

I assured him it would be a pleasure.

Surprisingly, at dinner that evening we had a full compliment. Emboldened by our acceptance of their Bible reading, even Mr. Pritheroe and his daughter joined us. He enjoyed commenting on the meal's richness, its overabundance. "Nothing will be wasted," Martha assured him. "Whatever is left will go downstairs and be consumed there."

"There is something to be said for that," the man grudgingly admitted, "but it might be better if you invited the servants to partake with you."

Martha laughed. "There are several reasons why that shouldn't happen. Everyone would be made uncomfortable and in any case there isn't enough room at the table."

Mr. Pritheroe opened his mouth, but then closed it again when he saw the determination on Martha's face. He wouldn't win this one. Miss Cartwright sat next to Richard, but used the occasion to ignore him. Instead, she chatted to Steven, who sat on her other side.

The conversation became more flirtatious and animated. Julia plied her fan so much she nearly had her glass over. Richard quietly moved it out of harm's way, but other than that, took little notice. He saw me across the table, and lifted his glass. I smiled back at him. Martha's head moved sharply when she saw the movement. I hoped she would ascribe it to a simple flirtation, but I felt secure enough now to tell her the truth if she should ask me.

Miss Cartwright turned a smiling face to Steven. "You have a charming wit, sir." I'd never found Steven witty. Quite the opposite, in fact. "It nearly makes up for the lack of it in other directions." She glanced at Richard, her gaze hard and sharp, though he took no notice. There were few lulls in the conversation because Miss Cartwright kept herself so busy with Steven. She might consider Steven relatively safe, as a man of the cloth. It was clear she was trying to make Richard jealous, as though the encounter with him the other day had never happened and they were still a couple. I guessed she was used to getting her own way, pampered and petted all her life. She would have driven Richard mad within six months. He had his own share of self-centredness, which wouldn't have worked well with hers.

I watched the flickering light from the candles reflected on the jewels and brocades the Kerres and Cartwrights wore, and felt, frankly, jealous. I longed to wear something a little more exciting than this unrelieved black. At least, in three months, I would be able to wear grey and white, pearls and simple jewellery.

Lizzie looked wonderful in black, even mourning black. With pursed lips, she too watched Miss Cartwright, either making mental notes or criticising her, I couldn't tell which.

At last, Miss Cartwright paused to draw breath, and I took my chance. "James, I don't know if you've seen the old coach in the stables?"

James stared at me, perplexed. He knew about it and he must know knew I couldn't have forgotten, but he said nothing. Pritheroe's head snapped round, little eyes narrowed. "The strap that broke—the one that caused the accident—I'm almost sure someone cut it." I stopped for dramatic effect.

Miss Cartwright waved her fan carelessly and Martha gasped, horrified. I didn't look around, because Richard, Gervase and Lizzie would be doing that.

James's puzzled expression told me he knew I was dissembling. "I've seen it, my dear. I've come to the same conclusion. I can't think who would have done such a thing." The air positively glittered with reaction. I could leave them to discuss it.

"I'm sure you must be mistaken, Miss Golightly." Miss

Cartwright seemed annoyed that any other female should take centre stage at any table she occupied.

I shook my head. "There's no mistake."

Julia Cartwright shrugged and turned back to Steven, but he watched me now, and she petulantly flicked open her fan and waved it before her face.

The elder Miss Cartwright ventured no opinion. James, realising this must be a subterfuge, put his hand over Martha's to warn her. She looked horrified, but sat silent. Richard watched quietly, turning his wine glass around and around on the table. He never spilled a drop, although I doubt he was aware he was doing it. The air filled with noisy speculation, except for the minister and his daughter. She sat next to him, her head down, gripping her table knife. It was impossible to guess at her thoughts, she sat so still in her place.

"A servant—it must have been a servant," Miss Cartwright said.

"Not necessarily," Richard answered. "It could have been anyone."

I glanced at the footman standing a little behind his chair, but I saw no sign of any emotion on his face. Still, it would be all around the servants' hall by bedtime, and since we had decided that the knowledge must enter the public domain, it must help us in our quest.

Mr. Pritheroe was the only person who still ate, and he showed no signs of letting up, but he could talk and eat, as he had shown us so graphically before. "Whoever did this thing flouted the will of God. We were within hours of breaking the entail and making this house a house of God."

Richard turned to him, every sign of interest on his face. I had learned not to trust that look. When he took a real interest in something, he didn't quirk a brow in quite that way and the gleam of mischief was absent from his eyes. "Is that what you would have done?"

"It was always intended that this house would become a centre for the religion some people called Prithism." I heard Lizzie giggle. Pritheroe ignored her. "We could have brought more people to the Word, and saved more souls in time for Armageddon."

And lived in luxury while you did it, I thought, but I wasn't bold enough to say it.

"I have always considered this as a temporary setback. I trust in the Lord. I know He will find a way."

"God helps those who help themselves."

The preacher stiffened in response to Gervase's remark. "Are you suggesting I did this dreadful thing, sir?"

"No, of course not," said Gervase. "There's no reason on earth why you should want the last two earls dead—is there?"

"Sir." Pritheroe's vehement response released some of his dinner back to where it came from—his plate. I looked away in disgust. "They were my benefactors, and God fearing people."

He addressed himself to his plate again. I hoped the exercise would be beneficial to him.

Martha hastily turned the conversation to other things, but my announcement had its effect. The trap had been set.

Later during the evening when Richard had the chance of a quiet word with me, he murmured, "Now—we watch."

Chapter Eighteen

We watched. All the next day at least one of us stayed in the sunny room in sight of the little parlour. Lizzie and I spent a lot of time there, with some sewing so Martha couldn't accuse us of being idle.

My sister took the opportunity to castigate my rashness. "You should have waited, Rose. Who knows what delights await us, with this change in our fortunes? We have new people to meet, much to see. You'll have saddled yourself with a husband and a scandal."

"But, Lizzie, you know I was never good in the marriage market," I protested.

She looked up from her work. "I used to think so, but I'm not so sure now. Steven had a partiality for you, and now you've dropped him in favour of someone better. Really, my dear, you could have had much more choice if you had only waited."

"But I wouldn't have fallen in love with any of them."

"Love!" She put as much scorn as she could muster into the word and applied herself to her work with great vigour, while I continued with mine more tranquilly. I felt very tranquil these days. "How long does love last?"

"We are good friends." I knew better than to argue. Lizzie had a low opinion of love.

"That's more like it. And," she continued, pensively, "he is a leader of fashion. Though heaven knows what this affair will do to it."

"He's still hopeful of bringing it off without scandal."

"How does he expect to work such a miracle?" Her needle flashed in and out of her work at a great pace.

"He'll talk to Miss Cartwright's father when he takes her home next week. He says, apart from idolising his only daughter, the man is sensible. Once he understands the fault lies all on my lord's side, he'll see reason. Any other way will hurt Miss Cartwright, you see. He's giving her the opportunity to cry off which is, after all, a perfectly proper thing for a young lady to do."

"From what I've heard he's more likely to create a disturbance about it." Lizzie worked for a few minutes in silence, tight lipped.

"You know Mr. Drury is repeating the most scandalous gossip about your Lord Strang, don't you?" Lizzie pushed the needle into the cloth, leaning forward conspiratorially.

My heart sank. "What sort of gossip?"

"He's seduced a maid under this very roof." Lizzie said with relish.

"I don't believe a word of it." Not a maid, but me.

Lizzie, met my gaze frankly "Neither do I. Oh, I don't know your Lord Strang well enough to judge his character, but Steven was sweet on you. It's probably some sort of revenge."

"James is going to send Steven away. Since James became Lord Hareton, Steven's attentions have become increasingly uncomfortable. He seems to think I made him some promises. I swear to you, Lizzie, I did no such thing. I spoke to James and he's finding Steven a comfortable living far away from here."

Lizzie looked up. "Was that your idea?"

"R—Strang's," I told her.

"Better than sending him home."

I put down one cloth and picked up another. I'd been doing plain sewing, but this looked more interesting—a cloth that had come unstitched on one corner. Quite an old one, from the look of the ladies embroidered on it. It would be difficult to match it with the bright modern silks at my disposal. I frowned over my work.

"A charming scene," came a voice from the door. Gervase bowed to us. "Delightful domesticity. I've come to take over from one of you ladies."

"Not quite the thing, sir," Lizzie pointed out. "Can you sew?"

"May I perhaps escort one of you in a short walk then? You must be in need of fresh air."

October grew old now, but since Lizzie had no desire to go out into the cold, I accepted Gervase's offer with relief. At home in Devonshire I walked out every day, but the lack of proper gardens to walk in, and the multitude of tasks needing to be done indoors had prevented me from taking my usual exercise.

Gervase waited while I fetched a cloak, hat and gloves. He gave me his arm as support, and took me to the little path we'd ridden down that first morning. "There's very little space to walk or ride. I've taken my horse out on some mornings, but I fear we have our task to do, thanks to Strang."

I smiled up at him. "This is just what I needed. I've wanted a breath of fresh air all morning. It's such a fine day." Indeed, it was one of those cold, sunny days that remind one of the spring to come, or the summer just passed.

"Yes." He changed the subject abruptly. "I hope you don't mind if I ask you a few questions. Do you really wish to marry my brother? No," he said, as he saw my mouth open to reply, "don't answer at once. He can be like a whirlwind, once he makes up his mind, scooping up everything and everyone in his path. I've seen it before. You should know he is autocratic, generous to a fault and loyal. He's been the best of brothers to me, but I've seen him so bemuse others they've done precisely what he wants without consideration of their own wishes. If you have doubts, you may be sure they'll go no further, unless you wish them to." He glanced at me as we continued to stroll down the path.

I knew my own mind. "No, sir. He swept me off my feet, as the saying goes, but I'm willing to be swept. I fell in love with him, Gervase. Although I felt completely confused and lost at first, I know I can trust him now."

Gervase smiled in relief. "I'm glad. I've not heard him laugh the way he does with you for a very long time. My mother said after I went away that she never heard him laugh again. For what my opinion's worth, I'm sure he's truly attached to you." This confirmation from his brother, who knew him best, meant a great deal to me. "When I came back from India, he had hardened, lost the gentleness he had as a boy. I knew much of it was my fault. My dreadful scandal marked him so much he'd taken the guilt on himself. He tried to wreak his revenge on the society that rejected me by seducing and gambling his way through it, making his mark, making them pay." He sighed. "I heard of his behaviour and I believe I was the only one who guessed its true significance. And of course, we missed each other. We'd never been apart for such a significant length of time before. Our parents never forbade communication, so we wrote a great deal but apart from a brief meeting in Rome at the beginning of my exile, we didn't see each other until I came home last year. When I first saw him in all his society glory, I hardly recognised him. It nearly broke my heart. If it hadn't been broken already. I thought I'd lost him until we arrived here at the Abbey."

I didn't know what to reply to this, but no answer seemed to be required. We paused. A bird sang in the silence "I've something to say to you, ma'am. I beg you'll hear it through and think hard about it." He stopped walking, turning to face me. I looked up at him. "I'd like to offer you my hand in marriage."

I gaped, something I hadn't done since I was a small girl. Would these brothers never fail to astonish? I couldn't speak for the thoughts racing through my head. Was Gervase in love with me, too? He'd never shown any sign, but some men don't.

"Let me explain. I'll tell you the whole, if I may." I nodded, still beyond speech. "Ten years ago, I created such a scandal it will probably never be forgotten, although it seems to have been forgiven. I fell in love with someone so unsuitable, and did it so openly people still talk about it when they see me. I eventually left the country for the Continent, as you have no doubt heard.

"We grew up with the Boughtons. Their land marched with

ours. Until they sold their property afterwards, they were our best friends. I slowly came to realise my feelings were more than affection. When they were reciprocated, my joy was, unfortunately, unconfined. We barely lived through the scandal. Scandal isn't just a social affair, it causes business relationships to falter, alliances with other families to fall and my father had to work hard to restore our reputation." I nodded. The effects in our local society could be as devastating, and scandals from a generation or so back were still remembered. "Believe me, ma'am, when our father gets wind of Richard's plans, he'll be incandescent with rage. You'll be able to hear his wrath over five counties. I think that's why Miss Cartwright is so stubborn. She believes Richard will give way under that rage, but I'm afraid she doesn't know Richard. He won't."

I felt apprehensive. I hated shouting and upsets. Not timidly, I would face what I had to but they made me physically unwell. "Also, our sister must be hurt by this. She's just had her come-out. Myself, I don't think the scandal will be as great as all that. Richard may succeed in persuading Mr. Cartwright to do the proper thing, but you should know it could cause great hurt to someone I think you love. But the scandal I caused will add to the one Richard will cause if he refuses to marry Julia Cartwright while the contract between them is still in force." A light breeze disturbed the fallen leaves, causing them to rattle against the dry earth and the path we stood on. Gervase came to the point, the real point, of his story. "You see, Miss Golightly, I didn't elope with Lady Mary." He swallowed. "I ran away with her husband, the boy I'd grown up with, Edward. I still love him, but we can never see each other again. They made him promise. He wasn't strong enough to bear it."

My hand flew to my mouth involuntarily, but he spared me the necessity of speaking by carrying on with his story. He watched me as he spoke, his eyes wary. "They hushed it up, saying that I had run off with Lady Mary. She went into hiding at one of my father's remoter estates where nobody knew her and they said Edward had pursued us abroad. Then they persuaded him to come back." His voice broke and he looked away. I pressed his sleeve in sympathy and listened, but I said nothing to break his flow. He looked so distraught that my heart went out to him.

Gervase cleared his throat. He must have gone over this tragedy over and over in his mind and he might be able to control it more readily, but he still faltered. I hadn't realised, hadn't even suspected, but it explained so much when I thought about it. *That* was why the old scandal was still so potent. It also explained why Richard wore that hard carapace over his sensitive nature. He must have grown it very quickly. Even his heavy maquillage would have served to hide his true feelings, making it easier for him to face people after Gervase had inadvertently done such a terrible thing to his brother.

"I'm telling you this because you have a right to know, but also to make you understand that you have nothing to fear from me. If you marry me, you'll still be Richard's, still see him as much as you wish. He won't go near Julia if he's compelled to marry her. If she keeps him to the contract, he'll go insane if he has to lose you. Probably return to the old Richard, the uncaring, restless one with no heart. He'll kill himself with debauchery. I can't watch that without trying to help. I owe him happiness and I want to see him achieve it." He forced a smile. "I've money enough for ten lifetimes, and we like each other, do we not?"

The power of speech returned to me. "And are you still of the same—inclination, sir?"

He laughed at my hesitation. "I'm afraid so, but much more discreet these days, of course. The problem is, everybody knows it. It's not said to my face, which is much more hurtful, you know, than if they pointed and sneered directly."

"Why should they? What has it to do with them?" This new information didn't affect my liking for Gervase at all. It made me angry on his behalf.

He smiled at me, looking so like his brother, but not possessing Richard's special qualities. "Nothing at all, dear ma'am. One solution is for me to find a complacent wife—one who wouldn't expect me to perform the impossible. Then there's the heir. Richard has taken such a dislike to Miss Cartwright, even if he's forced to marry her, it's unlikely he would ever consummate the marriage." I shuddered at the thought and what it would mean to him. "If you and he were...forgive me...intimate, the heir could still appear. Otherwise, the title passes out of the immediate family."

Gervase would acknowledge the child and it would be the legitimate heir. If Richard's marriage to Julia remained childless, any child Gervase and I produced would inherit. I began to see what Gervase meant, but the necessity for lifelong subterfuge made my heart weigh heavy in my chest. Still, it would be better than nothing, better than watching him kill himself with excess, better than watching him with another woman, or a plethora of them. "Would Richard agree to this?"

"He may have no choice. He's signed the contract and they're due to be married soon. After this visit, he is expected to return to our family seat at Eyton and settle a date. One of the main cards in his hand is that our father wants an heir, and it's obvious he won't get one from me. So if Richard refuses to consummate a marriage to a woman not of his choosing and holds out for you, he could win our father over. We would still face a scandal but our father's support would help to overcome it. But it's Richard's only chance. Please think of my offer. It's an answer of a sort. If you need it, come to me. Will you promise me that?"

I had to think of the practical. "I will promise to come to you if I'm hurt, if it becomes too much to bear. For the rest, I must think about it. Should we keep this from him?"

"I think so, for the time being. I've thought it might make him easier in his mind, but I'm not sure. It might make him extremely angry." I thought that, too. Richard refused to consider any alternative to marrying me but my more cautious nature demanded other courses and this was the best one I'd heard, so far.

Gervase had made me think of the other people involved in this mess, Richard's sister, his parents, Lizzie, James and Martha, even Miss Cartwright's family. It would be too selfish of us to cause hurt to them. I wouldn't feel easy if we did this and all those other people suffered.

Gervase offered a bizarre solution, but it offered a chance to avoid too much hurt to too many people. As to my own feelings about Gervase, I still considered him a kind, gentle and amusing friend. His preferences were his own business. If I married him, I need never know much about them, as long as he was discreet.

With a heavy heart, I had to agree that my marriage to Richard, which we both desired so dearly, might not be possible after all. I thanked Gervase for his concern. "It might work. I promise I'll think about it."

He smiled to reassure me. He saw my distress, despite the pain of recalling his story. "Don't be so downcast. Matters might never come to this."

I laughed, despite my hurt. "Please don't think me rude, sir—"

"Gervase, remember. Brother-in-law, husband or friend, but just Gervase."

"Gervase. I love Richard with all my heart. I'm still taken aback, confused, but I want him very much. I'm saddened to think I might not achieve my heart's desire, but many people don't, do they?" He smiled wryly. "Thank you very much for your offer. I promise, I will bear it in mind."

We went in. He'd brought me back to the earth I should never have left.

Chapter Nineteen

We watched the room for the next two days, but nothing out of the ordinary happened. Lady Hareton and her father spent all their time there, reading, sewing and waiting, as the minister put it, until his leg should be well enough for God to reveal His word. She did everything for her father. She fetched, carried and sewed, and the sewing she kept herself busy with was invariably one of his shirts.

Pritheroe tyrannised his daughter completely. He constantly reminded her of her duty. Rather than behaving like a mature, sensible woman, she bowed her head, saying, "Yes, Father." It was painful to watch. If the obeisance had been less pronounced, if he'd left her some dignity, given her private time of her own, it would have been better. Now she had no husband to order her, he treated her as though she was back under his jurisdiction.

Lizzie and Gervase made it difficult for Richard and me to have more than a few moments together. My feelings for him were the same, would never, ever change, and I still determined to have him, one way or another.

We snatched a rare half hour together on the second afternoon. I tried to tell him how I felt.

"You may have to marry Miss Cartwright. A breach of promise suit could bankrupt your family and drive them into disgrace." He looked at me, solemnly, but said nothing. "I want you. I can't give you up now. I'd be happy to become your mistress, to retire from society, if that would provide an answer.

James can disown me, and distance himself from my disgrace."

"I can't believe you said that. No one has shown me such generosity before." He slipped his arm about my shoulders and gave me a gentle kiss. "But it won't answer, my love. I don't want you just in my bed, but in my life. I want you as a friend and partner, not merely a bed companion. My dearest love, I don't want to embarrass you, but you know some women in certain parts of most cities are cheap. When one seeks a certain sort of relief, one body is very much like another, so long as it's clean. If that was all I wanted, I could find relief somewhere, but I don't want that. I want you. You have something they don't have, something none of the society women I've—known—possess. You're the only woman I want in my life, associated with me and my name. I won't marry Julia. If you come abroad with me, it will be difficult for her to pursue a suit against me. My family will be spared the worst of it."

I took his hand, thinking of my conversation with his brother. "I trust you. I love you," I said, but I could make no promises other than personal ones.

"I hear Gervase has spoken to you." I stiffened in his arms and he looked at me in concern. "Does it give you a dislike of him? I hope not, but many people do feel that way."

I relaxed. "No—nothing like that. I like him very much." I would keep Gervase's counsel and not tell Richard about his brother's astonishing proposal.

"My parents expended much time and money to keep the whole truth out of the public domain." His face froze. He held me loosely, as if he'd left me and gone somewhere else. "Yes, it was difficult, but it happened twelve years ago. Society has taken Gervase back to its viperous bosom. Being fabulously wealthy helps, of course."

"Is he really so rich?"

"Enormously rich. My brother could give Croesus odds. The strong and clever can make fortunes in India. Gervase had also lost his heart, so that helped him too, as he had no distractions. You'll be marrying the pauper in the family, my love, the poor brother left behind to look after family affairs.

Sometimes I think I should have followed him, but my father was so set on one of his sons marrying and begetting he wouldn't hear of it. Perhaps we will travel, now."

"You didn't think of it before?"

"I found the idea of letting someone into my life unthinkable. Until you."

"Julia?"

"Julia wouldn't have intruded on my life." He smiled down at me. "When I look at you I can hardly remember what she looks like." He drew me closer.

A sound outside made us separate quickly. He put one finger to his lips in a warning gesture and crossed the room to the door. For once, Mr. Pritheroe and his daughter hadn't appeared that morning. We had been alone.

Through the half open door, we saw Lady Hareton and Mrs. Peters opening the door to the small parlour. They didn't speak, and except for the rustling of their skirts, they didn't make a sound. They had their backs to us, otherwise they must have seen us, as the door of our room was only slightly closed, but they seemed intent on their errand. They might have decided to clean the room while Mr. Pritheroe was absent, but they carried no brushes, no cloths and they seemed intent on stealth.

The women closed the door behind them. Richard crossed the room, took the knife out of the drawer in the small table, and beckoned me to follow him.

We went across the hall and stopped outside the door of the small parlour, listening. Richard stood nearest the door and waited until we heard the sound we waited for—the click of the secret panel above the fireplace. Concealing the knife behind him, he opened the door and we went in.

The panel gaped open, and Mrs Peters and Lady Hareton stood before its empty depths. They spun around as we came in, and tried some semblance of the courtesies, both curtseying, trying to hide their confusion, but we didn't move.

"Didn't you find it?" said Richard.

A noise indicated Lizzie had returned with sewing. When

she saw us, she immediately dropped her work and followed us in.

"Close the door, if you please," said Richard.

Lizzie obeyed. They must have seen from our faces that we knew what they had been looking for but Mrs. Peters still tried to excuse them. "We found this door, sir. We wondered what might be inside."

"Treasure?" asked Richard, coolly, still holding the knife behind the skirts of his coat, "An overlooked will, perhaps? Or maybe just an ordinary item."

Lady Hareton gasped, hand to her mouth. She looked at Mrs. Peters, who glared at us balefully. "Whatever it might be, there's nothing to link it with anything." She put up her chin, ready, one would have thought, for the blow.

"You're quite right." Richard drew out the knife from behind his coat. It gleamed wickedly. "I thought you might be involved, Mrs. Peters. This knife is so clean there's not a mark on it. It must have taken a great deal of scrubbing to bring it back to this." He turned the knife, and it caught the pale November sun, glinting as he turned it.

"It did," the housekeeper said. "But I don't think I can be hung for cleaning a knife."

"One would have thought not," Richard agreed. "But if it was a particular knife, what then?"

"It has to be shown it was that knife," Mrs. Peters said, game to the last.

"Dear me, I believe we've discovered a mother hen. What has Lady Hareton to do with all this? Did she take pity on you, and agree to help you? Are you, perhaps, a relative?"

"Christ, no. If I were a member of that family, I might have turned the knife on myself."

"A sensible solution," Richard agreed urbanely.

Lizzie cried out, "Lady Hareton!"

Richard was only just in time to prevent her falling to the hard wooden floor. He lifted her and put her on one of the comfortless benches that were the only seating the room had to offer. He handed me the knife, and knelt next to the lady, while Lizzie went to the other room, returning with some of the cushions Martha had installed there. Richard lifted Lady Hareton's head, and placed one of them under it while Mrs. Peters poured a glass of water from the jug on the table.

Richard felt in his pocket, and handed her a small flask, which Mrs. Peters took and opened, sniffing the contents. She seemed satisfied, for she poured a small amount of the tawny liquid into the water, then took Richard's place by her mistress, and lifted Lady Hareton's head.

"Come, my lady, take some of this." Lady Hareton roused a little and did as she was told. She spluttered so much she had to be lifted to a sitting position, but when the housekeeper held the glass to her lips, she took some more.

"Do you think she can be—in the family way?" Lizzie said, and was surprised by the fierce response of the lady kneeling by her mistress.

Mrs. Peters lifted her head once, and said, "No," but the ravaged expression on her face told us what we needed to know. Then she went back to her charge.

Richard raised his eyebrows, and I took a step back.

Eventually, Lady Hareton regained some of her composure. Lizzie and I sat together on the other hard bench, and Richard stood by the fire. The secret compartment still gaped open behind his head for anyone to see.

"I did it." That quiet voice, so seldom heard now filled the room. "I cut the strap."

"No, my lady," Mrs. Peters said quickly, trying to drown out the quiet voice with her own louder one. "I told you, if you hold fast, they can prove nothing."

"She's quite right, you know," Richard said. "There's nothing to connect the two."

"Could you say it was shock, sir?" Mrs. Peters looked up at him. "Could you say she didn't know what she said?"

She and Richard stared at each other. "It might be possible for us to be conveniently deaf. Can you tell us the whole?"

Mrs. Peters thought for a long time then, and watched Richard. Then she sighed heavily. She seemed to sag from her usual upright posture. "I think we must. I have no choice but to trust you. It started when the old earl died. His son behaved properly until after the funeral but he came across the minister and he changed completely. He was pre-contracted to a society lady, but he managed to break it. Then he set about destroying everything his father had done. In one way, you can understand it, because the old man saw him as nothing but a way to preserve the family, not as a person. He whipped his children regularly and never allowed them to sit in his presence or express an opinion of their own."

I didn't understand how anyone couldn't love, or at least, care for their children.

Mrs. Peters continued with her narrative. "There were only the two boys, so he concentrated on them. They never knew when the summons came. Neither of them was strong enough to stand up to him. If they had, perhaps this needn't have happened. Two years after the old earl's death, his son saw Mr. Pritheroe preaching in the village, and brought him back here. The minute he passed through these doors, I thought the preacher was the old earl come back. Not in his appearance, but he had the same arrogance and singleness of purpose. Next day, Lord Hareton ordered the rooms shut up and most of the maids out. When they tried to pack up the treasures and cover the furniture, he told them to let it be and go, so they went.

"My lady here arrived and Lord Hareton said he would marry her. He did so the following month. Mr. Pritheroe left her here while he went about the country on his mission. Lord Hareton sent him what money he could, but he also devised a scheme to break the entail, to sell everything for the religion. He treated my lady as badly as he'd been treated by his own father."

She pushed up Lady Hareton's sleeve, exposing the scar of what must have been a severe and painful burn. Lizzie and I both cried out, and Richard grimaced, as we all saw the wound and imagined the pain that must have gone with it.

"He did that for something I can't even remember. With a fresh flat iron that sat by the fire in the kitchen, waiting for its proper use. I'm sorry, but I wanted to give you some idea of what went on here." Lady Hareton didn't resist, but looked up at us with her big brown eyes, unflinchingly. "If you want to know the whole," the housekeeper continued relentlessly, "there is no way on earth my lady can be with child, as she is still a maid."

Before we took in the terrible implications of that last sentence, the door crashed open, and Mr. Pritheroe came in. He complained loudly. He held a crutch under one arm, to support his broken limb, and he held his other hand to his head.

"What are you all doing in here?" He made so much noise he didn't hear the quiet click when Richard closed the secret door over the mantelpiece.

"Where is my daughter?" He looked over to where she lay on the bench, a pillow behind her head. "What are you doing there, girl, lounging around at this time of day? What's that you have?" He clumped over to her, took the glass out of her unresisting hand, and sniffed the contents. "Brandy!" he cried, and hurled the glass to the back of the fireplace. It shattered noisily.

Richard sighed at the needlessly dramatic gesture. "Sir, your daughter feels faint. The brandy was purely medicinal." Lady Hareton looked up at Richard, her face white. Violence glittered in her father's eyes. I'd heard him say women needed whipping frequently. I'd thought it as rhetorical as his other pronouncements, but now I knew it wasn't.

"Brandy is never medicinal." The minister looked only at his daughter.

"Father," she begged him, faintly. "Please."

"Please what? Get up this instant, girl. My head hurts, my leg is sore and I need something to eat."

Lady Hareton began to rise. Richard moved swiftly across to her and pressed the countess back to the bench. "Your daughter has been taken ill. It would be most unwise of her to undertake any exertion."

"Sir, you have no right to come between a man and his womenfolk," the so-called reverend protested. "I know what is right for my daughter."

"Legally, sir, you have a point," Richard replied. "Morally, however, your authority is questionable."

"How dare you?"

"Sir, it may be strange to you to meet people you cannot command," Richard said calmly. "It may be that you deliberately restrict yourself to the company of people you can dominate. Bullies often do, in my experience."

The explosion should have raised dust, if there had been any to raise. "Sir, I keep my company to people who deserve it."

"That, I doubt," Richard's eyes were ice cold, his demeanour took on the supercilious, aristocratic expression I hadn't seen since he stepped down from his carriage on the first day. It was a mask, purposely concealing the anger beneath, but I could feel his fury. The air bristled with it. "Very few people deserve your company, but if what I have just seen is any indication of her married life, the last but one Lord Hareton was one of the few."

"He treated her as a woman should be treated."

"He beat her, subdued her and kept her a maid," Richard said. "Women were meant for better things."

Pritheroe sneered, his mouth a hard, thin line. "Carnal relations, perhaps? Oh I've heard of your reputation, my lord, I know what you and your kind get up to."

"I doubt that." Richard remained calm, but I worried that tensions would erupt into violence. "We treat women as human beings."

"A woman needs taming," grunted Pritheroe. At least he had reduced the volume of his pronouncements. "Women are born sinners, they bear Eve's shame, and they must pay for it all their lives."

"I can't see us ever agreeing on that point," Richard said, "and I don't intend to get into any discussions with you on the subject. However, I will not see this happen to anyone who asks me for help."

"Has my daughter dared to ask you for help?"

"In every way but words." Richard glanced down to where Lady Hareton still lay, staring mutely at him. He gave her a small smile of reassurance. "I will do my best to see that you are kept away from her in future, that she is left in peace. She has suffered in silence too long. As Dowager Countess, she has rights."

The sneering tone remained in Mr. Pritheroe's voice. "You'll take her under your protection, perhaps?"

Richard chose not to take the insult. "In every way but the personal one."

"Marry her, maybe?"

"I'm unable to do so as I'm promised elsewhere. My protection will be limited to ensuring you come nowhere near her in future. I'm sure Lord Hareton will join me in this."

"Are you?" asked the odious man. "Well, I think if I took you to court, they might think differently."

Richard shook his head. "She is a widow; she has rights. Even if she did cause the death of her husband and his brother."

Chapter Twenty

We felt the pause before Lady Hareton wailed, a long, keening wail that released her troubles and pain. I thought she'd never stop.

The door burst open to admit Martha, on the warpath. She glared and stood arms akimbo, mutely demanding an explanation. James was out about the estate, or he would have followed his wife shortly after. Servants gathered outside. Without looking, Martha back heeled the door, slamming it shut.

No one could be heard over that terrible keening, the long, drawn-out wails coming over and over, increasing in volume. I closed my eyes, feeling Richard's hand touch my shoulder. I opened my eyes and nodded to him before he turned to Pritheroe and his daughter. Mrs. Peters leaned over her mistress and slapped her face, hard.

The noise shut off, like the lid of a box slamming closed, but the sound still reverberated in my ears. Lady Hareton put her hand to her face and burst into tears. Without hesitation, Mrs. Peters took her into her arms and rocked her like a baby.

"Please take her ladyship upstairs," Richard said, "and put her to bed. If you need something for her comfort, my man Carier should be able to help."

Mrs. Peters glanced up at him and nodded. Together, they helped Lady Hareton to her feet. Slowly, the housekeeper led her out of the room. Martha moved aside to let them pass, laying her hand on Lady Hareton's shoulder as she passed.

When the door had closed, she turned to us. "Tell me the whole."

Richard nodded. "The announcement at table the other night was a subterfuge. We had found the knife which may very well have cut the traces on the coach, and we wanted to bring whoever had done it out into the open. It took a day or two, but we discovered who it was, eventually. Lady Hareton has been treated appallingly by her father and her husband. I won't detail it here, but I will tell you later, should you wish it."

Martha nodded. She didn't take her gaze away from him. Pritheroe also watched him, his concentrated, fascinated gaze trance-like in its intensity. "She cut the strap on the coach. I don't think she realised what she was doing. If she'd been in her right mind, she'd have taken a surer step to murder. Perhaps she wanted to frighten them, or put a period to her own existence, since I took her place in the coach that day. It's impossible to say. I don't think she knows herself why she did it." He cleared his throat, the first indication of emotion he had shown, except when he'd looked at me to assure himself I was coping with all this. "I for one cannot condemn her, but the decision isn't mine. I have undertaken to ensure that her father doesn't approach her again, but it is up to Lord Hareton whether he prosecutes or not."

Martha opened her mouth to speak. Before she could, Pritheroe roared his anger. "My daughter? Is this true? Can you prove it?"

Richard turned to face him. "No. The knife is clean. There's nothing to connect it to the accident. Lady Hareton has admitted the act, and she has more than enough reason to do it. The evidence may not be enough for a court." He addressed Martha next. "If you choose to prosecute, you may have to make further enquiries. For myself, I am satisfied. I don't wish to take this any further, so if your husband should wish to, I'm afraid he must do it without me."

Martha managed to speak this time. "James won't prosecute. The lady has suffered enough. She's half out of her mind in any case. Not fit to stand trial."

Richard smiled. "Thank you."

He got no further as Pritheroe bellowed forth once more. "My daughter? I have no daughter. How dare she defy the laws of God and Man in this way?"

Richard waited until he stopped to draw breath. "Will you prosecute?"

"Me? No. Although she has cost me a fortune. If she did it, she should have waited until the signatures were on the entail."

Richard's smile was malicious. "Because she didn't want you to have it. Why should you be rewarded for what you did to her?"

"I brought her up as a good, God-fearing girl. The devil must have been in her from the first. I cannot acknowledge such a wicked child, such an evil spirit." He glared at Martha. "I and my servant will leave in the morning. I cannot stay in this house of iniquity any longer."

He stumped to the door and let himself out. No one moved to help him.

The spell was broken. I dived in my pocket for my handkerchief and applied it to my eyes. Martha said, "Thank God for that. I've wanted to throw him out since he left his sickbed. Normally I wouldn't let someone with that kind of injury leave, but I don't care. He can break the other one tomorrow and I'd still make sure he was gone in the morning."

Richard touched my shoulder again. "Miss Golightly, are you well?" The frightening, glittering temper was gone. Only concern adorned his face.

I mopped my eyes. "Quite well. But I have a strange dislike of voices raised in anger. I'm a coward, I suppose."

"Never that."

I favoured him with a watery smile. "I'm fine, really I am." I wiped away my tears, feeling my sister's arm around my shoulders.

"She's always been like that," Lizzie explained. "You have to be used to a lot of noise in our house, but Rose has never liked loud, angry voices."

"Or being the centre of attention," I added. "But the result was worthwhile. Will he really leave his daughter alone now?"

"She's cost him too much," Richard said.

Martha agreed. "She can move to the Dower House with Mrs. Peters to care for her. I've been to see it. It's a tidy property, much better than this barn. She'll be very comfortable there."

"May I perhaps put a man there?" Richard asked. "A groom perhaps, or a footman? I can obtain a useful man, one who will take care not to allow her father to come into her presence again."

Martha gave him a look of curiousity, but agreed.

Mrs. Peters returned, dropping a tight curtsey. "I've put her ladyship to bed and given her laudanum to help her sleep." She was pleased to hear that Pritheroe intended to leave without his daughter. "I've seen things no one should see. Her ladyship is very troubled. Peace and quiet will heal her."

"We'd like you to move with her to the Dower House," said Martha.

The housekeeper looked as though a burden had been removed from her. "Oh my lady, I think it would be for the best. I'm sure Lady Hareton didn't mean for it to happen. She was very sorry you were hurt, my lord. That was the worst of it for her."

"I have much to thank her for." Richard smiled. Only I knew what he meant and, perhaps, Lizzie.

Mrs. Peters held another surprise. "My lady, when we found that cupboard, it wasn't empty."

Martha looked at her, eyes wide, eyebrows raised.

"We found a document inside. Her ladyship can't read, but I read it." Mrs. Peters paused and looked around at us all. "It was a will, signed and witnessed. It left everything to Pritheroe."

"Was it conditional on the entail being broken?" Richard asked, sharply.

"No my lord. If it was broken, then everything was to go to the minister. If Sir James, as he was then, refused, everything not entailed was to go to Mr. Pritheroe."

"The house in London, the cash..." Martha began to list it.

"Indeed," Richard interrupted, smoothly. "Where is this document?"

"I burned it." Mrs. Peters showed no regret. I warmed to her.

"Good." Richard glanced at Martha's troubled face. "Don't worry. The last earl was half out of his mind. The will would have been contested. The only beneficiaries would have been the lawyers."

Martha smiled. "Would you please promise not to tell James? It would upset him to know about it."

We readily agreed. I appreciated what Martha was saying. James was thoroughly honest, and although he could do nothing, he would be upset to hear that the last incumbent of the earldom had other plans for the estate that had been foiled.

"I must return to my lady," said Mrs. Peters.

"Before you go, please take this. It doesn't belong here." Richard handed her the gleaming knife.

She took it with a smile. "Thank you my lord."

Mrs. Peters attended Lady Hareton in her room for the next day. She explained to me although she wasn't ill, she was exhausted and needed a good rest. "That father of hers has never given her a chance to think, so I'll give her that chance now."

I understood Mrs. Peters' reticence. She'd spent years in this dreadful place, watching the horrors unleashed on her lady, watching her spirit broken, her sanity risked. I couldn't have withstood such treatment for so long. I would most likely run away and taken my chances with poverty instead.

There was little to do but wait. The Misses Cartwright were packing to leave, Richard with them. Bereft, I thought my dream was at an end, though I knew, in my heart, he would return. I was glad Gervase intended to stay. "It's either here or go home," he confided in me, "and I don't want to be within a hundred miles of the place when Richard confronts our father."

"Will he be very angry?"

"Savage, I should think." Gervase grinned. "Richard always faced up to him, but I never could, I always gave in. That's why I ran away. I don't know what the outcome will be, mind, but Richard asked me to take particular care of you, and you know you'll have him, one way or the other." I put on a brave face, smiling. He was very kind.

The scandal hovering over my family had been lifted. Pritheroe would say nothing now.

Chapter Twenty-one

I sat at my ease in the drawing room the day after Pritheroe left, enjoying a dish of tea and a quiet moment. We'd had tea, but I lingered to pour myself a last dish and sit before the fire. My solitude seemed dearly bought when Steven entered. I must face him some time, I'd put it off too long. I put down my tea dish, and sat up in my chair.

Steven came and stood before me. I asked him to sit, but he shook his head. "Lord Hareton has just informed me that he's found me a living. Isn't that good news?"

"Excellent news. Congratulations."

His face remained solemn. "It's in Alnwick." He watched me closely.

I nodded. I didn't know what he expected me to say.

"Do you know where that is?"

I shook my head and watched him.

"It's north of here. The living itself is in the village of Colnwick, near to Alnwick."

He turned away from me then, took a turn about the room, then faced me. "I'd hoped Lord Hareton would need a chaplain here, but it seems not."

He stopped. From his expectant look, he required me to say something. "I'm very pleased for you." I tried to smile.

This was clearly not the expected response. "I'm very grateful to his lordship." He came closer to me. His face took on a look of eagerness I didn't like and apprehension rose in my throat. "Because he's given me what I most wanted—an opportunity to earn my own living, to have the means to support a wife."

I felt sick and my heart sank. Did he think I still cared for him? It seemed so. He kneeled in front of me in the most embarrassing way, and took one of my hands in his. "Dare I ask—would you consider being that wife? May I seek an interview with Lord Hareton?" His face wore a yearning expression. His beautiful brown eyes filled with pleading. "All those things we said—all the promises." I didn't answer him. "Will you make good on them now?"

I must speak, must try to let him down as lightly as I could, as I'd left it for so long and left him to wonder all this time. "I made you no promises. I'm sorry, Steven. If I ever cared for you, the passion didn't last."

He stared at me in disbelief. "After all we said? Can you remember last summer?"

"Yes, I remember it well. I remember the day you first approached me, when Lizzie had given you short shrift. I remember what you said, what I said, but I made you no promises, Steven. I don't consider myself bound to you."

He looked as if I had struck him. His eyes opened wide as they stared into mine. "Heartless!" he cried, rocking back on his heels. He dropped my hand.

That was overly dramatic, and if he stayed before the fire for very much longer, he would scorch his coat. "Please get up, sir. There is no need for histrionics."

He ignored me. "Can it be? Has another stolen you from me? Have you given way before a handsome face and good address?"

"No, that was you. Lord Strang is nowhere near as handsome as you." I gasped in dismay. I could have bitten my tongue out, I had told him far more than he needed to know.

He stood, and strode around the room. I was glad to see the skirts of his coat away from the fire. I watched him, compared my past feelings for him with the powerful feelings I had now for Richard; feelings that made me do things I'd never thought myself capable of. I would never have done those things with Steven.

"I'm sorry." I rose to leave.

Steven stood between me and the door. He deliberately barred my way.

"Strang." His handsome face contorted with rage. "I suspected as much, but I wasn't certain. You can't have him, he's betrothed already."

"He intends to break it," I informed him calmly.

"He wouldn't dare." He pushed his face close to mine. "He won't be allowed to. I thought if you had a *tendre* at all, it was for the younger brother. I might have let you go, if that was the case." Privately, I thought not. In any event, he had no right to "let me go" as he had never had me in the first place. "How could you, Rose, how could you?"

I opened my mouth to speak, but he threw up his hands. "No, I can't stay silent. I must tell you, my dear, I must. Strang is a rake, a libertine of the highest order."

With a sinking heart, I remembered what he'd seen upstairs that day. I realised he was about to relate it to me. I tried to stop him. "It makes no difference. Please, Steven, let me pass." I tried to pass him, but he stood firm.

"No." He flung out both his arms to prevent me leaving.

Tiring of his dramatics, I sighed and resigned myself to listen before I left.

"I'd rather you had spared me having to tell you. You should know on what you want to waste yourself. Last week, I was in the corridor above the State Rooms."

Struck by a sudden thought, something that hadn't occurred to me until that moment, I asked, "What were you doing there?"

He flushed. "That doesn't matter now. I heard a sound. Oh, God, how am I to tell you?" He seemed only too glad to tell me. A gleam of triumph lurked in his eyes. "I opened the door. I'm sorry, my darling, but I saw Lord Strang and he was not alone."

"Canoodling with the maids, was he?" I couldn't resist the

levity. All his dramatics demanded it.

"Worse." Steven covered his eyes. "Though how I can bear to tell you I do not know." He made the most of this. He let his hand drop, and took mine in it again, compelling me to look up into his eyes. "He was in bed with one of the maids."

I didn't hesitate. "A man must have his pleasures."

"Rose, you can't think that."

"No I can't, but I don't see what business it is of yours. I'll deal with it in my own way. I'm sorry, Steven, but it makes no difference to the way I feel about you. It's over—if it was ever anything in the first place, there's nothing left now."

My hair, my unmanageable hair had come loose from its neat knot, and I felt a strand on my shoulder. I put my hand up to push it back into position. Then I saw Steven staring at me in disbelief. "Your hair—that day—I saw—"

I remembered the way Richard had spread my hair to cover my face, the only part of me Steven had been able to see. My hair was of a deep chestnut colour, thick, wavy and distinctive.

"Rose, tell me it isn't true. No, no, I can't believe it."

I think he was truly shocked now, although I wasn't sure if it was his Christian principles, or his damaged pride when he found out Richard had succeeded where he had failed.

I thought of denying it, saying it was none of his business, but I tired of his histrionics. "Believe it." I used the same tones Richard had that day.

Then he knew for sure. With some fascination, I watched the expressions cross his handsome face. I think he was truly horrified, but I wasn't sure why. I don't think it was moral outrage—what *was* he doing on that corridor?—more that someone had got there first. I may be maligning him, but I don't think so. He stood before me, and looked down at me in sorrow and judgement. "Your brother must be told."

"What do you think he'll make me do? Marry Lord Strang perhaps?" Anger rose inside me. He had no right to question me in this way

He coloured red with genuine fury. I felt a little afraid. I'd steeled myself to cope with his displeasure, but the angry expression in his face promised more than words. "So the woman I thought so pure—the woman I was prepared to give my name to—is nothing but a common whore."

He had made me very angry now, and I wasn't prepared to take that last insult. "I thought you behaved like a whore in Devonshire by selling yourself to the highest bidder."

"How dare you, madam!" He went as white as he had been red a moment before. The shock of his discovery made him truly angry, but I wasn't fully prepared for his next move. "It disgusts me that you can do that with someone you have known barely a week. I courted you, I gave up everything else for you, and I even followed you here—" that was a bit rich, "—and you throw it all back in my face. Well, madam, what's good for the goose—"

He threw his arms around me, pinning my arms to my sides. He crushed my mouth painfully under his, while he pulled at my bodice. I'd thought it a sturdy one, but it was not, sadly, sturdy enough to withstand him. His hands seemed to be everywhere, fumbling, tugging, and prying in places where they had no right to be. My bodice gave way, and then as he pushed me hard, I fell backwards on to the floor, stunned by the unexpected abruptness of his attack and the knock my head received when it connected with the floor.

He put one hand on my mouth and leant across my body to stop me using my hands to free myself. He used his other hand to grope at my breasts, and drag them painfully out from my stays. I threw my head to one side in an effort to break free, but he had his hand clamped over my mouth so hard, I found it difficult to breathe.

He must have mistaken my frightened struggle for breath for a response to his obscene fumbling, for he said in a low, libidinous voice, charged by perverted passion, "You like that, hey? Let's see what else we can do." He pushed up my skirts.

That, and his arrogant assumption that I would enjoy such an insulting violation, was his mistake. With my legs free of my skirts, I could kick, and I did, as hard as I could. I didn't care where the kicks landed just so long as they found their mark somewhere on him. I managed to squirm free of him. Before he caught hold of me again, I took a deep breath and screamed, as loudly as I could.

"Bitch!" Steven caught me again, his expression nothing like I'd never seen on him before. A half smile, half leer marred his handsome features. In my despair, I thought no one had heard, but then the door crashed open, and suddenly the room filled with people.

Richard, Gervase and Miss Cartwright saw the truly unedifying spectacle of a man of the cloth rolling on the floor when I kicked him again. Richard ran across the room, a sword in his hand and I cried out, terrified. Not for Steven, but for Richard. It was only a dress sword but its long, thin blade could have killed Steven, wielded in the right way. Then he threw it in the air, caught it the other way around under the hilt, and used it to rap Steven smartly under the chin. It knocked him out cold.

Richard dropped the sword and reached into his pocket, but Gervase was there instantly. He gripped his brother's arm. "Richard, no."

Richard met his brother's hard look with one of his own, full of fury. No coldness there, none of the controlled anger he had turned on Pritheroe. After a moment he nodded, and pulled his hand back out of his pocket, empty.

He turned, his face white, and came to me. I was surprised to hear a feminine cry of "Steven!" because I certainly didn't call out.

Richard lifted me, tucked my breasts back into what was left of my bodice, smoothed my skirts back into place, laid me down on the couch and sat next to me. Richard had found my fichu, which Steven had torn off to get to my breasts, and he wrapped it around me to cover my ruined gown.

He never took his gaze away from my face. I was relieved, but ashamed as well. I believed I'd provoked this attack somehow. Perhaps I was a bitch, and a whore, and all the other things Steven had called me. Overwrought, out of breath, confused, I clutched his coat and burst into tears.

He lifted me and held me against his shoulder, making soothing noises. I'm afraid I must have ruined his beautiful blue coat with so many salty tears, but I was unable to stop. I must have grown hysterical, for he pushed me away after a while and gave me a little shake so that I stopped crying. Then he took a linen handkerchief from his pocket, and dried my tears himself as I rested thankfully against his shoulder. All the time he murmured soothingly, as though I was a child hurt by a fall. "Hush, my sweet. He'll never touch you again, I'll kill him first. Hush, now. There, there."

The room seemed full of people, and all of them talked and shouted at once. I looked across to the fireplace, where Steven was still stretched out at full length, but he began to stir now. Miss Cartwright stood next to him, staring from one to the other of us. Gervase was trying to talk to Martha, who had come in on the heels of James, indoors for once, as luck would have it.

I blushed. "I'm so sorry." His mobile eyebrows went up.

"Sorry? As far as I can see, you're not the one who'll make the apology. I shan't ask how you feel—you must feel wretched. And this room is far too full for my liking—"

There was an almighty row beginning.

Gervase had both hands on James's shoulders, while James called, "I'll kill him. How dare he touch my sister!"

"How can you blame Steven for all this? The girl's a hussy. She must have provoked him somehow." Julia glared at Richard.

Everyone saw the look of contempt Richard flashed her. "There is never an excuse for this kind of behaviour, madam." He stood and lifted me off the couch and then kicked the sword he had used on Steven out of the way across the floor. It clattered across the polished wooden floor in the sudden silence, as everyone stared at him.

"My lord, your arm."

"Perfectly well now, my precious love. I'm going to take you to your room, and I won't leave you until you feel more yourself again." He looked down at my face, openly loving, and it reassured me that he, at least, wasn't disgusted by me.

I was too weak and relieved to protest any more. "You promise?"

"I promise." He kissed me lightly on the mouth.

Martha and James stared at us, stunned. James stepped forward. "I'll take over now."

I clutched Richard's arm and looked up at his face. He smiled down at me. "It would be a great privilege to look after her. I promise you, no harm will come of it."

Miss Cartwright stood stock-still in the centre of the room, humiliated and ignored. I felt so sorry for her at that moment, despite her stupid comments shortly before. Still holding me, Richard turned to her. "I'm sorry you should find out in this way, Julia. Believe me, this isn't the only reason I wish to break our contract."

"I'll see you in hell, Richard Kerre." She said it quietly, but with such malice I feared for her sanity. Richard smiled as though she had made a polite remark, inclined his head to her in a courtly manner and left the room with me. I didn't see who opened the door for us. I kept my eyes on his face.

Although I protested I was quite able to walk, he didn't put me down until we reached my room. There he gently put me on my feet so he could open the door, took me inside and laid me on the bed. "Now." He looked around. "Ah yes—" He fetched my wrapper which lay on a chair near the fire—a poor thing compared to his magnificent item, but serviceable. I blushed when he began to undo my ruined gown and took the fichu away, but he smiled. "Think of me as your lady's maid, my love." That made me smile, and I sat up so he could help me slip the gown off my shoulders.

He deftly unlaced my stays for me, pulled them away and put my wrapper around my shoulders so I could thrust my arms into the sleeves. He pushed gently on my shoulders, made me lie down again, and talked calmly all the time to soothe me, fastening the garment for me at the front. Then he fetched a damp cloth from the washstand and wiped my face.

I caught his hand and kissed it. "You're too kind."

"You're too foolish if you think that." He put down the cloth and sat on the bed next to me. "Did he hurt you?"

"Not much." Now I was out of danger, I was unwilling to admit I might have hurt my foot in some way in my backwards fall. He considered me calmly. "You *are* hurt, aren't you? I'll kill him."

"No, no more dramatics today." I laid my hand on his sleeve. "But would you look at my foot, please? He pushed me back, and I think I caught it somehow."

Pushing my skirt back, he examined my ankle. He flexed the foot as I winced. "Did that hurt? I'm sorry, my sweet." He replaced my skirt, turning to face me. "No bones broken, I think, but it's a trifle swollen. I'll send Carier to you. I'd set him over any doctor. I think you should stay here for the rest of the day. I'll make sure you're left alone, but I'll send someone to you with a hot drink. And you might like a bath, later."

"Oh, Richard." I cried a little again, relief taking control of my wayward emotions. He seemed to have taken over my welfare. Normally I would have cavilled at such treatment, but at this time, it came as a relief, although I did wonder how he would deal with Martha.

He didn't go until he was sure he had properly comforted me, but when he had gone I indulged in the hearty bout of tears I'd been holding back, and then I promptly fell asleep.

Chapter Twenty-two

I woke later in the day to the sound of pouring water. Richard had been as good as his word, and ordered me a bath. The maid helped me as I lay against the warm towels in hot water and dreamed. I didn't allow myself to dwell on recent events. I felt too tired, drowsy, but he was right. After the bath, I felt much better, cleansed in more than body.

I relaxed in a chair by the fire while the maid brought a hot drink. Martha and Carier came in to me, Martha seeming to have regained her rightful place as my chaperone. Carier propped my swollen foot on a stool, probing the leg gently for injuries. He bound it and stood. "Only a sprain, ma'am. You'll recover in a few days. Don't put your weight on it more than you have to." He bowed and turned to go, but Martha stopped him.

"How long have you served Lord Strang, Carier?"

"Since he went on the Grand Tour at eighteen, my lady."

"Is he a good master?"

"The best, my lady." He waited until Martha nodded, dismissing him. He took the cup that had held the posset I'd drunk away with him.

Martha poured tea, then sat in a chair by the fire, her face serious. "You have been playing a dangerous game, haven't you?"

I looked at her over the rim of my tea dish. I'd known her all my life, but recently she had taken on a new sheen with her responsibilities. In a few years, she would become entirely the great lady.

"I didn't see it coming. Neither did Lord Strang. It's taken us both by surprise."

"No." Her gaze never left my face. "He explained things to us." She paused, frowning. "He's a difficult man, Rose. Are you sure he's what you want?"

Sincerely concerned, she thought I'd be unable to cope with such a difficult person in the longer term. After all, up until now I'd been the quiet, disregarded member of the family. I had no hidden depths anyone had noticed before, not even a private life of my own.

"Yes, Martha. I'm very sure."

Martha looked at me in silence, and then she nodded in her brisk way. "You're determined to have each other. There's not much I can say is there? Though I don't know what we're going to do about his betrothed. He says he'll go and talk to her father, and then speak to his."

"He wants us to marry quietly, then go to Venice. He owns a property there."

Martha frowned. "That's akin to elopement. You might find it very difficult, when you return."

"I can't say I don't care, because I know what it will do to you. But if that's the only way, then I'll do it."

"He might bring them around." We knew it was unlikely. "James seems reconciled to it. I like him. If he can persuade James to give you up to him, the rest should be easy."

We smiled, and sipped our tea.

"Lord Strang is very concerned for you, dear," Martha went on. "When you have rested, perhaps you may see him."

"Tell him I'm well. Please, Martha, may I see him soon?"

"Not until you've had a good night's sleep." I had to accept her advice, though I'd rather have seen him before I slept, but I was tired and conscious of not looking my best. My newfound vanity speaking to me again.

"What did he tell you?"

"Enough." Martha sipped her tea, then put the dish down.

"He's determined to make you his wife, and you have accepted him. Rose, that was a foolish thing to do. You know he's not in a position to propose to you."

"He hasn't formally proposed."

Concern stamped her homely features. "Rose, are you sure? You don't have to, not now. You don't have to marry at all if you don't wish to. James can provide you with everything you want. You used to talk about living independently, with your own household. In a few years, you can do so, if you wish. It's not desperation, is it?"

"No. I love him, Martha. I'm sure of it. I don't think life with him will be easy, but I want to try. I'll take him, Martha, under any circumstances."

She looked at me hard. "No, you won't. You'll take him when he's free to ask. He says he will be in a few weeks, but we must wait and see."

I couldn't argue with her. Martha had always been very aware of the proprieties. She'd have been appalled, had she known what we'd done. She might even refuse to let him come near me again and so drive us to a true elopement. I had every confidence Richard would conclude his contract with Miss Cartwright, whatever the cost. I remembered the look he'd given her when she'd tried to excuse Steven's behaviour. She'd be lucky if he consented to share a coach with her on the journey home now.

Martha sighed, looking at the small comforts we'd brought to the room. "I don't like this house."

"Will you stay here?"

"I don't think so, dear. The place is rotting around us. We've had a builder looking at the house and the timbers are rotting and the structure was thrown up with little regard to quality. It would take too much to restore it, almost a complete rebuild. We've been discussing it, James and I. We always wanted to extend the manor at home, and now we may do so. I miss my family and friends, too. We don't belong here."

"But the people who rely on the estate?"

Martha sighed. "We will do our best to help them. We're not abandoning the estate, just the house."

"Things will never be the same again. You have a title, a new way to make in the world."

"No, things won't be the same, but at least I can face it in the comfort of my own home, with my people about me. Exeter Assembly Rooms will be agog with it." Her eyes gleamed at the thought. The old tabbies who sat by the wall and gossiped would have a field day. Her real triumph would be when she confronted them. Any London success paled into insignificance compared to that.

I felt relaxed, quiet. The day's events receded as I remembered someone else in distress in this house.

"How is Lady Hareton?" I put down my empty cup and sat up.

Martha looked grave. "She's not at all well. Mrs. Peters is devoted to her. I don't want to upset you, dear, but she's had such a bad time of it. Her back is lined with scars you would only expect to see on a sailor from the beatings she received from her husband and father. We've kept her in her room. Mrs. Peters is attending to her. She's keeping her well dosed with laudanum."

I was appalled.

"She'll stay here, then move to the Dower House. Mrs. Peters said that with my authority, she'll do well with her ladyship. I believe she will." She smiled to reassure me. I was thinking of poor Lady Hareton. What despair she must have gone through with no one to turn to. I hadn't thought such cruelty existed, but despite knowing what she did was wrong, I was glad she'd enough spirit to do it.

My eyes were caught by something outside. It was dark now, but I saw a glow at the corner of the window. "What's that?"

Martha went over to close the curtains on the early winter night. "Just the old coach, my dear. James says it's beyond repair, so he ordered it burned. I'm glad because it was a melancholy thing." She turned back to me. "I don't know what the cut strap thing at dinner was, but you must have been mistaken. It probably gave way with old age, rotten for years like the rest of this place." I could swear that she winked at me.

"I suppose I saw an illusion," I agreed, pleased James had made that decision. Lady Hareton had suffered enough for the sins she'd been driven to commit.

I leaned back, yawning, and Martha noticed. "Back to bed now, dear." It was comforting to be tucked between the sheets like a child. I was very tired. "Sleep now."

I woke up at two in the morning, ravenously hungry and with a dry mouth. After checking the time on the pocket watch I kept by my bed, I turned over and tried to sleep, but it was no use. I was awake now. I swung my feet out of bed and tested my foot on the floor. It was tender, but I could bear it. Finding my wrapper, I thrust my arms into it and limped to the door. If I could find something downstairs without disturbing anyone, I could probably get back to sleep.

It took me some time to get downstairs, gripping the banister, taking a step at a time. Carefully, I limped to the dining room. Cordial and bread rolls awaited me on the sideboard. I sat, finishing my meagre repast, enjoying the solitude. Even the servants were abed.

When finished, I rested, considering the day's astonishing events. They'd take some time to sink in properly. Perhaps, I thought, with a smile, I should get up every night at two, just to think about things. It helped.

I recalled a large vase of walking sticks by the back door, resolving to fetch one before returning upstairs.

I shuffled carefully up the corridor, favouring my right foot as much as I could, because the ankle was getting progressively sore, and then I heard a sound, the unmistakable sound of footsteps. Too early for the maids to be up, and everyone else had gone to bed. I looked around wildly for somewhere to hide, but couldn't see anywhere. They'd hear the door open, and come to investigate. More dignified for me to face them.

As they rounded the corner, they came to a halt and stared

at me, as I did at them.

Steven and Julia.

"Oh God," breathed Steven. "Don't call out."

I remembered him saying that once before. I had been afraid of him then, but not now. "Good evening. Why should I call out?"

They were dressed for riding, but it was far too early for even the earliest morning ride, and Steven carried two bags. He bent and quietly put them down.

"Yes, why should you care?" said Julia Cartwright bitterly. "If it weren't for Steven I'd be utterly ruined."

"I think that might be putting it a bit high." I kept my voice down. "You could have given Richard the release he asked for. He wanted that before he met me."

Julia's lip curled in a sneer. "I could have brought him around. With the help of his father—and mine."

Angry, but still remembering to be quiet I demanded, "And what sort of life would that have been for him? Forced into marriage with someone he couldn't like?"

Julia gave me a look of contempt. "Like? What does that matter? I could have given him the children he needs, and left him to follow his own life. How will you feel when he takes his first mistress? He says he loves you. How long do you think that will last? He's never gone more than a month before, and I don't think he will this time."

She articulated some of my doubts, but I couldn't let her see it. I used the reasoning she would understand. "I'll be a viscountess. And someday a countess. I'll manage."

Julia turned triumphantly to Steven. "There? You see? You wanted to marry someone like that?"

Steven looked at me, a frown above his velvety eyes. "You really think that way, Rose? You'll take him anyway?"

"I'll take him." That much was true.

"Then Julia is truer than you, because she wants me, despite my poverty."

"Because of it, more like." I needed something to hold on to, but I wasn't about to show them my weakness.

"How so?"

"She can dominate you, you'll be her creature as Richard never would be." I had seen enough of how Julia operated to guess this was a strong motive. "She tried to manipulate him to her ways, but he wouldn't have it. You will."

"Hah." The look Steven gave Julia held the fondness he had previously reserved for me, a look I suspected he'd practiced before a mirror. Seizing her, he kissed her, their mouths opening hungrily on each other. I was meant to watch, but I chose to shuffle over to the stand and find a stick instead.

I felt much more secure now I could support myself properly. A crutch lay by the stand, but I left it. The stout hazel branch in my hand served me better.

When they emerged, a trifle breathless, Steven stared at me, his mouth curled in a sneer. "Who's in control now? Do you think you and Strang are the only people who can find quiet corners in this godforsaken house?"

I hadn't foreseen that, but when I thought about it, it made sense. That was why Steven was on that deserted corridor that afternoon, that was why he hadn't pursued me as vigorously as he might. He had his hands full, in more ways than one, with Julia Cartwright.

"You're lovers?"

"Why not? You are."

"So we are. And—now what?"

"We're leaving," Steven said defiantly. "Going to Gretna."

"Congratulations." Steven had snagged a rich wife, after all. Julia was a considerable heiress. After the marriage, Steven could count the money as his own.

"Why not wait to do it properly?" I could have kicked myself, except I would have fallen over.

"Because," Julia said, bitterly, "if I stay, let Strang take me home, my father will bring a breach of promise suit against him and I'll be the laughing stock of society. And I still won't have him, so what's the point? The only reason would be to get even with you, but I'd hurt myself just as much. Oh don't worry," she continued, as despite my good intentions, I sighed in relief, "I'll get even."

"Why bother, if you have what you want in Steven?" I hated this pettiness, this tit-for-tat mentality.

"Because you have done me a wrong, and I'll see you punished for it."

Steven shrugged. He'd gained a greater prize, in losing me. Even with an enhanced dowry, my fortune was no match for Julia's. She was the only child of a rich man. Her prospects were mouth watering to a fortune hunter like Steven.

I knew I should have stopped them, called out, but I couldn't think of one good reason why I should do so. I was between them and the back door, so I moved aside. "Godspeed."

They moved past me. Julia produced a key, unlocking the door. "We're riding to York to hire a carriage there. Now, you know, will you have us stopped? Will you send people after us?"

"Not me." I was going back to bed.

"Thanks for that, at least," she said.

Cold air gusted through the open door. "This isn't the end." She gave me the key. Without a backward glance, they left.

I locked the door after them. I got upstairs without waking anyone and fell at once into a dreamless sleep.

Chapter Twenty-three

I felt much better the next day. When Lizzie put her head around the door at nine o' clock, I was comfortably propped on pillows, in bed with some hot chocolate.

She came in and sat on the bed. "Good morning."

"Good morning." As children, we'd shared a bed. Every day we'd say "Good morning" to each other. It was good to be reminded of it.

"How are you feeling?"

"Much better, thank you."

Lizzie took my hand. "Two months ago, if you'd told me I'd be sitting in a great house, with my sister who had—well, all the things you have done in so short a time."

I yawned. "I feel like it happened to someone else. Two proposals of marriage—one conditional—"

She interrupted me. "Two?"

"Richard and Gervase."

"Both? Both of them asked you?"

"Gervase only asked me so I could be with Richard, in case Miss Cartwright kept him to the contract." I didn't feel I could tell her Gervase's real feelings. I hadn't the right. "He says he owes his brother a great deal." The excuse sounded lame to me, but I didn't want to let anyone else in.

"Then it's no use my making a push." She smiled, not really concerned. "In any case, Martha has said we can go to London next year. Oh, Rose. It's just what I always dreamed of." She caught her hands together in delight.

"Yes, I know." I sipped my chocolate. "Did Martha say I might get up?"

"If you wish, she says," my sister replied. "She won't let anyone see you until you are ready to see them."

"You mean Richard, don't you?"

"Yes." She looked at me for a few moments consideringly. "I would never have thought of you doing those things."

"What things?" I said sharply.

"Accepting him without referring him to James, and when he's still contracted to somebody else..." Then she burst out with, "I know I'm not supposed to excite you, but, really my dear, I have to tell you."

This sudden burst of excitement from her woke me out of my lethargy and I sat up straight. I knew what she was about to tell me. "What now?"

"Martha said I could tell you if you seemed ready, and I think you look well enough."

I finished my drink and put my cup down.

She took both my hands in hers. "They put Steven in his room last night, to make sure he came nowhere near you. James said he would send him away without a character this very morning. He wouldn't have him under his roof any longer, and you should have seen how wild Drury was."

"Furious, I imagine."

Lizzie continued with her story. "Lord Strang put his man Carier outside to guard him. You know Carier came and dressed your foot?"

"Yes."

"Well, while he did that, Mr. Drury got a note to Miss Cartwright, and it seems they have run off together."

"What?" Completely restored, I threw the covers aside and made to get out of bed, but my swollen ankle reminded me forcibly of its presence and I was compelled to put my hand back on the bed for support. The adventure last night must have made it worse.

Lizzie grinned, delighted at the response she had received. "I thought you would be interested. They must have left quite early, because when James sent a rider to the village, it seems they were seen before dawn, riding towards York. James has sent people to every inn there, but they seem to have got well away. They might have caught the mail, or bespoken a carriage, but if they did, they didn't use their real names. We don't even know if they've gone north or south."

I knew.

I tried to take my weight on my foot, but it felt very tender this morning. "Lizzie, don't stop, but will you help me to dress? Just a loose gown or something, but I must get up."

Lizzie collected petticoats, stays, gown, stockings and shoes and talked. "They both left notes." I threw off my night rail and put on a fresh shift. "Lord Strang has them," Lizzie told me, lacing my stays for me at the back. "James and his lordship spent half the evening closeted together last night, but they seem to be in accord this morning. I've seen them say good morning to each other, but they're both a bit stiff, even after the excitement of finding Drury missing. I think this is new to both of them."

"I hope so," I said, with a smile.

Barely half an hour later Lizzie had me ensconced in the sunny room near the small parlour. A manservant had carried me downstairs, but I had taken my sturdy hazel stick. I sat on a sofa that was new to the room, my ankle up on a stool, staring into the fire when the door opened on the one face I wanted to see most.

Richard came straight over to me, took my hand, and looked for a long time into my face. Reassured by what he saw there, he sat by my side without taking his gaze away from mine. "Miss Golightly, would you do me the honour of becoming my wife?"

"Yes."

An end and a beginning. I was glad he had been so direct, made it easy for me, so different to Steven's histrionics of the

239

day before. He gave me a gentle kiss, cherishing me. "Thank you."

"You're welcome." That made him smile, and his smile made me smile.

"I shall give you a ruby for a ring. It would suit you."

"Get me a ring from a fair if you like, I don't care."

"You want a gypsy? I should disappoint you then."

We didn't speak for a while. When we did, I was leaning against his shoulder, his arm comfortably about me. He took me in another kiss and I had no doubt that if he could ensure we wouldn't be interrupted, he'd be making love to me soon.

"I asked Carier to give you a sleeping draught. These experiences can return to haunt one, and you needed the rest."

I was taken aback to be so peremptorily treated, and said so.

"I'm sorry, my love, but you were very distressed. Believe me, it was the best way."

Since I did feel much better this morning, and I was now so happy, I couldn't do anything but forgive him instantly, but I warned him not to try that again. We kissed.

"Well then," he said eventually. "When Carier came to care for you I was going to see Drury, but Gervase stopped me. I had every intention of killing him, but Gervase made me see it wouldn't do. It would be doing us both a disservice. Didn't I tell you other people's problems were easier? If it had been anyone else, I would have been far calmer, but that he should do that to you—" He broke off. I saw the diamond pin fastening his neckcloth glitter as he took a few deep breaths. "But he won't touch you any more." He looked at me gravely. "Did Drury hurt you very much, my love?"

"Not very much. Though if I hadn't screamed he might have done. I kicked him and screamed."

"Very resourceful."

"Well if I'd panicked, he might have been able to—to do what he wanted. I think," I continued thoughtfully, "he might not have been entirely aware of what he was doing. He seemed beside himself with rage."

"That seemed to be Julia's main reaction. They deserve each other. Julia was very upset. I went to see her after she had gone to her room, but it did no good. I was in no mood to be conciliatory. She was in a temper and I couldn't reason with her, so I left." He shrugged. I found I didn't want to imagine that scene. "This morning, at about seven, when the maids went up to light the fires they discovered they had both gone. There are notes, one from Drury to you, the other from Julia to me." He leaned forward to reach into his coat pocket and bring out the notes in question. They had both been opened.

"Your brother took the view he didn't want to see you insulted by him any further, so he opened Drury's letter. It contains invective, but I asked him to give it to me, so you could see it if you wanted to." I held out my hand, and silently he put the note into it. There, within the protective arc of his arm, I read the letter.

"Dear Rose,

We've meant a great deal to each other, but I'm afraid we must part. I loved you truly. I never meant to hurt you, but the thought of you with that man overwhelmed me. I lost my head. I can't ask your forgiveness. It was only my right, and you did this to yourself. You acted with such wantonness..."

I looked up at Richard. "And James saw this?"

"I told him Drury had seen you in my arms. I didn't say we were both naked at the time."

I looked hastily at the letter, memories of past delights coming back too richly for me. I read on.

"I'd become aware Miss Julia Cartwright was sadly neglected by Lord Strang. He took no more notice of her than he would his servant. I attempted to comfort her in her loneliness, and I think she may have become fonder of me than I meant. I certainly became more aware of her charms than can be thought proper."

"They've been meeting in secret."

"Undoubtedly. Julia said they'd been meeting for some

time. She said she found him attractive, but she would still forgive me if I sought her pardon properly." He stopped, and smiled down at me. "So I didn't ask her pardon."

I continued to read.

"After the insult delivered to her yesterday, she was in such distress, she felt quite overcome. Strang visited her later, trying to force his attentions upon her. This overset her so much, she was insistent she must get away. I volunteered to take her, and accordingly, we intend to make for Gretna Green. I'm sorry we must part like this, but I see no other way.

Yours in sorrow,

Steven Drury."

I looked up in amazement. "You didn't do that, I'm sure. Force your attentions on her?"

"Her aunt can vouch that I didn't, as she was there the whole time. They didn't think to take the elder Miss Cartwright, so I fear they are sadly compromised. If they don't reach Gretna in time, she may very well be a wronged woman before too long, if she isn't already." He smiled. "Much as you are, my sweet life."

I smiled back. "Not at all as I am,"

He tipped my chin up with his finger. "Not at all as you will be," he promised. I'd have dropped the letter, but he drew back after one gentle, loving kiss.

"I have something to tell you. I woke up in the night. My mouth was dry." I proceeded to tell him about my encounter with Steven and Julia. He listened in silence until I had done.

"First, you should never have gone down alone. There was a maid within call—I made sure of it. You should have sent her."

"But then I would never have met them. And I'm not used to having maids within call at night."

"You'll have more than a maid soon enough," he reminded me, tenderly. I blushed, and he laughed softly. Touching my cheek, he said, "I can't wait."

"I don't suppose we can marry before I'm out of mourning."

"No," he said, regretfully. "Hareton insists on waiting until April."

"April." My breath caught. He smiled at my eagerness. "I still can't believe it."

"I'll make you believe it." Another gentle kiss, then he drew back. "What made you confront them last night? I should be angry with you, especially after what he did to you."

"I wasn't in danger. And I didn't plan it, it just happened. When they came down, there was nowhere to hide."

"You should have called out."

"And awakened everyone? They'd have been returned to their rooms. You'd still have to return Julia to her father and face a breach of promise suit."

He smiled. "So I would."

"Should I have called out, roused the house?"

"Only if you were in danger. They've put themselves in the wrong. Hareton is no longer required to find a living for a man I can't help thinking would make a most unsuitable vicar, and Julia has reneged on our contract. Even if they catch them, she is disgraced, and I can't be expected to go through with it now." He caressed my neck. "Clever girl," he murmured, and kissed me again. "But had he hurt you again, this time I would have killed him."

"Oh, Richard."

"What is it, my love?"

"I love you so much, it makes me afraid sometimes."

"Don't be. I'll care for you, love you, make you happy. I worked hard to convince Hareton. He's a good man. He's still not entirely convinced, but he knows it's what you want, so he'll give his blessing."

"What happens now?"

"Now?" He leaned back, and caught sight of the hazel stick. "Now, I go upstairs and fetch you something more suitable to support you while your foot is getting better." That made me laugh, and he looked at my face once more and smiled. "I have a malacca cane you might like. Then, I'll stay a few more days before I go to Eyton. I won't be gone above a week, it's not far, and I don't have to take the detour to Surrey, where Julia's father lives. I've written a letter to my father, explaining Julia's actions, asking him to cancel the contract. I won't tell him about you until I see him. I think he'll be pleased."

"How so?"

"My love, I could marry a chambermaid, if she'll give him an heir. The way I feel about you—"

I blushed, so he didn't continue.

"Martha wants to go home. She's decided to rebuild in Devonshire, rather than continue here."

"I can't blame her. This place is a mausoleum. Even your redoubtable sister-in-law would have her work cut out to make it a comfortable family home." I looked at him speculatively and he laughed. "Are you thinking about Eyton?" I nodded. "Don't worry. You won't be needed there for some years yet, and in any case, it's both smaller and more comfortable. I have a couple of places, but if you don't like them, we'll buy somewhere else. No need to worry about that now." He kissed me again. "Gervase will look after you while I'm gone. So will you go back to Devonshire with your family?"

"Until April." I hooked an arm about his neck. "Then, we'll see." I pulled him to me for a more passionate kiss, but he drew back after a short time.

"Hareton said I wasn't to over excite you, and I have to agree with him. You've had a great shock. You must have time to recover."

"What did Julia say in her letter?"

"Mainly invective. You may read it, if you like, but I wouldn't recommend it. She was in a fine temper when she wrote it, and very little of it makes much sense."

I leaned forward as far as I could without hurting my foot, rolled Steven's note into a ball, and tried to throw it into the fire, but it fell short. Laughing, Richard leaned forward and retrieved it, crumpling up Miss Cartwright's letter with it. He threw them into the heat of the flame. We watched them curl, flare up, blacken and fall into ash.

"I doubt Mr. Cartwright would care to see what language his daughter has acquired. I wish Drury joy of her, and her fortune." He turned to me decisively. "That's enough of that sordid adventure." He took my hand again.

"April," I whispered.

"I can begin to repay your gift then."

I lost no time in convincing him that would be most welcome.

About the Author

To learn more about Lynne Connolly, please visit www.lynneconnolly.com. Send an email to lynneconnollyuk@yahoo.co.uk or join her Yahoo! group to join in the fun with other readers! http://groups.yahoo.com/group/lynneconnolly. She can also be found at MySpace, Facebook and the Samhain Café.

Breinigsville, PA USA
13 October 2009
225754BV00001B/2/P